BRAT FARRAR

SPECTATOR: 'Suspense is achieved by unexpected twists and extremely competent story-telling . . . credible and convincing.' (*Marghanita Laski*)

NEW STATESMAN: 'Miss Tey has a wonderful gift for portraying impostors; and the character of Brat Farrar, combining charm with deceit, is a triumph of her art.' (*Ralph Partridge*)

CONDITIONS OF SALE

BRAT FARRAR

JOSEPHINE TEY

UNABRIDGED

PAN BOOKS LTD : LONDON

First published 1949 by Peter Davies Ltd.
This edition published 1954 by Pan Books Ltd.,
33 Tothill Street, London, S.W.1

ISBN 0 330 10293 1

2nd Printing 1957
3rd Printing 1959
4th Printing 1961
5th Printing 1964
6th Printing 1965
7th Printing 1968
8th Printing 1972

Printed in Great Britain by
Cox & Wyman Ltd., London, Reading and Fakenham

1

"AUNT BEE," said Jane, breathing heavily into her soup, "was Noah a cleverer back-room boy than Ulysses, or was Ulysses a cleverer back-room boy than Noah?"

"Don't eat out of the point of your spoon, Jane."

"I can't mobilise the strings out of the side."

"Ruth does."

Jane looked across at her twin, negotiating the vermicelli with smug neatness.

"She has a stronger suck than I have."

"Aunt Bee has a face like a very expensive cat," Ruth said, eyeing her aunt sideways.

Bee privately thought that this was a very good description, but wished that Ruth would not be quaint.

"No, but which was the cleverest?" said Jane, who never departed from a path once her feet were on it.

"Clever-*er*," said Ruth.

"Was it Noah or Ulysses? Simon, which was it, do you think?"

"Ulysses," said her brother, not looking up from his paper.

It was so like Simon, Bee thought, to be reading the list of runners at Newmarket, peppering his soup, and listening to the conversation at one and the same time.

"Why, Simon? Why Ulysses?"

"He hadn't Noah's good Met service. Whereabouts was Firelight in the Free Handicap, do you remember?"

"Oh, away down," Bee said.

"A coming-of-age is a little like a wedding, isn't it, Simon?" This was Ruth.

"Better on the whole."

"Is it?"

"You can stay and dance at your own coming-of-age. Which you can't at your wedding."

"I shall stay and dance at *my* wedding."

"I wouldn't put it past you."

Oh, dear, thought Bee, I suppose there are families that have *conversation* at meals, but I don't know how they manage it. Perhaps I haven't been strict enough.

She looked down the table at the three bent heads, and Eleanor's still vacant place, and wondered if she had done right by them. Would Bill and Nora be pleased with what she had made of their children? If by some miracle they could walk in now, young and fine-looking and gay as they had gone to their deaths, would they say: "Ah, yes, that is just how we pictured them: even to Jane's ragamuffin look?"

Bee's eyes smiled as they rested on Jane.

The twins were nine-going-on-ten and identical. Identical, that is to say, in the technical sense. In spite of their physical resemblance there was never any doubt as to which was Jane and which was Ruth. They had the same straight flaxen hair, the same small-boned face and pale skin, the same direct gaze with a challenge in it; but there the identity stopped. Jane was wearing rather grubby jodhpurs and a shapeless jersey festooned with pulled ends of wool. Her hair was pushed back without aid of mirror and held in the uncompromising clasp of a kirby-grip so old that it had reverted to its original steel colour, as old hairpins do. She was slightly astigmatic and, when in the presence of Authority, was in the habit of wearing horn-rimmed spectacles. Normally they lived in the hip pocket of her breeches, and they had been lain-upon, leant-upon, and sat-upon so often that she lived in a permanent state of bankruptcy; breakages over the yearly allowance having to be paid for out of her money-box. She rode to and fro to lessons at the Rectory on Fourposter, the old white pony; her short legs sticking out on either side of him like straws. Fourposter had long ago become a conveyance rather than a ride, so it did not matter that his great barrel was as manageable as a feather-bed and almost as wide.

Ruth, on the other hand, wore a pink cotton frock, as fresh as when she had set off on her bicycle that morning for the Rectory. Her hands were clean and the nails unbroken, and somewhere she had found a pink ribbon and had tied the two side-pieces of her hair in a bow on the top of her head.

Eight years, Bee was thinking. Eight years of contriving, conserving, and planning. And in six weeks' time her steward-ship would come to an end. In little more than a month Simon would be twenty-one and would inherit his mother's fortune, and the lean years would be over. The Ashbys had never been rich but while her brother lived there was ample to keep Latch-etts—the house and the three farms on the estate—as it should

6

be kept. Only his sudden death had accounted for the near-poverty of those eight years. And only Bee's own resolution accounted for the fact that her sister-in-law's money would, next month, come to her son intact. There had been no borrowing on the strength of that future inheritance. Not even when Mr Sandal, of Cosset, Thring and Noble, had been prepared to countenance it. Latchetts must pay its way, Bee had said. And Latchetts, after eight years, was still self-supporting and solvent.

Beyond her nephew's fair head she could see, through the window, the white rails of the south paddock, and the flick of old Regina's tail in the sunlight. It was the horses that had saved them. The horses that had been her brother's hobby had proved the salvation of his house. Year after year, in spite of all the ills, accidents, and sheer cussedness that afflict horseflesh, the horses had shown a profit. The swings had always paid a little more than the roundabouts. When the original small stud that had been her brother's delight seemed likely to be a doubtful prop, Bee had added the small hardy children's ponies to occupy the colder pastures half-way up the down. Eleanor had schooled doubtful hacks into "safe rides for a lady", and had sold them at a profit. And now that the manor was a boarding-school she was teaching others to ride, at a very respectable price per hour.

"Eleanor is very late, isn't she?"

"Is she out with La Parslow?" Simon asked.

"The Parslow girl, yes."

"The unhappy horse has probably dropped dead."

Simon got up to take away the soup plates, and to help out the meat course from the sideboard, and Bee watched him with critical approval. At least she had managed not to spoil Simon; and that, given Simon's selfish charm, was no small achievement. Simon had an air of appealing dependence that was quite fallacious, but it had fooled all and sundry since he was in the nursery. Bee had watched the fooling process with amusement and something that was like a reluctant admiration; if she herself had been gifted with Simon's particular brand of charm, she felt, she would in all likelihood have made it work for her as Simon did. But she had seen to it that it did not work with her.

"It would be nice if a coming-of-age had something like bridesmaids," Ruth observed, turning over her helping with a fastidious fork.

7

This fell on stony ground.

"The Rector says that Ulysses was probably a frightful nuisance round the house," said the undeviating Jane.

"Oh!" said Bee, interested in this sidelight on the classics. "Why?"

"He said he was 'without doubt a—a gadget-contriver', and that Penelope was probably very glad to be rid of him for a bit. I wish liver wasn't so *smooth*."

Eleanor came in and helped herself from the sideboard in her usual silent fashion.

"Pah!" said Ruth. "What a smell of stables."

"You're late, Nell," Bee said, inquiring.

"She'll never ride," Eleanor said. "She can't even bump the saddle yet."

"Perhaps loony people can't ride," Ruth suggested.

"Ruth," Bee said, with vigour. "The pupils at the Manor are not lunatic. They are not even mentally deficient. They are just 'difficult'."

"Ill-adjusted is the technical description," Simon said.

"Well, they *behave* like lunatics. If you behave like a lunatic how is anyone to tell that you're not one?"

Since no one had an answer to this, silence fell over the Ashby luncheon table. Eleanor ate with the swift purposefulness of a hungry schoolboy, not lifting her eyes from her plate. Simon took out a pencil and reckoned odds on the margin of his paper. Ruth, who had stolen three biscuits from the jar on the Rectory sideboard and eaten them in the lavatory, made a castle of her food with a moat of gravy round it. Jane consumed hers with industrious pleasure. And Bee sat with her eyes on the view beyond the window.

Over that far ridge the land sloped in chequered miles to the sea and the clustered roofs of Westover. But here, in this high valley, shut off from the Channel gales and open to the sun, the trees stood up in the bright air with a midland serenity: with an air, almost, of enchantment. The scene had the bright perfection and stillness of an apparition.

A fine inheritance; a fine rich inheritance. She hoped that Simon would do well by it. There were times when she had—no, not been afraid. Times perhaps when she had wondered. Simon had far too many sides to him; a quick-silver quality that did not go with a yeoman inheritance. Only Latchetts, of all the surrounding estates, still sheltered a local family and Bee hoped that it would go on sheltering Ashbys for centuries to come. Fair, small-boned, long-headed Ashbys like the ones round the table.

"Jane, must you splash fruit juice round like that?"

"I don't like rhubarb in inches, Aunt Bee, I like it in mush."

"Well, mush it more carefully."

When she had been Jane's age she had mushed up her rhubarb too, and at this same table. At this same table had eaten Ashbys who had died of fever in India, of wounds in the Crimea, of starvation in Queensland, of typhoid at the Cape, and of cirrhosis of the liver in the Straits Settlements. But always there had been an Ashby at Latchetts; and they had done well by the land. Here and there came a ne'er-do-well—like her cousin Walter—but Providence had seen to it that the worthless quality had been confined to younger sons, who could practise their waywardness on subjects remote from Latchetts.

No queens had come to Latchetts to dine; no cavaliers to hide. For three hundred years it had stood in its meadows very much as it stood now; a yeoman's dwelling. And for nearly two of those three hundred years Ashbys had lived in it.

"Simon, dear, see to the cona."

Perhaps its simplicity had saved it. It had pretended to nothing; had aspired to nothing. Its goodness had been dug back into the earth; its sap had returned to its roots. Across the valley the long white house of Clare stood in its park, gracious as a vicereine, but there were no Ledinghams there now. The Ledinghams had been prodigal of their talents and their riches; using Clare as a background, as a purse, as a decoration, as a refuge, but not as a home. For centuries they had peacocked over the world: as pro-consuls, explorers, court jesters, rakes, and revolutionaries; and Clare had supported their extravagances. Now only their portraits remained. And the great house in the park was a boarding-school for the unmanageable children of parents with progressive ideas and large bank accounts.

But the Ashbys stayed at Latchetts.

2

As Bee poured the coffee the twins disappeared on ploys of their own, this being their half-holiday; and Eleanor drank hers hastily and went back to the stables.

"Do you want the car this afternoon?" Simon asked. "I half promised old Gates that I would bring a calf out from Westover in one of our trailers. His own has collapsed."

"No, I don't need it," Bee said, wondering what had prompted Simon to so dull a chore. She hoped it was not the Gates daughter; who was very pretty, very silly, and very commonplace. Gates was the tenant of Wigsell, the smallest of the three farms; and Simon was not normally tolerant of his opportunism.

"If you really want to know," Simon said as he got up, "I want to see June Kaye's new picture. It's at the Empire."

The disarming frankness of this would have delighted anyone but Beatrice Ashby, who knew very well her nephew's habit of throwing up two balls to divert your attention from the third.

"Can I fetch you anything?"

"You might get one of the new bus timetables from the Westover and District offices if you have time. Eleanor says they have a new Clare service that goes round by Guessgate."

"Bee," said a voice in the hall. "Are you there, Bee?"

"Mrs Peck," Simon said, going out to meet her.

"Come in, Nancy," Bee called. "Come and have coffee with me. The others have finished."

And the Rector's wife came into the room, put her empty basket on the sideboard, and sat down with a pleased sigh. "I could do with some," she said.

When people mentioned Mrs Peck's name they still added: "Nancy Ledingham that was, you know"; although it was a decade since she had stunned the social world by marrying George Peck and burying herself in a country rectory. Nancy Ledingham had been more than the "débutante of her year"; she had been a national possession. The penny Press had done for her what the penny postcard had done for Lily Langtry: her beauty was common property. If the public did not stand on chairs to see her pass they certainly stopped the traffic; her appearance as bridesmaid at a wedding was enough to give the authorities palpitations for a week beforehand. She had that serene unquestionable loveliness that defeats even a willing detractor. Indeed the only question seemed to be whether the ultimate coronet would have strawberry leaves or not. More than once the popular Press had supplied her with a crown, but this was generally considered mere wishful thinking; her public would settle for strawberry leaves.

And then, quite suddenly—between a *Tatler* and a *Tatler*, so to speak—she had married George Peck. The shattered Press, doing the best they could for a shattered public, had pulled out the *vox humana* stop and quavered about romance, but George had defeated them. He was a tall, thin man with the face of a very intelligent and rather nice ape. Besides, as the society editor of the *Clarion* said: "A clergyman! I ask you! I could get more romance out of a cement-mixer!"

So the public let her go, into her chosen oblivion. Her aunt, who had been responsible for her coming-out, disinherited her. Her father died in a welter of chagrin and debts. And her old home, the great white house in the park, had become a school.

But after thirteen years of rectory life Nancy Peck was still serenely and unquestionably beautiful; and people still said: "Nancy Ledingham that was, you know."

"I've come for the eggs," she said, "but there's no hurry, is there? It's wonderful to sit and do nothing."

Bee's eyes slid sideways at her in a smile.

"You have such a nice face, Bee."

"Thank you. Ruth says it is a face like a very expensive cat."

"Nonsense. At least—not the furry kind. Oh, I know what she means! The long-necked, short-haired kind that show their small chins. Heraldic cats. Yes, Bee, darling, you have a face like a heraldic cat. Especially when you keep your head still and slide your eyes at people." She put her cup down and sighed again with pleasure. "I can't think how the Nonconformists have failed to discover coffee."

"Discover it?"

"Yes. As a snare. It does far more for one than drink. And yet no one preaches about it, or signs pledges about it. Five mouthfuls and the world looks rosy."

"Was it very grey before?"

11

"A sort of mud colour. I was so happy this week because it was the first week this year that we hadn't needed sitting-room fires and I had no fires to do and no fireplaces to clean. But nothing—I repeat, nothing—will stop George from throwing his used matches into the fireplace. And as he takes fifteen matches to light one pipe——! The room swarms with waste-paper baskets and ash-trays, but no, George must use the fireplace. He doesn't even *aim*, blast him. A fine careless flick of the wrist and the match lands anywhere from the fender to the farthest coal. And they have all got to be picked out again."

"And he says: Why don't you leave them."

"He does. However, now that I've had some Latchetts coffee I have decided not to take a chopper to him after all."

"Poor Nan. These Christians."

"How are the coming-of-age preparations getting on?"

"The invitations are about to go to the printers; which is a nice definite stage to have arrived at. A dinner for intimates, here; and a dance for everyone in the barn. What is Alec's address, by the way?"

"I can't remember his latest one off-hand. I'll look it up for you. He has a different one almost every time he writes. I think he gets heaved out when he can't pay his rent. Not that I hear from him often, of course. He has never forgiven me for not marrying well, so that I could keep my only brother in the state to which he had been accustomed."

"Is he playing just now?"

"I don't know. He had a part in that silly comedy at the Savoy but it ran only a few weeks. He is so much a type that his parts are necessarily limited."

"Yes, I suppose so."

"No one could cast Alec as anything but Alec. You don't know how lucky you are, Bee, to have Ashbys to deal with. The incidence of rakes in the Ashby family is singularly low."

"There was Walter."

"A lone wolf crying in the wilderness. What became of Cousin Walter?"

"Oh, he died."

"In an odour of sanctity?"

"No. Carbolic. A workhouse ward, I think."

"Even Walter wasn't bad, you know. He just liked drink

12

and hadn't the head for it. But when a Ledingham is a rake he is plain bad."

They sat together in a comfortable silence, considering their respective families. Bee was several years older than her friend: almost a generation older. But neither could remember a time when the other was not there; and the Ledingham children had gone in and out of Latchetts as if it were their home, as familiar with it as the Ashbys were with Clare.

"I have been thinking so often lately of Bill and Nora," Nancy said. "This would have been such a happy time for them."

"Yes," Bee said, reflectively; her eyes on the window. It was at that view she had been looking when it happened. On a day very like this and at this time of the year. Standing in the sitting-room window, thinking how lovely everything looked and if they would think that nothing they had seen in Europe was half as lovely. Wondering if Nora would look well again; she had been very pulled down after the twins' birth. Hoping she had been a good deputy for them, and yet a little pleased to be resuming her own life in London tomorrow.

The twins had been asleep, and the older children upstairs grooming themselves for the welcome and for the dinner they were to be allowed to stay up for. In half an hour or so the car would swing out from the avenue of lime trees and come to rest at the door and there they would be; in a flurry of laughter and embracing and present-giving and well-being.

The turning on of the wireless had been so absent-minded a gesture that she did not know that she had done it. "The two o'clock plane from Paris to London," said the cool voice, "with nine passengers and a crew of three crashed this afternoon just after crossing the Kent coast. There were no survivors."

No. There had been no survivors.

"They were so wrapped up in the children," Nancy said. "They have been so much in my mind lately, now that Simon is going to be twenty-one."

"And Patrick has been in mine."

"Patrick?" Nancy sounded at a loss. "Oh, yes, of course. Poor Pat."

Bee looked at her curiously. "You had almost forgotten, hadn't you?"

"Well, it is a long time ago, Bee. And—well, I suppose one's mind tidies away the things it can't bear to remember. Bill and

Nora—that was frightful, but it *was* something that happened to people. I mean, it was part of the ordinary risks of life. But Pat—that was different." She sat silent for a moment. "I have pushed it so far down in my mind that I can't even remember what he looked like any more. Was he as like Simon as Ruth is like Jane?"

"Oh, no. They weren't identical twins. Not much more alike than some brothers are. Though oddly enough they were much more in each other's pockets than Ruth and Jane are."

"Simon seems to have got over it. Do you think he remembers it often?"

"He must have remembered it very often lately."

"Yes. But it is a long way between thirteen and twenty-one. I expect even a twin grows shadowy at that distance."

This gave Bee pause. How shadowy was he to her: the kind solemn little boy who should have been coming into his inheritance next month? She tried to call up his face in front of her but there was only a blur. He had been small and immature for his age, but otherwise he was just an Ashby. Less an individual than a family resemblance. All she really remembered, now she thought about it, was that he was solemn and kind.

Kindness was not a common trait in small boys.

Simon had a careless generosity when it did not cost him inconvenience; but Patrick had had that inner kindness that not only gives but gives up.

"I still wonder," Bee said unhappily, "whether we should have allowed the body that was found on the Castleton beach to be buried over there. A pauper's burial, it was."

"But, Bee! It had been months in the water, hadn't it? They couldn't even tell what sex it was; could they? And Castleton is miles away. And they get all the corpses from the Atlantic founderings, anyhow. I mean, the nearer ones. It is not sense to worry over—to identify it with——" Her dismayed voice died into silence.

"No, of course it isn't!" Bee said briskly. "I am just being morbid. Have some more coffee."

And as she poured the coffee she decided that when Nancy had gone she would unlock the private drawer of her desk and burn that pitiful note of Patrick's. It was morbid to keep it, even if she had not looked at it for years. She had never had the heart to tear it up because it had seemed part of Patrick.

14

But of course that was absurd. It was no more part óf Patrick than was the despair that had filled him when he wrote: "I'm sorry, but I can't bear it any longer. Don't be angry with me. Patrick." She would take it out and burn it. Burning it would not blot it from her mind, of course, but there was nothing she could do about that. The round schoolboy letters were printed there for always. Round, careful letters written with the stylograph that he had been so attached to. It was so like Patrick to apologise for taking his own life.

Nancy, watching her friend's face, proffered what she considered to be consolation. "They say, you know, that when you throw yourself from a high place you lose consciousness almost at once."

"I don't think he did it that way, Nan."

"No!" Nancy sounded staggered. "But that was where the note was found. I mean, the coat with the note in the pocket. On the cliff-top."

"Yes, but by the path. By the path down the Gap to the shore."

"Then what do you——?"

"I think he swam out."

"Till he couldn't come back, you mean?"

"Yes. When I was *in loco parentis* that time, when Bill and Nora were on holiday, we went several times to the Gap, the children and I; to swim and have a picnic. And once when we were there Patrick said that the best way to die—I think he called it the lovely way—would be to swim out until you were too tired to go any farther. He said it quite matter-of-factly, of course. In those days it was—a mere academic matter. When I pointed out that drowning would still be drowning, he said: 'But you would be so tired, you see; you wouldn't care any more. The water would just take you.' He loved the water."

She was silent for a little and then blurted out the thing that had been her private nightmare for years.

"I've always been afraid that when it was too late to come back he may have regretted."

"Oh, Bee, no!"

Bee's sidelong glance went to Nancy's beautiful, protesting face.

"Morbid. I know. Forget I said it."

"I don't know now how I *could* have forgotten," Nancy said, wondering. "The worst of pushing horrible things down into

15

one's subconscious is that when they pop up again they are as fresh as if they had been in a refrigerator. You haven't allowed time to get at them to—to mould them over a little."

"I think a great many people have almost forgotten that Simon had a twin," Bee said, excusing. "Or that he has not always been the heir. Certainly no one has mentioned Patrick to me since the coming-of-age celebrations have been in the air."

"Why was Patrick so inconsolable about his parents' death?"

"I didn't know he was. None of us did. All the children were wild with grief to begin with, of course. Sick with it. But none more than another. Patrick seemed bewildered rather than inconsolable. 'You mean: Latchetts belongs to me now?' I remember him saying, as if it were some strange idea, difficult to understand. Simon was impatient with him, I remember. Simon was always the brilliant one. I think that it was all too much for Patrick; too strange. The adrift feeling of being suddenly without his father and mother, and the weight of Latchetts on his shoulders. It was too much for him and he was so unhappy that he—took a way out."

"Poor Pat. Poor darling. It was wrong of me to forget him."

"Come; let us go and get those eggs. You won't forget to let me have Alec's address, will you? A Ledingham must have an invitation."

"No, I'll look up it when I go back, and telephone it to you. Can your latest moron take a telephone message?"

"Just."

"Well, I'll stick to basic. You won't forget that he is Alec Loding on the stage, will you?" She picked up her basket from the sideboard. "I wonder if he would come. It is a long time since he has been to Clare. A country life is not Alec's idea of amusement. But an Ashby coming-of-age is surely something that would interest him."

3

But Alec Loding's main interest in the Ashby coming-of-age was to blow the celebrations sky-high. Indeed, he was at this moment actively engaged in pulling strings to that end.

Or, rather, trying to pull strings. The strings weren't pulling very well.

He was sitting in the back room at the Green Man, the remains of lunch spread before him, and beside him sat a young man. A boy, one would have said, but for something controlled and still that did not go with adolescence. Loding poured coffee for himself and sugared it liberally; casting a glance now and then at his companion, who was turning an almost empty beer glass round and round on the table. The movement was so deliberate that it hardly came under the heading of fidgeting.

"Well?" said Loding at last.

"No."

Loding took a mouthful of coffee.

"Squeamish?"

"I'm not an actor."

Something in the unaccented phrase seemed to sting Loding and he flushed a little.

"You're not asked to be emotional, if that is what you mean. There is no filial devotion to be simulated, you know. Only dutiful affection for an aunt you haven't seen for nearly ten years—which one would expect to be more dutiful than affectionate."

"No."

"You young idiot, I'm offering you a fortune."

"Half a fortune. And you're not offering me anything."

"If I'm not offering it to you, what am I doing?"

"Propositioning me," said the young man. He had not raised his eyes from his slowly-turning beer.

"Very well, I'm propositioning you, to use your barbarous idiom. What is wrong with the proposition?"

"It's crazy."

"What is crazy about it, given the initial advantage of your existence?"

"No one could bring it off."

"It is not so long since a famous general whose face was a household word—if you will forgive the metaphor—was impersonated quite successfully by an actor in broad daylight and in full view of the multitude."

"That's quite different."

"I agree. You aren't asked to impersonate anyone. Just to be yourself. A much easier task."

"No," said the young man.

Loding kept his temper with a visible effort. He had a pink, collapsed face that reminded one of the underside of fresh mushrooms. The flesh hung away from his good Ledingham bones with a discouraged slackness, and the incipient pouches under his eyes detracted from their undoubted intelligence. Managers who had once cast him for gay young rakes now offered him nothing but discredited roués.

"My God!" he said suddenly. "Your teeth!"

Even that did not startle the young man's face into any expression. He lifted his eyes for the first time, resting them incuriously on Loding. "What's the matter with my teeth?" he asked.

"It's how they identify people nowadays. A dentist keeps a record of work, you know. I wonder where those kids went. Something would have to be done about that. Are those front teeth your own?"

"The two middle ones are caps. They were kicked out."

"They went to someone here in town, I remember that much. There was a London trip to see the dentist twice a year; once before Christmas and once in the summer. They went to the dentist in the morning and to a show in the afternoon: pantomime in the winter and the Tournament at Olympia in the summer. These are the kind of things you would have to know, by the way."

"Yes?"

The gentle monosyllable maddened Loding.

"Look, Farrar, what are you frightened of? A strawberry mark? I bathed with that kid in the buff many a time and he hadn't as much as a mole on him. He was so ordinary that you could order him by the dozen from any prep school in England. You are more like his brother at this moment than that kid ever was, twins though they were. I tell you, I thought for a moment that you *were* young Ashby. Isn't that good enough for you? You come and live with me for a fortnight and by the end of it there won't be anything you don't know about the village of Clare and its inhabitants. Nor anything about Latchetts. I know every last pantry in it. Nor anything about the Ashbys. Can you swim, by the way?"

The young man nodded. He had gone back to his glass of beer.

"Swim well?"

"Yes."

"Don't you ever qualify a statement?"

"Not unless it needs it."

"The kid could swim like an eel. There's the matter of ears, too. Yours look ordinary enough, and his must have been ordinary too or I should remember. Anyone who has worked in a life-class notices ears. But I must see what photographs of him exist. Front ones wouldn't matter, but a real close-up of an ear might be a give-away. I think I must take a trip to Clare and do some prospecting."

"Don't bother on my account."

Loding was silent for a moment. Then he said, reasonably: "Tell me, do you believe my story at all?"

"Your story?"

"Do you believe that I am who I say I am, and that I come from a village called Clare, where there is someone who is practically your double? Do you believe that? Or do you think that this is just a way of getting you to come home with me?"

"No, I didn't think it was that. I believe your story."

"Well, thank heaven for that, at least," Loding said with a quirk of his eyebrow. "I know that my looks are not what they were, but I should be shattered to find that they suggested the predatory. Well, then. That settled, do you believe that you are as like young Ashby as I say?"

For a whole turn of the glass there was no answer. "I doubt it."

"Why?"

"On your own showing it is some time since you saw him."

"But you don't have to *be* young Ashby. Just look like him. And believe me you do! My God, how you do! It's something I wouldn't have believed unless I saw it with my own eyes; something I have imagined only happened in books. And it is worth a fortune to you. You have only to put out your hand and take it."

"Oh, no, I haven't."

"Metaphorically speaking. Do you realise that except for the first year or so your story would be truth? It would be your own story; able to stand up to any amount of checking." His voice twisted into a comedy note. "Or would it?"

"Oh, yes, it would check."

"Well, then. You have only to stow away on the *Ira Jones*

19

out of Westover instead of going for a day trip to Dieppe, *et voilà*!"

"How do you know there was a ship called the *Ira Jones* at Westover about then?"

"'About then'! You do me scant justice, *amigo*. There was a ship of that repellent title at Westover the day the boy disappeared. I know because I spent most of the day painting her. On canvas, not on her plates, you understand. And the old scow went out before I had finished; bound for the Channel Islands. All my ships go out before I have finished painting them."

There was silence for a little.

"It's in your lap, Farrar."

"So is my table napkin."

"A fortune. A charming small estate. Security. A——"

"*Security*, did you say?"

"After the initial gamble, of course," Loding said smoothly.

The light eyes that looked at him for a moment held a faint amusement.

"Hadn't it occurred to you at all, Mr Loding, that the gamble was yours?"

"Mine?"

"You're offering me the sweetest chance for a double-cross that I ever heard of. I take your coaching, pass the exam, and forget about you. And you wouldn't be able to do a thing about it. How did you figure to keep tabs on me?"

"I hadn't. No one with your Ashby looks could be a double-crosser. The Ashbys are monsters of rectitude."

The boy pushed away the glass.

"Which must be why I don't take kindly to the idea of being a phoney. Thank you for my lunch, Mr Loding. If I had known what you had in mind when you asked me to lunch with you, I wouldn't have——"

"All right, all right. Don't apologise. And don't run away; we'll go together. You don't like my proposition: very good: so be it. But you, on the other hand, fascinate me. I can hardly take my eyes off you, or believe that anything so unique exists. And since you are sure that my improper proposal to you has nothing of the personal in it, there is nothing against our walking as far as the Underground together."

Loding paid for their lunch, and as they walked out of the

Green Man he said: "I won't ask where you are living in case you think I want to hound you. But I shall give you my address in the hope that you will come to see me. Oh, no; not about the proposition. If it isn't your cup of tea then it isn't your cup of tea; and if you felt like that you certainly wouldn't make a success of it. No, not about the proposition. I have something in my rooms that I think would interest you."

He paused artistically while they negotiated a street crossing.

"When my old home, Clare, was sold—after my father's death—Nancy bundled together all the personal things in my room and sent them to me. A whole trunkful of rubbish, which I have never had the energy to get rid of, and a large proportion of it consists of snapshots and photographs of the companions of my youth. I think you would find it very interesting."

He glanced sideways at the uncommunicative profile of his companion.

"Tell me," he said as they stopped at the entrance to the Underground, "do you play cards?"

"Not with strangers," said the young man pleasantly.

"I just wondered. I had never met the perfect poker face until now, and I should be sorry if it was being wasted on some nonconformist abstainer. Ah, well. Here is my address. If by any chance I have fled from there the *Spotlight* will find me. I am truly sorry I couldn't sell you the idea of being an Ashby. You would have made an excellent master of Latchetts, I feel. Someone who was at home with horses, and used to an outdoor life."

The young man, who had made a gesture of farewell and was in the act of turning away, paused. "Horses?" he said.

"Yes," Loding said, vaguely surprised. "It's a stud, you know. Very well thought of, I understand."

"Oh." He paused a moment longer, and then turned away.

Loding watched him as he went down the street. "I missed something," he was thinking. "There was some bait he would have risen to, and I missed it. Why should he have nibbled at the word horse? He must be sick of them."

Ah, well; perhaps he would come to see what his double looked like.

4

THE boy lay on his bed in the dark, fully dressed, and stared at the ceiling.

There were no street lamps outside to illuminate this back room under the slates; but the faint haze of light that hangs over London at night, emanation from a million arcs and gas-lights and paraffin lamps, shone ghost-like on the ceiling so that its cracks and stains showed like a world map.

The boy was looking at a map of the world, too, but it was not on the ceiling. He was examining his odyssey; conducting a private inventory. That meeting today had shaken him. Somewhere, it seemed, there was another fellow so like him that for a moment they could be mistaken for each other. To one who had been very much alone all his life that was an amazing thought.

Indeed, it was the most surprising thing that had happened to him in all his twenty-one years. In a way it was as if all those years that had seemed so full and exciting at the time had been merely leading up to that moment when the actor chap had caught himself short in the street and said: "Hello, Simon."

"Oh! Sorry!" he had said at once. "Thought you were a friend of——" And then he had stopped and stared.

"Can I do something for you?" the boy had asked at last, since the man showed no sign of moving on.

"Yes. You could come and have lunch with me."

"Why?"

"It's lunch-time, and that's my favourite pub behind you."

"But why me?"

"Because you interest me. You are so like a friend of mine. My name is Loding, by the way. Alec Loding. I act a bad part in a bad farce at that very bad old theatre over there." He had nodded across the street. "But Equity, God bless them, has ordained a minimum fee for my labours, so the hire is considerably better than the part, I rejoice to say. Do you mind telling me your name?"

"Farrar."

"Farrell?"

"No. Farrar."

"Oh." The amused, considering look was still in his eye. "Is it long since you came to England?"

"How did you know I had been out of it?"

"Your clothes, my boy. Clothes are my business. I have dressed too many parts not to recognise American tailoring when I see it. Even the admirably conservative tailoring that you so rightly wear."

"Then what makes you think I'm not American?"

At that the man had smiled quite broadly. "Ah, *that*," he said, "is the eternal mystery of the English. You watch a procession of monks in Italy and your eye singles out one and you say: 'Ha! An Englishman.' You come across five hoboes wrapped in gunny sacks sheltering from the rain in Wisconsin, and you notice the fifth and think: 'Dear goodness, that chap's English.' You see ten men stripped to the buff for the Foreign Legion doctor to pass judgment on, and you say—— But come to lunch and we can explore the subject at leisure."

So he had gone to lunch, and the man had talked and been charming. But always behind the lively puffy eyes there had been that quizzical, amused, almost unbelieving look. That look was more eloquent than any of his subsequent argument. Truly he, Brat Farrar, *must* be like that other fellow to bring that look of half-incredulous amusement into someone's eyes.

He lay on the bed and thought about it. This sudden identification in an unbelonging life. He had a great desire to see this twin of his; this Ashby boy. Ashby. It was a nice name: a good English name. He would like to see the place too: this Latchetts, where his twin had grown up in belonging quiet while he had bucketed round the world, all the way from the orphanage to that moment in a London street, belonging nowhere.

The orphanage. It was no fault of the orphanage that he had not belonged. It was a very good orphanage; a great deal happier than many a home he had seen in passing since. The children had loved it. They had wept when they left and had come back for visits; they had sent contributions to the funds; they had invited the staff to their marriages, and brought their subsequent children for the matron's approval. There was never a day when some old girl or boy was not cluttering up the front door. Then why had he not felt like that?

Because he was a foundling? Was that why? Because no visitors ever came for him; no parcels or letters or invitations? But they had been very wise about that; very determined to prop his self-esteem. If anything he had been privileged beyond the other children by his foundling status. His Christmas present from Matron, he remembered, had been looked upon with envy by children whose only present came from an aunt or uncle; a mere relation, as it were. It was Matron who had taken him off the doorstep; and who saw to it that he heard how well-dressed and cared-for he had been. (He heard about this at judicious intervals for fifteen years but he had never been able to feel any satisfaction about it.) It was Matron who had determined his name with the aid of a pin and the telephone directory. The pin had come down on the word Farrell. Which had pleased Matron considerably; her pin had once, long ago, come down on the word Coffin, and she had had to cheat and try again.

There had never been any doubt about his first name, since he had arrived on the doorstep on St Bartholomew's day. He had been Bart from the beginning. But the older children had changed that to Brat, and presently even the staff used the more familiar name (another device of Matron's to prevent his feeling "different"?) and the name had followed him to the grammar school.

The grammar school. Why had he not "belonged" there, then?

Because his clothes were subtly different? Surely not. He had not been thin-skinned as a child; merely detached. Because he was a scholarship boy? Certainly not: half his form were scholarship boys. Then why had he decided that the school was not for him? Decided with such un-boylike finality that all Matron's arguments had died into ultimate silence, and she had countenanced his going to work.

There was no mystery about his not liking the work, of course. The office job had been fifty miles away, and since no ordinary lodgings could be paid for out of his salary he had had to stay in the local "boys' home". He had not known how good the orphanage was until he had sampled the boys' home. He could have supported either the job or the home, but not the two simultaneously. And of the two the office was by far the worse. It was, as a job, comfortable, leisurely, and graced with certain, if far-off prospects; but to him it had been a prison.

He was continually aware of time running past him; time that he was wasting. This was not what he wanted.

He had said good-bye to his office life almost accidentally; certainly without premeditation. "DAY RETURN TO DIEPPE" a bill had said, plastered against the glass of a newsagent's window; and the price, in large red figures, was exactly the amount of his savings to the nearest half-crown. Even so, he would have done nothing about it if it had not been for old Mr Hendren's funeral. Mr Hendren was the "retired" partner, and on the day of his funeral the office shut down "out of respect". And so, with a week's pay in his pocket and a whole week-day free, he had taken his savings and gone to see "abroad". He had had a grand time in Dieppe, where his first-year French was no deterrent to enjoyment, but it had not even crossed his mind to stay there until he was on his way home. He had reached the harbour before the shocking idea took hold of him.

Was it native honesty, he thought, staring at the Pimlico ceiling, or his good orphanage training that had made his unpaid laundry bill bulk so large in the subsequent mental struggle? A boy who had no money and no bed for the night should hardly have been concerned with the ethics of bilking a laundry of two-and-threepence.

The camion, rolling up from the harbour, had been his salvation. He had held up his thumb, and the brown, sweaty brigand at the wheel had grinned at this international gesture and slowed as he passed. He had run at the moving cliff-face, snatched and clung, and been hauled aboard. And all his old life was behind him.

He had planned to stay and work in France. Debated with himself during the long run to Havre, when gesture had given out and the driver's patois proved unintelligible, how best he might earn enough to eat. It was his neighbour in the Havre *bistro* who enlightened him. "My young friend," the man had said, fixing him with melancholy spaniel's eyes, "it is not sufficient to be a man in France in order to work. One has also to have papers."

"And where," he had asked, "does one not have papers? I mean, in what country? I can go anywhere." He was suddenly conscious of the world, and that he was free of it.

"God knows," the man had said. "Mankind grows every day more like sheep. Go to the harbour and take a ship."

"Which ship?"

"It is immaterial. Have you in English a game that——"
He made descriptive gestures.

"A counting-out game? Oh, yes. Eenie, meenie, minie,
moe."

"Good. Go to the harbour and do 'Eenie, meenie, minie,
moe.' And when you go aboard 'moe' see that no one is looking. On ships they have a passion for papers that amounts to a
madness."

"Moe" was the *Barfleur*, and he had not needed papers after
all. He was the gift from heaven that the *Barfleur's* cook had
been looking for for years.

Good old *Barfleur*; with her filthy pea-green galley smelling of
over-used olive oil, and the grey seas combing up mountains
high, and the continuous miracle of their harmless passing, and
the cook's weekly drunk that left him acting unpaid cook, and
learning to play a mouth-organ, and the odd literature in the
fo'c'sle. Good old *Barfleur*!

He had taken a lot away with him when he left her, but most
important of all he took a new name. When he had written his
name for the Captain, old Bourdet had taken the final double-L
to be an R, and copied the name Farrar. And he had kept it so.
Farrell came out of a telephone directory; and Farrar out of a
tramp skipper's mistake. It was all one.

And then what?

Tampico and the smell of tallow. And the tally-man who
had said: "You Englishman? You want shore job?"

He had gone to inspect the "job", expecting dish-washing.

Odd to think that he might still be living in that great quiet
house with the tiled patio, and the bright scentless flowers, and
the bare shadowed rooms with the beautiful furniture. Living
in luxury, instead of lying on a broken-down bedstead in Pimlico. The old man had liked him, had wanted to adopt him;
but he had not "belonged". He had enjoyed reading the
English newspapers to him twice a day, the old man following
with a slender yellow forefinger on his own copy; but it was not
the life he was looking for. ("If he doesn't understand English, what's the good of reading English to him?" he had asked
when the job was first explained to him; and they had made him
understand that the old man knew "reading" English, having
taught himself from a dictionary, but did not know how to pro-
nounce it. He wanted to listen to it spoken by an Englishman.)

26

No, it had not been for him.   It had been like living in a film set.

So he had gone as cook to a collection of botanists.   And as he was packing to go the butler had said consolingly: "Better you go, after all.   If you stay his mistress poison you."

It was the first he had heard of a mistress.

He had cooked his way steadily to the New Mexico border. That was the easy way into the States: where there was no river to stop you.   He enjoyed this absurd, brilliant, angular country but, like the old aristocrat's home near Tampico, it was not what he was looking for.

After that it had been a slow crescendo of satisfaction.

Assistant cook for that outfit at Las Cruces.   Their intolerance of any variation from the food they knew, and their delight in his accent.   ("Say it again, Limey."   And then their laughter and their delighted "Whaddya know!")

Cook to the Snake River round-up.   And his discovery of horses.   And the feeling it gave him of having come home.

Riding herd for the Santa Clara.   And the discovery that "ornery" horses were less ornery when ridden by the limey kid.

A spell with the shoesmith at the Wilson ranch.   He had had his first girl there, but it hadn't been half as exciting as seeing what he could do with the "hopeless lot" in the corral.   "Nothing but shooting for them," the boss had said.   And when he had suggested trying to do something about them, the boss had said unenthusiastically: "Go ahead; but don't expect me to pay hospital bills.   You're hired as help to the farrier."

It was from that lot that Smoky came: his beautiful Smoky. The boss gave it him as a reward for what he had done with the hard cases.   And when he went to the Lazy Y he took Smoky with him.

Breaking horses for the Lazy Y.   That had been happiness. That had been happiness full up and running over.   Nearly two years of it.

And then.   That momentary slowness on his part; drowsy with heat or dazzled by the sun.   And seeing the writhing brown back turning over on him.   And hearing his thigh-bone crack.

The hospital at Edgemont.   It had not been at all like the hospitals in films.   There were no pretty nurses and no handsome internes.   The ward had sage-green walls, the fittings were old and dingy, and the nurses overworked. They alternately spoiled and ignored him.

The sudden stoppage of letters from the boys.

The sweat-making business of learning to walk again, and the slow realisation that his leg had mended "short". That he was going to be permanently lame.

The letter from the boss that put an end to the Lazy Y.

Oil. They had struck oil. The first derrick was already going up not two hundred yards from the bunk house. The enclosed cheque would look after Brat till he was well again. Meanwhile, what should be done with Smoky?

What would a lame man do with a horse in an oil field?

He had cried about Smoky; lying in the dark of the ward. It was the first time he had cried about anyone.

Well, he might be too slow to break horses any more, but he would be no servant to oil. There were other ways of living with horseflesh.

The dude ranch. That had not been like the films either.

Ungainly women in unseemly clothes punishing the saddles of broken-spirited horses until he wondered that they didn't break in two.

The woman who had wanted to marry him.

She had been not at all the kind of woman you'd imagine would want a "kept man". Not fat or silly or amorous. She was thin, and tired-looking, and rather nice; and she had owned the place up the hill from the dude ranch. She would get his leg put right for him, she said. That was the bait she had offered.

The one good thing about the dude ranch was that you made money at it. He had never had so much money in his life as when he finished there. He planned to go East and spend it. And then something had happened to him. The smaller, greener country in the East, the smell of spring gardens, woke in him a nostalgia for England that dismayed him. He had no intention of going back to England for years yet.

For several restless weeks he fought the longing—it was a baby thing to want to go back—and then quite suddenly gave in. After all, he had never seen London. Going to see London was quite a legitimate reason for going to England.

And so to the back room in Pimlico and that meeting in the street.

5

HE got up and took his cigarettes from the pocket of the coat that was hanging on the back of the door.

Why hadn't he been more shocked when Loding made his suggestion?

Because he had guessed that a proposition would be coming? Because the man's face had been warning enough that his interests would be shady? Because it quite simply had nothing to do with him, was not anything that he was likely to touch?

He had not been indignant with the man; had not said: "You swine, to think of cheating your friend out of his inheritance!" or words to that effect. But then he had never been interested in other people's concerns: their sins, their griefs, or their happiness. And anyhow, you couldn't be righteous with a man whose food you were eating.

He moved over to the window and stood looking out at the dim frieze of chimney-pots against the luminous haze. He was not broke yet but he had gone the length of prospecting for a job, and the prospects were anything but encouraging. It seemed that there were far more people interested in stable jobs in England than stables to accommodate them. The horse world contracted as the horse lovers expanded. All those men who had lost their main interest in living when the cavalry was put down were still hale and active, and besieged stable entrances at the mere whiff of a vacancy.

Besides, he didn't want just to "do his two a day". If road engineering interested you you didn't pine to spend your days putting tar on the surface.

He had tried a few contacts, but none of the good places was interested in a lame stranger without references. Why should they be? They had their pick of England's best. And when he had mentioned that his experience of breaking had been in the States, that seemed to settle it. "Oh, cattle horses!" they said. They said it quite kindly and politely—he had forgotten until he came back how polite his countrymen were—but they had implied in one way or another that Western kill-or-cure methods were not theirs. Since they never said so openly he could not explain that they were not his either. And anyhow, it wouldn't have been any good. They wanted to know something about you before they took you to work with them in this country. In America, where a man moved on every so often, it was different; but here a job was for life, and what you were mattered almost as much as what you could do.

The solution, of course, was to leave the country. But the real, the insurmountable trouble was that he didn't want to go. Now that he was back he realised that what he had thought of as free, purposeless wandering had merely been a long way round on the way back to England. He had come back, not via Dieppe, but via Las Cruces and points east; that was all. He had found what he wanted when he found horses; but he had no more sense of "belonging" in New Mexico than he had at the grammar school. He had liked New Mexico better, that was all.

And better still, now that he looked at it, he liked England. He wanted to work with English horses in an English greenness on English turf.

In any case, it was much more difficult to get out of this country than to get into it, if you were broke. He had shared a table at the Coventry Street Lyons one day with a man who had been trying for eighteen months to work his passage somewhere or other. "Cards!" the little man had snarled. "That's all they ever say. Where is your card? If you don't happen to belong to the Amalgamated Union of Table-napkin Folders you can't as much as help a steward set a table. I'm just waiting to see them let a ship sink under them because no one aboard has the right card for manning a pump with."

He had looked at the Englishman's furious blue eyes and remembered the man in the Havre *bistro*. "One has also to have papers." Yes, the world was cluttered up with paper.

It was a pity that Loding's proposition was so very criminal.

Would he have listened to it with any more interest if Loding had mentioned the horses earlier?

No, of course not; that was absurd. The thing was criminal and he wouldn't touch it.

"It would be quite safe, you know," said a voice in him. "They wouldn't prosecute you even if they found out, because of the scandal. Loding said that."

"Shut up," he said. "The thing's criminal."

It might be amusing to go and see Loding act, one night.

He had never met an actor before. It would be a ne
to sit and watch the performance of someone you l
How would Loding be as a partner?

"A very clever partner, believe me," said the voice.

"A plain bad lot," he said. "I don't want any part of him."

"You don't need any part of any of it," said the voice. "You have only to go to Latchetts and say: Take a look at me. Do I remind you of anyone? I was left on a doorstep on such-and-such a date, and as from today I want a job."

"Blackmail, 'm? And how much do you think I'd enjoy a job I'd blackmailed out of anyone? Don't be silly."

"They owe you something, don't they?"

"No, they don't. Not a bean."

"Oh, come off it! You're an Ashby and you know it."

"I don't know it. There have been doubles before. Hitler had several. *Lots* of famous people have doubles. The papers are for ever printing photographs of the humble doubles of great men. They all look like the great men with the character sponged out."

"Bunk. You're an Ashby. Where did you get your way with horses?"

"Lots of people have a way with horses."

"There were sixty-two kids at that orphanage, and did any of them go about spurning good jobs, and adoption by rich parents, so that they could find their way to horses?"

"I didn't know I was looking for horses."

"Of course you didn't know. Your Ashby blood knew."

"Oh, shut up."

Tomorrow he would go down to Lewes and have a go at that jumping stable. He might be lame but he could still ride any-thing on four legs. They might be interested in someone who could ride at ten stone and didn't mind risking his neck.

"Risk your neck when you might be living in clover?"

"If it was clover I wanted I could have had it long ago."

"Ah, but not clover with horses in it."

"Shut up. You're wasting your time."

He began to undress, as if movement might put an end to the voice. Yes; he would go down to Lewes. It was a little too near his calf country, but no one would recognise him after those six years. It wouldn't really matter, of course, if they did; but he didn't want to go backwards.

31

"You could always say: Sorry, my name is Ashby," mocked the voice.

"Will you be quiet!"

As he hung his jacket over the back of the chair he thought about that young Ashby who had bowed out. With everything in the world to live for he had gone and thrown himself off a cliff. It didn't make sense. Did parents matter all that much?

"No, he was a poor thing, and you'd make a much better job of Latchetts in his place."

He poured cold water into the basin and washed vigorously; an orphanage training being almost as lasting as a Regular Service one. And as he towelled himself on the thin turkish—so old that it was limp-wet before he was dry—he thought: "I wouldn't like it, anyhow. Butlers, and things." His idea of English middle-class life being derived from American films.

Anyhow, the thing was unthinkable.

And he'd better stop thinking about it.

Someone had said that if you thought about the unthinkable long enough it became quite reasonable.

But he would go sometime and see those photographs of Loding's. There was no harm in that.

He must see what his "twin" looked like.

He didn't like Loding much, but just going to see him could do no harm, and he did want to see photographs of Latchetts.

Yes, he would go to see Loding.

The day after tomorrow perhaps; after he had been to Lewes. Or even tomorrow.

6

MR SANDAL, of Cosset, Thring and Noble, was nearing the end of his afternoon's work and his mind was beginning its daily debate as to whether it should be the 4.55 or the 5.15 that should bear him home. This was almost the only debate that ever exercised Mr Sandal's mind. The clients of Cosset, Thring and Noble were of two kinds only: those who made up their own minds about a problem and told their solicitors in firm tones what they wanted done, and those who had no problems. The even pulse of the Georgian office in the shadow of the plane trees was never quickened by unexpected news or untoward happenings. Even the death of a client was not news: clients were expected to die; the appropriate will would be in the appropriate deed-box and things would go on as before.

Family solicitors; that is what Cosset, Thring and Noble were. Keepers of wills and protectors of secrets; but not wrestlers with problems. Which is why Mr Sandal was by no means the best person to take what was coming to him.

"Is that all, Mercer?" he said to his clerk, who had been showing a visitor out.

"There's one client in the waiting-room, sir. Young Mr Ashby."

"Ashby? Of Latchetts?"

"Yes, sir."

"Oh, good; good. Bring in a pot of tea, Mercer, will you?"

"Yes, sir." And to the client: "Will you come in, sir?"

The young man came in.

"Ah, Simon, my dear boy," Mr Sandal said, shaking hands with him, "I am delighted to see you. Are you up on business, or are you just——"

His voice died away uncertainly, and he stared, the gesture of his arm towards a chair arrested mid-way.

"God bless my soul," he said, "you are not Simon."

"No. I am not Simon."

"But—but you *are* an Ashby."

"If you think that, it makes things a whole lot easier for me."

"Yes? Do forgive me if I am a little confused. I didn't know that there were Ashby cousins."

"There aren't, as far as I know."

"No? Then—forgive me—which Ashby are you?"

"Patrick."

Mr Sandal's neat mouth opened and shut like a goldfish's.

He stopped being a green thought in a green shade and became a very worried and staggered little lawyer.

For a long moment he looked into the light Ashby eyes so near his own without finding any words that seemed adequate to the occasion.

"I think we had better both sit down," he said at last. He indicated the visitors' chair, and subsided into his own with an air of being glad of an anchorage in a world suddenly at sea.

"Now, let us clarify the situation," he said. "The only Patrick Ashby died at the age of thirteen, some—let me see—eight years ago, it must be."

"What makes you think he died?"

"He committed suicide, and left a farewell note."

"Did the note mention suicide?"

"I am afraid I cannot recall the wording."

"Nor can I, exactly. But I give you the sense of it. It said: 'I can't stand it any longer. Don't be angry with me.'"

"Yes. Yes, that was the tenor of the message."

"And where in that is the mention of suicide?"

"The suggestion surely is—one would naturally infer—the letter was found on the cliff-top with the boy's coat."

"The cliff path is the short cut to the harbour."

"The harbour? You mean——"

"It was a running-away note; not a suicide one."

"But—but the coat?"

"You can't leave a note on the open down. The only way to leave it is in the pocket of something."

"Are you seriously suggesting that—that—that you are Patrick Ashby, and that you never committed suicide at all?"

The young man looked at him with those unrevealing eyes of his. "When I came in," he said, "you took me for my brother."

"Yes. They were twins. Not identical twins, but of course very——" The full implication of what he was saying came home to him. "God bless my soul, so I did. So I did."

He sat for a moment or two staring in a helpless fashion. And while he stared Mercer came in with the tea.

"Do you take tea?" Mr Sandal asked, the question being merely a reflex conditioned by the presence of the tea-tray.

"Thank you," said the young man. "No sugar."

"You do realise, don't you," Mr Sandal said, half-appealingly, "that such a very startling and—and serious claim must be investigated? One cannot, you understand, merely accept your statement."

"I don't expect you to."

"Good. That is good. Very sensible of you. At some later date it may be possible—the fatted calf—but just now we have to be sensible about it. You do see that. Milk?"

"Thank you."

"For instance: you ran away, you say. Ran away to sea, I take it."

"Yes."

"On what ship?"

"The *Ira Jones*. She was lying in Westover harbour."

"You stowed away, of course."

"Yes."

"And where did the ship take you?" asked Mr Sandal, making notes and beginning to feel that he wasn't doing so badly after all. This was quite the worst situation he had ever been in, and there was no question of catching the 5.15 now.

"The Channel Islands. St Helier."

"Were you discovered on board?"

"No."

"You disembarked at St Helier, undiscovered?"

"Yes."

"And there?"

"I got the boat to St Malo."

"You stowed away again?"

"No, I paid my fare."

"You remember what the boat was called?"

"No; it was the regular ferry service."

"I see. And then?"

"I went bus-riding. Buses always seemed to me more exciting than that old station-wagon at Latchetts, but I never had a chance of riding in them."

"The station-wagon. Ah, yes," said Mr Sandal; and wrote: "Remembers car." "And then?"

"Let me see. I was garage-boy for a while at an hotel in a place called Villedieu."

"You remember the name of the hotel, perhaps?"

"The Dauphin, I think. From there I went across country and fetched up in Havre. In Havre I got a job as galley-boy on a tramp steamer."

"The name? You remember it?"

"I'll never forget it! She was called the *Barfleur*. I joined her as Farrar. F-a-r-r-a-r. I stayed with her until I left her in Tampico. From there I worked my way north to the States. Would you like me to write down for you the places I worked at in the States?"

"That would be very kind of you. Here is—ah, you have a pen. If you would just write them here, in a list. Thank you. And you came back to England——?"

"On the 2nd of last month. On the *Philadelphia*. As a passenger. I took a room in London and have lived there ever since. I'll write the address for you; you'll want to check that too."

"Yes. Thank you. Yes." Mr Sandal had an odd feeling that it was this young man—who after all was on trial, so to speak—who was dominating the situation and not, as it certainly should be, himself. He pulled himself together.

"Have you attempted to communicate with your—I mean, with Miss Ashby?"

"No, is it difficult?" said the young man gently.

"What I mean is——"

"I've done nothing about my family, if that is what you mean. I thought this was the best way."

"Very wise. Very wise." There he was again, being forced into the position of chorus. "I shall get in touch with Miss Ashby at once, and inform her of your visit."

"Tell her that I'm alive, yes."

"Yes. Quite so." Was the young man making fun of him? Surely not.

"Meanwhile you will go on living at this address?"

"Yes, I shall be there." The young man got up, again taking the initiative from him.

"If your credentials prove to be good," Mr Sandal said with an attempt at severity, "I shall be the first to welcome you back to England and to your home. In spite of the fact that your desertion of it has caused deep grief to all concerned. I find it inexplicable that you should not have communicated with your people before now."

"Perhaps I liked being dead."

"Being dead!"

"Anyhow you never did find me very explicable, did you?"

"Didn't I?"

"You thought it was because I was afraid that I cried, that day at Olympia, didn't you?"

"Olympia?"

"It wasn't, you know. It was because the horses were so beautiful."

"Olympia! You mean . . . But that was . . . You remember, then——"

"I expect you'll let me know, Mr Sandal, when you have checked my statements."

"What? Oh, yes; yes, certainly." Good heavens, even he himself had forgotten that children's party at the Tournament.

Perhaps he had been altogether too cautious. If this young man—the owner of Latchetts—dear me! Perhaps he should not have been so——

"I hope you don't think——" he began.

But the young man was gone, letting himself out with cool decision and a brief nod to Mercer.

Mr Sandal sat down in the inner office and mopped his brow.

And Brat, walking down the street, was shocked to find himself exhilarated. He had expected to be nervous and a little ashamed. And it had not been in the least like that. It had been one of the most exciting things he had ever done. A wonderful, tight-rope sort of thing. He had sat there and lied and not even been conscious that he was lying, it had been so thrilling. It was like riding a rogue; you had the same wary, strung-up feeling; the same satisfaction in avoiding an unexpected movement to destroy you. But nothing he had ever ridden had given him the mental excitement, the subsequent glow of achievement, that this had given him. He was drunk with it.

And greatly surprised.

So this, he thought, was what sent criminals back to their old ways when there was no material need. This breathless, step-picking excitement; this subsequent intoxication of achievement.

He went to have tea, according to Loding's instructions; but he could not eat. He felt as if he had already had food and drink. No previous experience of his had had this oddly satisfying effect. Normally, after the exciting things of life—riding, love-making, rescue, close calls—he was ravenously hungry. But now he just sat and looked at the food in front of him in a daze of content. The glow inside him left no room for food.

No one had followed him into the restaurant, and no one seemed to be taking any interest in him.

He paid his bill and went out. No one was loitering anywhere; the pavement was one long stream of hurrying people. He went to a telephone at Victoria.

"Well?" said Loding. "How did it go?"

"Wonderful."

"Have you been drinking?"

"No. Why?"

"That is the first time I have ever heard you use a superlative."

"I'm just pleased."

"My God, you must be. Does it show?"

"Show?"

"Is there any faint change in that poker face of yours?"

"How should I know? Don't you want to know about this afternoon?"

"I already know the most important thing."

"What is that?"

"You haven't been given in charge."

"Did you expect me to be?"

"There was always the chance. But I didn't really expect it. Not with our combined intelligences."

"Thanks."

"Did the old boy fall on your neck?"

"No. He nearly fell over. He's being very correct."

"Everything to be verified."

"Yes."

"How did he receive you?"

"He took me for Simon."

He heard Loding's amused laughter.

"Did you manage to use his Tournament party?"

"Yes."

"Oh, my God, don't go monosyllabic on me. You didn't have to rake it up, did you?"

"No. It fitted very neatly."

"Was he impressed?"

"It had him on the ropes."

"It didn't convince him, though?"

"I didn't wait to see. I was on my way out."

"You mean, that was your exit line? My boy, I take off my hat to you. You're a perishing marvel. After living in your pocket for the last fortnight I thought I was beginning to know you. But you're still surprising me to death."

"I surprise myself, if it's any consolation to you."

"I don't detect any bitterness in that line, do I?"

"No. Just surprise. Neat."

"Ah, well; we shall not be meeting for some time to come. It has been a privilege to know you, my boy. I shall never hear Kew Gardens mentioned without thinking tenderly of you. And I look forward, of course, to further privileges from knowing you in the future. Meanwhile, don't ring me up unless there is absolutely no alternative. You are as well briefed as I can make you. From now on you're on your own."

Loding was right: it had been a wonderful briefing. For a whole fortnight, from early morning till seven in the evening, rain or shine, they had sat in Kew Gardens and rehearsed the ways of Latchetts and Clare, the histories of Ashbys and Ledinghams, the lie of a land he had never seen. And that too had been exciting. He had always been what they called "good at exams"; and had always come to an examination paper with the same faint pleasure that an addict brings to a quiz party. And those fourteen days in Kew Gardens had been one glorified quiz party. Indeed, the last few days had had some of the tight-rope excitement that had characterised this afternoon. "Which arm did you bowl with?" "Go to the stables from the side door." "Did you sing?" "Could you play the piano?" "Who lived in the lodge at Clare?" "What colour was your mother's hair?" "How did your father make his money, apart from the estate?" "What was the name of his firm?" "What was your favourite food?" "The name of the tuck-shop owner in the village?" "Where is the Ashby pew in the church?" "Go from the great drawing-room to the butler's pantry in Clare." "What was the housekeeper's name?" "Could you ride a bicycle?" "What do you see from the south window in the attic?" Loding fired the questions at him through the long days, and it had been first amusing and then exciting to avoid being stumped.

Kew had been Loding's idea. "Your life since you came to London must be subject to the most searching scrutiny, if you will forgive the cliché. So you can't come and live with me as I suggested. You can't even be seen with me by anyone we know. Nor can I come to your Pimlico place. You must go on being unvisited there as you have been up till now." So the Kew scheme had been evolved. Kew Gardens, Loding said, had perfect cover and a wonderful field of fire. There was nowhere in London where you could see approaching figures at such a distance and still be unnoticed yourself. Nowhere in London that offered the variety of meeting-places, the undisturbed quiet, that Kew did.

So each morning they had arrived separately, by different gates; had met at a new point and gone to a different region;

and there for a fortnight Loding had primed him with photographs, maps, plans, drawings, and pencilled diagrams. He had begun with a one-inch Ordnance Survey map of Clare and its surroundings, progressed to a larger size, and thence to plans of the house; so that it was rather like coming down from above in a plane. First the lie of the country, then the details of fields and gardens, and then the close-up of the house so that the thing was whole in his mind from the beginning, and the details had merely to be painted on a picture already etched. It was methodical, careful teaching, and Brat appreciated it.

But the highlight, of course, was provided by the photographs. And it was not, oddly enough, the photograph of his "twin" that held his attention once he had seen them all. Simon, of course, was extraordinarily like him; and it gave him a strange, almost embarrassed, feeling to look at the pictured face so like his own. But it was not Simon who held his interest; it was the child who had not lived to grow up; the boy whose place he was going to take. He had an odd feeling of identity with Patrick.

Even he himself noticed this, and found it strange. He should have been filled with guilt when he considered Patrick. But his only emotion was one of partisanship; almost of alliance.

Crossing the courtyard at Victoria after telephoning, he wondered what had prompted him to say that about Patrick crying. Loding had told him merely that Patrick had cried for no known reason (he was seven then) and that old Sandal had been disgusted and had never taken the children out again. Loding had left the story with him to be used as and when he thought fit. What had prompted him to say that Patrick had cried because the horses were so beautiful? Was that, perhaps, why Patrick *had* cried?

Well, there was no going back now, whether he wanted to or not. That insistent voice that had talked to him in the dark of his room had fought for its head and got it. All he could do was sit in the saddle and hope for the best. But at least it would be a breath-taking ride; a unique, heart-stopping ride. Danger to life and limb he was used to; but far more exciting was this new mental danger, this pitting of wits.

This danger to his immortal soul, the orphanage would call it. But he had never believed in his immortal soul.

He couldn't go to Latchetts as a blackmailer, he wouldn't go as a suppliant, he would damn well go as an invader.

7

THE telegraph wires swooped and the earth whirled round the carriage window; and Bee's mind swooped and whirled with them.

"I would have come down to see you, of course," Mr Sandal had said on the telephone. "It is against all my principles to deal with such grave matters by telephone. But I was afraid that my presence might suggest to the children that there was something serious afoot. And it would be a pity to upset them if there is a chance that—that the trouble is temporary."

Poor dear old Sandal. He had been very kind; had asked her if she were sitting down, before he broke the news; and had said: "You're not feeling faint, are you, Miss Ashby?" when his shock had been administered.

She had not fainted. She had sat for a long time letting her knees get back their strength, and then she had gone to her room and looked for photographs of Patrick. Except for a studio group taken when Simon and Patrick were ten and Eleanor nine, she seemed to have nothing. She was not a snap-shot-keeper.

Nora had been a passionate collector of her children's photographs, but she had spurned photograph albums, which she held to be "a great waste of time and space". (Nora had never wasted anything; it had been as if she was half conscious that her allotted time was short.) She had kept them all in a tattered and bursting manila envelope with O.H.M.S. on it, and the envelope went everywhere with her. It had gone to Europe on that holiday with her, and had made part of that blaze on the Kent coast.

Balked of photographs, Bee went up to the old nursery, as if there she would get nearer to the child Patrick, although she knew very well that nothing of Patrick's remained there. Simon had burned them all. It was the only sign he had given that his twin's death was more than he could well bear. Simon had gone away to school after Patrick's death, and when he came back for the summer holidays he had behaved normally, if one took it for granted that not mentioning Patrick was in the circumstances normal enough. And then one day Bee had come on him tending a bonfire where the children had made their "Red Indian" and camp-fires, beyond the shrubbery, and on the fire were Patrick's toys and other small belongings. Even exercise books, she noticed, had been brought down to feed the flames. Books and childish paintings and the silly horse that had hung at the end of his bed; Simon was burning them all.

He had been furious when he saw her. He had moved between her and the fire, standing at bay, as it were, and glared at her.

"I don't want them around," he said, almost shouting.

"I understand, Simon," she had said, and had gone away.

So there was nothing of Patrick in the old nursery under the eaves; and not very much of the other children, after all. When this had been Bee's own nursery it had been ugly and individual and furnished largely with rejections from the other parts of the house. It had patterned linoleum, and a rag rug, and a cuckoo clock, and crazy basket chairs, and a clotheshorse, and a deal table covered with a red rep tablecloth trimmed with bobbles and marked with inkstains; and coloured prints of "Bubbles" and similar masterpieces hung against a cabbage-rose wallpaper. But Nora had done it over, so that it became an illustration from a homemaker magazine, in powder-blue and white, with a wallpaper of nursery-rhyme characters. Only the cuckoo clock had stayed.

The children had been happy there, but had left no mark on it. Now that it was empty and tidy, it looked just like something in a furniture shop window.

She had gone back to her own room, baffled and sick at heart, and had packed a small bag for her use in the morning. Tomorrow she must go up to town and face this new emergency in the history of the Ashbys.

"Do you believe, yourself, that it is Patrick?" she had asked.

But Mr Sandal could give her no assurance.

"He has not the air of a pretender," he allowed. "And if he is not Patrick, then who is he? The Ashby family resemblance has always been abnormally strong. And there is no other son of this generation."

"But Patrick would have written," she said.

That is the thought she always went back to. Patrick would

never have left her in grief and doubt all those years. Patrick would have written. It couldn't be Patrick.

Then if it wasn't Patrick, who *was* it?

Round and round went her mind, swooping and whirling.

"You will be the best judge," Mr Sandal had said. "Of those now living you are the one who knew the boy best."

"There is Simon," she had said.

"But Simon was a boy at the time and boys forget, don't they? You were grown up."

So the onus was being put upon her. But how was *she* to know? She who had loved Patrick but now could hardly remember what he looked like at thirteen. What test would there be?

Or would she know at once when she saw him that he was Patrick? Or that he—wasn't?

And if he wasn't and yet insisted that he was, what would happen? Would he bring a claim? Make a court action of it? Drag them all through the publicity of the daily Press?

And if he was Patrick, what of Simon? How would he take the resurrection of a brother he had not seen for eight years? The loss of a fortune. Would he be glad about it, fortune or no, or would he hate his brother?

The coming-of-age celebrations would have to be postponed, that was clear. They were much too close now for anything to be decided by that time. What excuse should they make?

But oh, if it *could*, by some miracle, be Patrick, she would be free of that haunting horror, that thought of the boy who regretted too late to come back.

Her mind was still swooping and swirling as she climbed the stairs to the offices of Cosset, Thring and Noble.

"Ah, Miss Ashby," Mr Sandal said. "This is a shocking dilemma. A most unprecedented—— Do sit down. You must be exhausted. A dreadful ordeal for you. Sit down, sit down. Mercer, some tea for Miss Ashby."

"Did he say why he didn't write, all those years?" she asked; this being the all-important thing in her mind.

"He said something about 'perhaps preferring to be dead'."

"Oh."

"A psychological difficulty, no doubt," Mr Sandal said, proffering comfort.

"Then you believe it *is* Patrick?"

"I mean, if it is Patrick, his 'preferring to be dead' would no

43

doubt arise from the same psychological difficulty as did his running away."

"Yes. I see. I suppose so. Only—it is so unlike Patrick. Not to write, I mean."

"It was unlike Patrick to run away."

"Yes; there is that. He certainly wasn't a runner-away by nature. He was a sensitive child but very brave. Something must have gone very wrong." She sat silent for a moment. "And now he is back."

"We hope so; we hope so."

"Did he seem quite normal to you?"

"Excessively," said Mr Sandal, with a hint of dryness in his tone.

"I looked for photographs of Patrick, but there is nothing later than this." She produced the studio group. "The children had studio portraits taken regularly every three years, from the time they were babies. This was the last of them. The new one would have been taken in the summer of the year Bill and Nora were killed; the year Patrick—disappeared. Patrick is ten there."

She watched while Mr Sandal studied the small immature face.

"No," he said at last. "It is impossible to say anything from so early a photograph. As I said before, the family likeness is very strong. At that age they are just young Ashbys, aren't they? Without any great individuality." He looked up from studying the photograph and went on: "I am hoping that when you yourself see the boy—the young man—you will have no doubt one way or another. After all, it is not entirely a matter of likeness, this recognition, is it? There is an aura of—of personality."

"But—but if I am not sure? What is to happen if I am not sure?"

"About that: I think I have found a way out. I dined last night with my young friend Kevin Macdermott."

"The K.C.?"

"Yes. I was greatly distressed, of course, and told him of my difficulty, and he comforted me greatly by assuring me that identification would be a quite simple matter. It was merely an affair of teeth."

"Teeth? But Patrick had quite ordinary teeth."

"Yes, yes. But he had no doubt seen a dentist, and dentists

44

have records. Indeed, most dentists have a sort of visual memory, I understand, of mouths they have treated—a very grim thought—and would almost recognise one at sight. But the record will certainly show——" He caught the look on Bee's face and paused. "What is the matter?"

"The children went to Hammond."

"Hammond? Well? That is simple, isn't it? If you don't definitely identify the boy as Patrick, we have only to——" He broke off. "Hammond!" he said quietly. "Oh!"

"Yes," Bee said, agreeing with the tone of the monosyllable.

"Dear me, how unfortunate. How very unfortunate."

Into the subsequent silence Mr Sandal said miserably: "I think I ought to tell you that Kevin Macdermott thinks the boy is lying."

"What could Mr Macdermott possibly know about it?" said Bee angrily. "He has not even seen him!" And as Mr Sandal went on sitting in miserable silence, "Well?"

"It was only Kevin's opinion on the hypothesis."

"I know, but why did he think that?"

"He said it was a—a 'phoney thing to come straight to a lawyer'."

"What nonsense! It was a very sensible thing to do."

"Yes. That was his point. It was too sensible. Too pat. Everything, Kevin said, was too pat for his liking. He said a boy coming home after years away would go home."

"Then he doesn't know Patrick. That is just what Patrick would have done: broken it gently by going to the family lawyer first. He was always the most thoughtful and unselfish of creatures. I don't think much of the clever Mr Macdermott's analysis."

"I felt it only right to tell you everything," Mr Sandal said, still miserably.

"Yes, of course," Bee said kindly, recovering her temper. "Did you tell Mr Macdermott that Patrick—that the boy had remembered crying at Olympia? I mean, that he had volunteered the information."

"I did; yes."

"And he still thought the boy was lying?"

"That was part of the 'patness' he professed not to like."

Bee gave a small snort. "What a mind!" she said. "I suppose that is what a court practice does."

"It is a detached mind, that is all. One not emotionally

engaged in the matter, as we are. It behoves us to keep our minds detached."

"Yes, of course," Bee said, sobered. "Well, now that poor old Hammond is to be no help to us—they never found him, did you know? Everything was just blown to dust."

"Yes. Yes, so I heard; poor fellow."

"Now that we have no physical evidence, I suppose we have to rely on the boy's own story. I mean, on checking it. I suppose that can be done."

"Oh, quite easily. It is all quite straightforward, with dates and places. That is what Kevin found so—— Yes. Yes. Of course it can be checked. And of course I am sure that it *will* check. He would not have offered us information which would be proved nonsense."

"So really there is nothing to wait for."

"No, I—— No."

Bee braced herself.

"Then how soon can you arrange for me to meet him?"

"Well—I have been thinking about it, and I don't think, you know, that it should be arranged at all."

"What?"

"What I should like to do—with your permission and co-operation—would be to, as it were, walk in on him. Go and see him unannounced. So that you would see him as he is and not as he wants you to see him. If we made an appointment here at the office, he would——"

"Yes, I see. I understand. I agree to that. Can we go now?"

"I don't see why not. I really don't see why not," Mr Sandal said in that regretful tone that lawyers use when they cannot see any reason why not. "There is, of course, the chance that he may be out. But we can at least go and see. Ah, here is your tea! Will you drink it while Mercer asks Simpson to ask Willett to get us a taxi?"

"You haven't got anything stronger, have you?" Bee asked.

"I'm afraid not; I'm afraid not. I have never succumbed to the transatlantic custom of the bottle in the office. But Willett will get you anything you may——"

"Oh, no, thank you; it's all right. I'll drink the tea. They say the effects are much more lasting, anyway."

Mr Sandal looked as though he would like to pat her encouragingly on the shoulder, but could not make up his mind to it. He was really a very kind little man, she thought, but just—just not much of a *prop*.

"Did he explain why he chose the name Farrar?" she asked, when they were seated in the taxi.

"He didn't explain anything," Mr Sandal said, falling back on his dry tone.

"Did you gather that he was badly off?"

"He did not mention money, but he seemed very well-dressed in a slightly un-English fashion."

"There was no suggestion of a loan?"

"Oh, no. Oh, dear me, no."

"Then he hasn't come back just because he is broke," Bee said, and felt somehow pleased. She sat back and relaxed a little. Perhaps everything was going to be all right.

"I have never quite understood why Pimlico descended so rapidly in the social scale," said Mr Sandal, breaking the silence as they travelled down the avenues of pretentious porches. "It has fine wide streets, and little through-traffic, and no more smuts than its neighbours. Why should the well-to-do have deserted it and yet stayed in Belgravia? Very puzzling."

"There is a sort of suction about desertion," Bee said, trying to meet him on the small-talk level. "The local Lady Almighty occasions the draught by leaving, and the rest, in descending order of importance, follow in her wake. And the poorer people flood in from either side to fill the vacuum. Is this the place?"

Her dismay took possession of her again as she looked at the dismal front of the house; at the peeling paint and the stained stucco, the variety of drab curtains at the windows, the unswept doorway and the rubbed-out house-number on the horrible pillar.

The front door was open and they walked in.

A different card on each door in the hallway proclaimed the fact that the house was let out in single rooms.

"The address is 59κ," Mr Sandal said. "I take it that κ is the number of the room."

"They begin on the ground floor and work upwards," Bee said. "This is B on my side." So they mounted.

"H," said Bee, peering at a first-floor door. "It's up the next flight."

The second floor was also the top one. They stood together

47

on the dark landing listening to the silence. He is out, she thought, he is out, and I shall have to go through all this again.

"Have you a match?" she said.

"ι and ɪ." she read on the two front-room doors.

Then it was the back one.

They stood in the dark for a moment staring at it. Then Mr Sandal moved purposively forward and knocked.

"Come in!" said a voice. It was a deep, boy's voice; quite unlike Simon's light sophisticated tones.

Bee, being half a head taller than Mr Sandal, could see over his shoulder; and her first feeling was one of shock that he should be so much more like Simon than Patrick ever was. Her mind had been filled with images of Patrick: vague, blurred images that she strove to make clear so that she could compare them with the adult reality. Her whole being had been obsessed with Patrick for the last twenty-four hours.

And now here was someone just like Simon.

The boy got up from where he had been sitting on the edge of the bed and with no haste or embarrassment pulled from off his left hand the sock he had been darning. She couldn't imagine Simon darning a sock.

"Good morning," he said.

"Good morning," said Mr Sandal. "I hope you don't mind: I've brought you a visitor." He moved aside to let Bee come in. "Do you know who this is?"

Bee's heart hammered on her ribs as she met the boy's light calm gaze and watched him identify her.

"You do your hair differently," he said.

Yes, of course; hairdressing had changed completely in those eight years; of course he would see a difference.

"You recognise her, then?" Mr Sandal said.

"Yes, of course. It's Aunt Bee."

She waited for him to come forward to greet her, but he made no move to. After a moment's pause he turned to find a seat for her.

"I'm afraid there is only one chair. It is all right if you don't lean back on it," he said, picking up one of those hard chairs with a black curved back and a tan seat with small holes in it. Bee was glad to sit down on it.

"Do you mind the bed?" he said to Mr Sandal.

"I'll stand, thank you, I'll stand," Mr Sandal said hastily.

The details of the face were not at all like Simon's, she

thought; watching the boy stick the needle carefully in the sock. It was the general impression that was the same; once you really looked at him the startling resemblance vanished, and only the family likeness remained.

"Miss Ashby could not wait for a meeting at my office, so I brought her here," Mr Sandal said. "You don't seem particularly——" He allowed the sentence to speak for itself.

The boy looked at her in a friendly unsmiling way and said: "I'm not very sure of my welcome."

It was a curiously immobile face. A face like a child's drawing, now she came to think of it. Everything in the right place and with the right proportions, but without animation. Even the mouth had the straight uncompromising line that is a child's version of a mouth.

He moved over to lay the socks on the dressing-table, and she saw that he was lame.

"Have you hurt your leg?" she asked.

"I broke it. Over in the States."

"But should you be walking about on it if it is still tender?"

"Oh, it doesn't hurt," he said. "It's just short."

"Short! You mean, permanently short?"

"It looks like it."

They were sensitive lips, she noticed, for all their thinness; they gave him away when he said that.

"But something can be done about that," she said. "It just means that it was mended badly. I expect you didn't have a very good surgeon."

"I don't remember a surgeon. Perhaps I passed out. They did all the correct things: hung weights on the end of it, and all that."

"But Pat——" she began, and failed to finish his name.

Into the hiatus he said: "You don't have to call me anything until you are sure."

"They do miracles in surgery nowadays," she said, covering her break. "How long ago is it since it happened?"

"I'd have to think. About a couple of years now, I think."

Except for the flat American _a_, his speech was without peculiarity.

"Well, we must see what can be done about it. A horse, was it?"

"Yes. I wasn't quick enough. How did you know it was a horse?"

"You told Mr Sandal that you had worked with horses. Did you enjoy that?" Just like railway-carriage small-talk, she thought.

"It's the only life I do enjoy."

She forgot about small-talk. "Really?" she said, pleased. "Were they good horses, those Western ones?"

"Most of them were commoners, of course. Very good stuff for their work—which, after all, is being a good horse, I suppose. But every now and then you come across one with blood. Some of those are beauties. More—more individual than I ever remember English horses being."

"Perhaps in England we 'manner' the individuality out of them. I hadn't thought of it. Did you have a horse of your own at all?"

"Yes, I had one. Smoky."

She noticed the change in his voice when he said it. As audible as the flat note in the cracked bell of a chime.

"A grey?"

"Yes, a dark grey with black points. Not that hard, iron colour, you know. A soft, smoky colour. When he had a tantrum he was just a whirling cloud of smoke."

A whirling cloud of smoke. She could see it. He must love horses to be able to see them like that. He must particularly have loved his Smoky.

"What happened to Smoky?"

"I sold him."

No trespassers. Very well, she would not trespass. He had probably had to sell the horse when he broke his leg.

She began to hope very strenuously that this was Patrick.

The thought recalled her to the situation which she had begun to lose sight of. She looked doubtfully at Mr Sandal.

Catching the appeal in her glance, Mr Sandal said: "Miss Ashby is no doubt prepared to vouch for you, but you will understand that the matter needs more clarification. If it were a simple matter of a prodigal's homecoming, your aunt's acceptance of you would no doubt be sufficient to restore you to the bosom of your family. But in the present instance it is a matter of property. Of the ultimate destination of a fortune. And the law will require incontrovertible evidence of your identity before you could be allowed to succeed to anything that was Patrick Ashby's. I hope you understand our position."

"I understand perfectly. I shall, of course, stay here until you have made your inquiries and are satisfied."

"But you can't stay *here*," Bee said, looking with loathing at the room and the forest of chimney-pots beyond the window.

"I have stayed in a great many worse places."

"Perhaps. That is no reason for staying here. If you need money we can give you some, you know."

"I'll stay here, thanks."

"Are you just being independent?"

"No. It's quiet here. And handy. And bung full of privacy. When you have lived in bunk houses you put a high value on privacy."

"Very well, you stay here. Is there anything else we can—can stake you to?"

"I could do with another suit."

"Very well. Mr Sandal will advance you whatever you need for that." She suddenly remembered that if he went to the Ashby tailor there would be a sensation. So she added: "And he will give you the address of his tailor."

"Why not Walters?" said the boy.

For a moment she could not speak.

"Aren't they there any more?"

"Oh, yes; but there would be too many explanations if you went to Walters." She must keep a hold on herself. Anyone could find out who the Ashby tailor had been.

"Oh, yes. I see."

She fell back on small-talk and began to take her leave.

"We have not told the family about you," she said, as she prepared to go. "We thought it better not to, until things are —are what Mr Sandal calls clarified."

A flash of amusement showed in his eyes at that. For a moment they were allied in a secret laughter.

"I understand."

She turned at the door to say good-bye. He was standing in the middle of the room watching her go, leaving Mr Sandal to shepherd her out. He looked remote and lonely. And she thought: "If this *is* Patrick, Patrick come home again, and I am leaving him like this, as if he were a casual acquaintance——" It was more than she could bear, the thought of the boy's loneliness.

She went back to him, took his face lightly in her gloved hand, and kissed his cheek. "Welcome back, my dear," she said.

8

So Cosset, Thring and Noble began their investigations, and Bee went back to Latchetts to deal with the problem of postponing the coming-of-age celebrations.

Was she to tell the children now, before the thing was certain? And if not, what excuse could she possibly put forward for not celebrating at the proper time?

Mr Sandal was against telling the children yet. The unknown Kevin's verdict had left a mark on him, it seemed; and he was entirely prepared to find a flaw in the so-complete dossier that had been handed to them. It would be inadvisable, he thought, to bring the children into this until the claim had been sifted through the finest mesh.

With that she agreed. If this thing passed—if that boy in the back room in Pimlico was not Patrick—they need never know anything about it. Simon would probably have to be told, so that he could be warned against future attempts at fraud, but by that time it would be of no more than academic interest; a quite impersonal affair. Her present difficulty was how to reconcile the children's ignorance with the postponing of the celebrations.

The person who rescued her from this dilemma was Great-uncle Charles, who cabled to announce his (long overdue) retirement, and his hope to be present at his great-nephew's coming-of-age party. He was on his way home from the Far East, and, since he refused to fly, his home-coming was likely to be a protracted one, but he hoped Simon would keep the champagne corked till he came.

Great-uncles do not normally cut much ice in the families in which they survive, but to the Ashbys Great-uncle Charles was much more than a great-Uncle: he was a household word. Every birthday had been made iridescent and every Christmas a tingling expectation by the thought of Great-uncle Charles's present. There were reasonable bounds to the possible presents of parents; and Father Christmas's were merely the answer to indents.

But neither reason nor bounds had any connection with presents from Great-uncle Charles. Once he had sent a set of chopsticks, which upset nursery discipline for a week. And once it had been the skin of a snake; the glory of owning the skin of a snake had made Simon dizzy for days. And Eleanor still ran to and from her bath in a pair of odd-smelling leather slippers that had come on her twelfth birthday. At least four times every year Great-uncle Charles became the most important factor in the Ashby family; and when you have been of first importance four times a year for twenty years your importance is pretty considerable. Simon might grumble and the others protest a little, but they would without doubt wait for Great-uncle Charles.

Besides, she had a shrewd idea that Simon would not be willing to offend the last-surviving Ashby of his generation. Charles was not rich—he had been far too liberal a giver all his life—but he was comfortably off; and Simon, for all his careless good nature and easy charm, was an exceedingly practical person.

So the postponement was taken by the family with resignation, and by Clare with equanimity. It was held to be a very proper thing that the Ashbys should wait until the old boy could be present. Bee spent her after-dinner leisure altering the date on the invitation cards, and thanking heaven for the mercifulness of chance.

Bee was at odds with herself these days. She wanted this boy to be Patrick; but it would be so much better for all concerned, she felt, if he proved not to be Patrick. Seven-eighths of her wanted Patrick back; warm, and alive, and dear; wanted it passionately. The other eighth shrank from the upheaval of the happy Ashby world that his return would bring with it. When she caught this renegade eighth at its work she reproved it and was suitably ashamed of herself; but she could not destroy it. And so she was distrait and short-tempered, and Ruth, commenting on it to Jane, said:

"Do you think she can have a Secret Sorrow?"

"I expect the books won't balance," Jane said. "She's a very bad adder-up."

Mr Sandal reported from time to time on the progress of the investigations, and the reports were uniform and monotonous. Everything seemed to confirm the boy's story.

"The most heartening thing, using the word in its sense of reassurance," Mr Sandal said, "is that the young man seems to have no contacts since he came to England. He has lived at that address since the *Philadelphia's* arrival, and he has had neither letters nor visitors. The woman who owns the house occupies one of the front rooms on the ground floor. She is one of those women who has nothing to do but sit back and watch her neighbours. The lives of her tenants seem to be an open book to the good lady. She is also accustomed to waiting for the postman and collecting the letters he drops. Nothing escapes her. Her description of myself was, I understand, hardly flattering but quite touching in its fidelity. The young man could therefore have hardly had visitors without her being aware of it. He was out all day, of course; as any young man in London would be. But there is no trace of that intimacy which would suggest connivance. He had no friends."

The young man came willingly to the office and answered questions freely. With Bee's consent, Kevin Macdermott had "sat in" at one of these office conferences, and even Kevin had been shaken. "What shakes me," Kevin had said, "is not the fellow's knowledge of the subject—all good con men are glib—but the general cut of his jib. He's quite frankly not what I expected. After a little while in my job you develop a smell for a wrong 'un. This chap has me baffled. He doesn't smell like a crook to me, and yet the set-up stinks."

So the day came when Mr Sandal announced to Bee that Cosset, Thring and Noble were now prepared to accept the claimant as Patrick Ashby, the eldest son of William Ashby of Latchetts, and to hand over to him everything that was due to him. There would be legal formalities, of course, since the fact of his death eight years ago had been presumed; but they would be automatic. As far as they, Cosset, Thring and Noble, were concerned, Patrick Ashby was free to go home whenever he pleased.

So the moment had come, and Bee was faced with breaking the news to the family.

Her instinct was to tell Simon first, privately; but she felt that anything that set him apart from the others in this matter of welcoming back his brother was to be avoided. It would be better to take for granted that for Simon, as for the others, the news would be a matter for unqualified happiness.

It was after lunch on a Sunday that she told them.

"I have something to tell you that will be rather a shock to you. But a nice kind of shock," she said. And went on from there. Patrick had not committed suicide, as they had thought.

54

He had merely run away. And now he had come back. He had been living for a little in London because, of course, he had to prove to the lawyers that he was Patrick. But he had had no difficulty in doing that. And now he was going to come home.

She had avoided looking at their faces as she talked; it was easier just to talk into space, impersonally. But in the startled silence that followed her story she looked across at Simon; and for a moment did not recognise him. The shrunk white face with the blazing eyes had no resemblance to the Simon she knew. She looked away hastily.

"Does it mean that this new brother will get all the money that is Simon's?" asked Jane, with her usual lack of finesse.

"Well, I think it was a horrible thing to do," Eleanor said bluntly.

"What was?"

"Running away and leaving us all thinking he was dead."

"He didn't know that, of course. I mean: that we would take his note to mean that he was going to kill himself."

"Even so. He left us all without a word for—for—how long is it? Seven years? Nearly eight years. And then comes back one day without warning, and expects us to welcome him."

"Is he nice?" asked Ruth.

"What do you mean by nice?" Bee asked, glad for once of Ruth's interest in the personal.

"Is he nice to look at? And does he talk nicely or has he a frightful accent?"

"He is exceedingly nice to look at, and he has no accent whatsoever."

"Where has he been all this time?" Eleanor asked.

"Mexico and the States, mostly."

"Mexico!" said Ruth. "How romantic! Does he wear a black sailor hat?"

"A what? No, of course he doesn't. He wears a hat like anyone else."

"How often have you seen him, Aunt Bee?" Eleanor asked.

"Just once. A few weeks ago."

"Why didn't you tell us about it then?"

"It seemed better to wait until the lawyers were finished with him and he was ready to come home. You couldn't all go rushing up to London to see him."

"No, I suppose not. But I expect Simon would have liked to go up and see him, wouldn't you, Simon?—and we wouldn't have minded. After all, Patrick was his twin."

"I don't believe for one moment that it is Patrick," Simon said, in a tight, careful voice that was worse than shouting.

"But, Simon!" Eleanor said.

Bee sat in a dismayed silence. This was worse than she had anticipated.

"But, Simon! Aunt Bee has seen him. She must know."

"Aunt Bee seems to have adopted him."

Much worse than she had anticipated.

"The people who *have* adopted him, Simon, are Cosset, Thring and Noble. A not very emotional firm, I think you'll agree. If there had been the faintest doubt of his being Patrick, Cosset, Thring and Noble would have discovered it during those weeks. They have left no part of his life, since he left England, unaccounted for."

"Of *course* whoever it is has had a life that can be checked! What did they expect? But what possible reason can they have for believing that he is Patrick?"

"Well, for one thing, he is your double."

This was clearly unexpected. "My double?" he said vaguely.

"Yes. He is even more like you than when he went away."

The colour had come back to Simon's face and the stuff on the bones had begun to look like flesh again; but now he looked stupid, like a boxer who is taking too much punishment.

"Believe me, Simon dear," she said, "it *is* Patrick!"

"It isn't. I know it isn't. You are all being fooled!"

"But, Simon!" Eleanor said. "Why should you think that? I know it won't be easy for you to have Patrick back—it won't be easy for any of us—but there's no use making a fuss about it. The thing is there and we just have to accept it. You are only making things worse by trying to push it away."

"How did this—this creature who says he is Patrick, how did he get to Mexico? How did he leave England? And when? And where?"

"He left from Westover in a ship called the *Ira Jones*."

"Westover! Who says so?"

"He does. And according to the harbourmaster, a ship of that name did leave Westover on the night that Patrick went missing."

56

Since this seemed to leave Simon without speech, she went on: "And everything he did from then on has been checked. The hotel he worked at in Normandy is no longer there, but they have found the ship he sailed from Havre in—it's a tramp, but it belongs to a firm in Brest—and people have been shown photographs and identified him. And so on, all the way back to England. Till the day he walked into Mr Sandal's office."

"Is that how he came back?" Eleanor asked. "Went to see old Mr Sandal?"

"Yes."

"Well, I should say that proves that he is Patrick, if anyone is in any doubt about it. But I don't know why there should be doubt at all. After all, it would be very easy to catch him out if he wasn't Patrick, wouldn't it? All the family things he wouldn't know . . ."

"It *isn't* Patrick."

"It is a shock for you, Simon, my dear," Bee said, "and, as Eleanor says, it won't be easy for you. But I think it will be easier when you see him. Easier to accept him, I mean. He is so undeniably an Ashby, and so very like you."

"Patrick *wasn't* very like me."

Eleanor saved Bee from having to reply to that. "He was, Simon. Of course he was. He was your twin."

"If *I* ran away for years and years, would you believe I was me, Jane?" Ruth asked.

"You wouldn't stay away for years and years, anyhow," Jane said.

"What makes you think I wouldn't?"

"You'd come home in no time at all."

"Why would I come home?"

"To see how everyone was taking your running away."

"When is he coming, Aunt Bee?" Eleanor asked.

"On Tuesday. At least that is what we had arranged. But if you would like to put it off a little—until you grow more used to the idea, I mean . . ." She glanced at Simon, who was looking sick and baffled. In her most apprehensive moments she had never pictured a reaction as serious as this.

"If you flatter yourself that I shall grow used to the idea, you are wrong," Simon said. "It makes no difference to me when the fellow comes. As far as I'm concerned he is not Patrick and he never will be."

And he walked out of the room. Walking, Bee noticed, not very steadily, as if he were drunk.

"I've never known Simon like that before," Eleanor said, puzzled.

"I should have broken it to him differently. I'm afraid it is my fault. I just—didn't want to make him different from anyone else."

"But he loved Patrick, didn't he? Why shouldn't he be glad about it? Even a *little* glad!"

"I think it is horrid that someone can come and take Simon's place, without warning, like that," Jane said. "Simply horrid. And I don't wonder that Simon is angry."

"Aunt Bee," said Ruth, "can I wear my blue on Tuesday when Patrick comes?"

9

BEE waited until Evensong would be over, and then walked across the fields to the Rectory. Ostensibly, she was going to tell them the news; actually she was going to pour out her troubles to George Peck. When George could withdraw his mind sufficiently from the classic world to focus it on the present one, he was a comfortable person to talk to. Unemotional and unshockable. Bee supposed that an intimate acquaintance with classic on-goings, topped-off with a cure of souls in a country parish, had so conditioned him to shocks that he had long ago become immune from further attack. Neither ancient iniquity nor modern English back-sliding surprised him. So it was not to Nancy, her friend, that she was taking her unquiet heart, but to the Rector. Nancy would wrap her round with warm affection and sympathy, but it was not sympathy she needed; it was support. Besides, if she was to find understanding it would not be with Nancy, who had forgotten Patrick's very existence, but with George Peck, who would most certainly remember the boy he had taught.

So she walked in the sunlight over the fields, through the churchyard, and into the Rectory garden through the little iron gate that had caused that terrific row in 1723. Very peaceful it all was tonight, and very peaceful were the rival smiths, sleeping within twelve feet of each other over there in the corner in good

Clare earth. Some day quite soon, she thought, pausing with her hand on the delicate iron scroll, my trouble too will be just an old song; one must try to keep things in proportion. But it was her head talking to her heart, and her heart would not listen.

She found the Rector where she knew he would be. Always after Evensong it was his habit to go and stare at something in the garden; usually at something at the farther end of the garden from which he could not be too easily recalled to the trivialities of social obligation. This evening he was staring at a purple lilac and polluting the fragrant air with a pipe that smelt like a damp bonfire. "There should be a by-law against pipes like George's," his wife had said, and the present sample was no exception. It depressed Bee still further.

He glanced up as she came down the path and went back to staring at the lilac. "Wonderful colour, isn't it," he said. "Odd to think that it is just an optical illusion. What colour is a lilac when you are not looking at it, I wonder?"

Bee remembered that the Rector had once broken it to the twins that a clock does not tick if no one is in the room. She had found Ruth being surreptitious in the hall, and Ruth, when asked what this noiseless progress was occasioned by, had said that she was "trying to sneak up on the drawing-room clock." She wanted to catch it not ticking.

Bee stood by the Rector in silence for a little, looking at the glory and trying to arrange her thoughts. But they would not arrange.

"George," she said at length, "you remember Patrick, don't you?"

"Pat Ashby? Of course." He turned to look at her.

"Well, he didn't die at all. He just ran away. That is what the note meant. And he is coming back. And Simon isn't pleased." A great round shameless tear slipped out of her eye and ran down her cheek. She brushed it off her chin and went on staring at the lilac.

George extended a bony forefinger and gently speared the front of her shoulder with it.

"Sit down," he said.

She sat down on the seat behind her, under the arch of the young green honeysuckle, and the Rector sat down beside her. "Now, tell me," he said; and she told him. All the bewildering story, in the proper order and with full detail; Mr Sandal's telephone call, the journey to town, the top-floor-back in Pimlico, the investigations of Cosset, Thring and Noble, the rescue by Great-uncle Charles, the ultimate facing of the facts and announcing them to the family, the family reaction.

"Eleanor is a little cold about it, but reasonable as she always is. The thing is there and she is going to make the best of it. Jane, of course, is partisan, and sorry for Simon, but she will get over that when she meets her brother in the flesh. She is a friendly soul by nature."

"And Ruth?"

"Ruth is planning her wardrobe for Tuesday," Bee said tartly.

The Rector smiled a little. "The happy ones of the earth, the Ruths."

"But Simon . . . How can one account for Simon?"

"I don't think that that is very difficult, you know. Simon would have had to be a saint to welcome back a brother who was going to supplant him. A brother, moreover, who has been dead to him since the age of thirteen."

"But, George, his twin! They were inseparable."

"I think that thirteen is further removed from twenty-one than almost any other equidistant points in life. It is a whole lifetime away. An association that ended at thirteen has little but sentimental value for the boy of twenty-one. Latchetts has been Simon's for—what is it?—eight years; he has known for eight years that he would come into his mother's money at twenty-one; to be deprived of all that without warning would upset a stronger character than Simon's."

"I expect I did it badly," Bee said. "The way I told them, I mean. I should have told Simon first, privately. But I did so want to keep them all on the same level. To pretend that they would all be equally glad. Taking Simon apart and telling him before the others would have—would have——"

"Anticipated the trouble."

"Yes. Something like that, I suppose. I suppose I had known quite well that his reaction would be—different from the others. And I just wanted to minimise the difference. I had never imagined for a moment, you see, that his reaction would be so violent. That he would go to the length of denying that Patrick was alive."

"That is only his method of pushing the unwelcome fact away from him."

60

"Unwelcome," Bee murmured.

"Yes, unwelcome. And very naturally unwelcome. You make things difficult for yourself if you don't accept that fundamental fact. *You* remember Patrick with your adult mind, and are rejoiced that he is still alive." He turned his head to look at her. "Or—are you?"

"Of *course* I am!" she said, a shade too emphatically. But he let it go.

"Simon doesn't remember him with an adult mind or adult emotions. To Simon he is a remembered emotion; not a present one. He has no present love to fight his present—hatred with."

"Oh, George."

"Yes; it is best to face it. It would take an almost divine love to combat the resentment that Simon must be feeling now; and there has never been anything in the least divine about Simon. Poor Simon. It is a wretched thing to have happened to him."

"And at the very worst moment. When we were all ready for celebration."

"At least this is the answer to something that has puzzled me for eight years."

"What is that?"

"The fact of Patrick's suicide. I could never reconcile it with the Patrick I knew. Patrick was a sensitive child, but he had a tremendous fund of good common sense; a balance. A far better equilibrium, for instance, than the less sensitive but more brilliant Simon. He had also, moreover, a great sense of obligation. If Latchetts was suddenly and unaccountably his he might be overwhelmed to the point of running away, but not unbalanced to the point of taking his life."

"Why did we all so unquestioningly accept the suicide theory?"

"The coat on the cliff-top. The note—which did read like a suicide one, undoubtedly. The complete lack of anyone who had seen him after old Abel met him between Tanbitches and the cliff. The persistence with which suicides use that particular part of the coast for their taking-off. It was the natural conclusion to come to. I don't remember that we ever questioned it. But it had always stayed in my mind as an unaccountable thing. Not the method, but the fact that Patrick should have taken his own life. It was unlike everything I

61

knew about Patrick. And now we find that, after all, he did no such thing."

"I shut my eyes and the lilac is no colour; I open them and it is purple," Bee was saying to herself; which was her way of keeping her tears at bay. Just as she counted objects when in danger of crying at a play.

"Tell me, are you pleased with this adult Patrick who has come back?"

"Yes. Yes, I am pleased. He is in some ways very like the Patrick who went away. Very quiet. Self-contained. Very considerate. Do you remember how Patrick used to turn and say: 'Are you all right?' before he began whatever he was planning to do on his own? He still thinks of the other person. Didn't try to—rush me, or take his welcome for granted. And he still keeps his bad times to himself. Simon always came flying to one with his griefs and grievances, but Patrick dealt with his own. He seems still to be able to deal with his own."

"Has he had a bad time, then, do you think?"

"I gather it hasn't been a bed of roses. I forgot to tell you that he is lame."

"Lame!"

"Yes. Just a little. Some accident with a horse. He is still mad about horses."

"That will make you happy," George said. He said it a little wryly, being no horseman.

"Yes," agreed Bee with a faint smile for the wryness. "It is good that Latchetts should go to a real lover."

"You rate Simon as a poor lover?"

"Not poor. Indifferent, perhaps. To Simon horses are a means of providing excitement. Of enhancing his prestige. A medium for trade; for profitable dickering. I doubt if it goes further than that. For horses as—people, if you know what I mean, he has little feeling. Their sicknesses bore him. Eleanor will stay up for nights on end with a horse that is ill, sharing the nursing fifty-fifty with Gregg. The only time Simon loses sleep is when a horse he wants to ride, or jump, or hunt, has a 'leg'."

"Poor Simon," the Rector said reflectively. "Not the temperament to make a successful fight against jealousy. A very destructive emotion indeed, jealousy."

Before Bee could answer, Nancy appeared.

"Bee! How nice," she said. "Were you at Evensong, and did you see the latest contingent from our local school for scandalisers? Two adolescents who are 'studying the prevalent English superstitions': to wit, the Church of England. A boy, very hairy for fourteen, it seemed to me; and a girl with eleven combs keeping up her not very abundant wisps. What would you say a passion for combs was an indication of? A sense of insecurity?"

"Beatrice has come with a very wonderful piece of news," the Rector said.

"Don't tell me Simon has got himself engaged."

"No. It is not about Simon. It's about Patrick."

"Patrick?" Nancy said uncertainly.

"He is alive." And he told her how.

"Oh, Bee, my dear," Nancy said, putting her arms round her friend, "how glorious for you. Now you won't have to wonder any more."

That Nancy's first reaction was to remember that private nightmare of hers broke Bee down altogether.

"You need a drink," Nancy said, briskly. "Come along in and we'll finish what's left in the sherry bottle."

"A deplorable reason for drinking sherry," the Rector said.

"What is?"

"That one 'needs a drink'."

"An even more deplorable reason is that if we don't drink it Mrs Godkin will. She has had most of the rest of the bottle. Come along."

So Bee drank the Rectory sherry and listened while George enlightened Nancy on the details of Patrick Ashby's return. Now that her weight of knowledge was shared with her own generation, the burden was suddenly lighter. Whatever difficulties lay ahead, there would be George and Nancy to support and comfort her.

"When is Patrick coming?" Nancy asked; and the Rector turned to Bee.

"On Tuesday," Bee told them. "What I can't decide is the best way of spreading the news in the district."

"That's easy," Nancy said. "Just tell Mrs Gloom."

Mrs Gloom kept the sweets-tobacco-and-newspaper shop in the village. Her real name was Bloom, but her relish for disaster caused her to be known, first by the Ledingham and Ashby children, and later by all and sundry, as Mrs Gloom.

"Or you could send yourself a postcard. The post office is almost as good. That is what Jim Bowden did when he jilted the Heywood girl. Sent his mother a telegram announcing his wedding. The fuss was all over before he came back."

"I'm afraid we are going to be at the exact centre of the fuss until the nine days' wonder is over," Bee said. "One must just put up with it."

"Ah, well, my dear, it's a *nice* sort of fuss," Nancy said, comforting.

"Yes. But the situation is so—so incalculable. It's like—like——"

"I know," Nancy said, agreeing. "Like walking on jelly."

"I was going to say picking one's way over a bog, but I think the jelly is a better description."

"Or one of those uneven floors at fun fairs," the Rector said unexpectedly, as Bee took her leave.

"How do you know about fun fairs, George?" his wife asked.

"They had one at the Westover Carnival a year or two ago, I seem to remember. A most interesting study in masochism."

"You see now why I have stuck to George," Nancy said, as she walked with Bee to the garden gate. "After thirteen years I am still finding out things about him. I wouldn't have believed that he even knew what a fun fair was. Can you picture George lost in contemplation of the Giant Racer?"

But it was not of Nancy's George that she was thinking as she walked away through the churchyard, but of the fun-fair floor that she was doomed to walk in the days ahead. She turned in at the south porch of the church and found the great oak door still unlocked. The light of the sunset flooded the grey vault with warmth, and the whole building held peace as a cup holds water. She sat down on a bench by the door and listened to the silence. A companionable silence which she shared with the figures on the tombs, the tattered banners, the names on the wall, the Legion's garish Union Jack, and the slow ticking of a clock. The tombs were all Ledingham ones: from the simple dignity of the Crusader to the marble family that wept with ostentatious opulence over the eighteenth-century politician. The Ashbys had no crusaders and no opulence. Their memorials were tablets on the wall. Bee sat there and read them for the thousandth time. "Of Latchetts" was the refrain. "Of Latchetts in this parish." No field-marshals, no chancellors, no poets, no reformers. Just the yeoman simplicity of Latchetts; the small-squire sufficiency of Latchetts.

And now Latchetts belonged to this unknown boy from half a world away.

"A great sense of obligation," the Rector had said, speaking of the Patrick he remembered. And that had been the Patrick that she, too, remembered. And that Patrick would have written to them.

Always she came back to that in her mind. The Patrick they knew would never have left them in grief and doubt for eight years.

"Some psychological difficulty," Mr Sandal had said. And after all, he *had* run away. A sufficiently unlikely thing for Patrick to do. Perhaps he had been overcome by shame when he came to himself.

And yet. And yet.

That kind child who so automatically asked: "Are you all right?"

That child with the "great sense of obligation"?

10

AND while Bee sat and stared at the Ashby tablets in the church at Clare, Brat Farrar was standing in the back room in Pimlico in a brand-new suit and a state of panic.

How had he got himself into this? What could he have been thinking of? He, Brat Farrar. How did he ever think that he could go through with it? How had he ever in the first place consented to lend himself to such a plan?

It was the suit that had shocked him into realisation. The suit was wrong-doing made concrete and manifest. It was a wonderful suit. The kind of suit that he had dreamed of possessing; so unremarkable, so unmistakable once you had remarked it; English tailoring at its unobtrusive best. But he stood looking at himself in the mirror in a kind of horror.

He couldn't do it, that was all. He just couldn't do it.

He would duck, before it was too late.

He would send back the goddamned suit to the tailor, and send a letter to that woman who had been so nice, and just duck out of sight.

"What!" said the voice. "And pass up the greatest adventure of your life? The greatest adventure that has happened to any man within living memory?"

"Adventure my foot. It's plain false pretences."

They wouldn't bother to look for him. They would be too relieved to have him out of their hair. He could duck without leaving a ripple.

"And leave a fortune behind?" said the voice.

"*Yes*, and leave a fortune behind. Who wants a fortune, anyhow?"

They would have his letter to insure them against any further nuisance from his side, and they would just let him go. He would write to that woman who, because she was kind, had kissed him before she was sure, and confess, and say he was sorry, and that would be that.

"And pass up the chance of owning a stud?"

"Who wants a stud?   The world's lousy with horses."

"And you are going to own some, perhaps?"

"I may, some day.   I may."

"Pigs may fly."

"Shut up."

He would write to Loding and tell him that he would be no party to his criminal schemes.

"And waste all that knowledge? All that training?"

"I should never have started it."

"But you did start it.   You finished it.   You are primed to the gills with knowledge worth a fortune.   You can't waste it, surely?"

Loding would have to whistle for that fifty per cent. How could he ever have thought of letting himself be an instrument in the hands of a crook like Loding!

"A very amusing and intelligent crook.   On the highest level of crookery.   Nothing to be ashamed of, believe me."

He would go to a travel agency tomorrow morning and get a berth out of the country.   Anywhere out of the country.

"I thought you wanted to stay in England?"

He would put the sea between him and temptation.

"Did you say temptation?   Don't tell me that you're still wavering!"

He hadn't enough left for a fare to America, but he had enough to take him quite a distance.   The travel agency would offer him a choice of places.   The world was wide and there was a lot of fun left in it.   By Tuesday morning he would be out of England, and this time he would stay out.

"And never see Latchetts at all?"

He would find some—— "What did you say?"

"I said: And never see Latchetts at all?"

He tried to think of an answer.

"Stumped you, haven't I?"

There must be an answer.

"Money, and horses, and fun, and adventure are common change. You can have them anywhere in the world. But if you pass up Latchetts now you pass it up for good. There won't be any going back."

"But what has Latchetts to do with me?"

"You ask that? You, with your Ashby face, and your Ashby bones, and your Ashby tastes, and your Ashby colouring, and your Ashby blood."

"I haven't any evidence at all that——"

"And your Ashby blood, I said. Why, you poor little brute of a foundling, Latchetts is your belonging-place, and you have the immortal gall to pretend that you don't care a rap about it!"

"I didn't say I didn't care. Of course I care."

"But you'll walk out of this country tomorrow, and leave Latchetts behind? For always? Because that is what it amounts to, my boy. That is the choice before you. Take the road of high adventure and on Tuesday morning you will see Latchetts. Duck, and you will never see it at all."

"But I'm not a crook! I can't do something that is criminal."

"Can't you? You've been giving a pretty good imitation of it these last few weeks. And enjoying it too. Remember how you enjoyed that tight-rope business on that first visit to old Sandal? How you enjoyed all the others? Even with a K.C. sitting across the table and doing a sort of mental X-ray on you. You loved it. All that is wrong with you just now is cold feet. Nerves. You want to see Latchetts as you have never wanted anything before. You want to live at Latchetts as an Ashby. You want horses. You want adventure. You want a life in England. Go to Latchetts on Tuesday and they are all yours."

"But——"

"You came half across the world to that meeting with Loding. Was that just chance? Of course not. It was all meant. Your destiny is at Latchetts. Your destiny. What you were born for. Your destiny. At Latchetts. You're an Ashby. Half across a world to a place you never heard of. Destiny. You can't pass up destiny. . . ."

Brat got slowly out of the brand-new suit, and hung it up with orphanage neatness on its fine new hanger. Then he sat down on the edge of his bed and buried his face in his hands.

He was still sitting there when the darkness came.

11

It was a beautiful day, the day that Brat Farrar came to Latchetts, but a restless little wind kept turning the leaves over so that in spite of the sunlight and the bright air the world was filled with a vague unease and a promise of storm.

"Much too shiny!" thought Bee, looking at the landscape from her bedroom window after breakfast. "'Tears before night', as Nanny used to say of too exuberant children. However. At least he will arrive in sunshine."

She had been greatly exercised in her mind over that arrival. It was to be as informal as possible; that was a thing that was agreed to by all concerned. Someone would meet him at the station and bring him home, and there would be luncheon with only the family present. The question was: Who was to meet him? The twins had held that the whole family should go to the station, but that, of course, was not to be thought of. The prodigal could hardly be welcomed publicly on the platform at Guessgate for the entertainment of the railway staff and casual travellers between Westover and Bures. She herself could not go without giving the returning Patrick an air of being her protégé; which was something to be avoided at all costs. She had not forgotten Simon's sneer about her "adoption" of Patrick. Simon—the obvious choice for the role of welcomer —was not available; since her announcement on Sunday he had slept at home but had not otherwise taken part in Latchett's activities, and Bee's attempt to talk to him in his room late on Monday night had been futile.

So she had been relieved when Eleanor offered to drive the four miles to the station at Guessgate and bring Patrick back.

The present load on her mind was that family meal after his arrival. If Simon did not turn up how was his absence to be explained? And if he did turn up what was that lunch going to be like?

She turned to go down for one more rehearsal with the cook

—their third cook in the last twelve months—when she was waylaid by Lana, their "help". Lana came from the village, and had gilt hair and varnished fingernails and the local version of the current make-up. She "obliged" only because her "boy-friend" worked in the stables. She would sweep and dust, she explained when she first came, because that was "all right", but she would not wait at table because that was "menial". Bee had longed to tell her that no one with her hands, or her breath, or her scent, or her manners, would ever be allowed to hand an Ashby a plate; but she had learned to be politic. She explained that there was, in any case, no question of waiting at table; the Ashbys always waited on themselves.

Lana had come to say that the "vacuum was vomiting instead of swallowing", and domestic worries closed once more over Bee's head and swamped domestic drama. She came to the surface in time to see Eleanor getting into her little two-seater.

"Aren't you taking the car?" she asked. The "car" was the family vehicle, Eleanor's disreputable little conveyance being known as "the bug".

"No. He'll have to take us as we are," Eleanor said.

Bee noticed that she had not bothered to change into a dress. She was wearing the breeches and gaiters in which she had begun the morning.

"Oh, take me, take me!" Ruth said, precipitating herself down the steps and on to the car, but taking good care, Bee noticed, to keep "her blue" away from the bug's dusty metal.

"No," Eleanor said firmly.

"I'm sure he would like me to be there. One of my generation, I mean. After all, he knows you. It won't be exciting for him to see you the way it would be for him to see——"

"No. And keep off if you don't want that dazzling outfit of yours to be mucked up."

"I do think it is selfish of Eleanor," Ruth said, dusting her palms as she watched the car grow small between the lime trees. "She just wants to keep the excitement to herself."

"Nonsense. It was arranged that you and Jane should wait here. Where is Jane, by the way?"

"In the stables, I think. She isn't interested in Patrick."

"I hope she comes in in good time for lunch."

"Oh, she will. She may not be interested in Patrick, but she is always ready for her meals. Is Simon going to be there, at lunch?"

"I hope so."

"What do you think he will say to Patrick?"

If the peace and happiness of Latchetts was going to break down into a welter of discord the twins must go away to school. They would be going to school in a year or two, anyhow; they had much better go now than live in an atmosphere of strain and hatred.

"Do you think there will be a scene?" Ruth asked, hopefully.

"Of course not, Ruth. I wish you wouldn't dramatise things."

But she wished, too, that she could count on there being no scene. And Eleanor, on her way to the station, was wishing the same thing. She was a little nervous of meeting this new brother, and annoyed with herself for being nervous. Her everyday clothes were her protest against her own excitement; a pretence that nothing of real moment was about to happen.

Guessgate, which served three villages but no town, was a small wayside station with a fairly heavy goods business but little passenger traffic, so that when Brat climbed down from his carriage there was no one on the platform but a fat country-woman, a sweating porter, the ticket-collector, and Eleanor.

"Hullo," she said. "You are very like Simon." And she shook hands with him. He noticed that she wore no make-up. A little powdering of freckles went over the bridge of her nose.

"Eleanor," he said, identifying her.

"Yes. What about your luggage? I have just the small car but the dickey holds quite a lot."

"I have just this," he said, indicating his "grip".

"Is the rest coming later?"

"No, this is all I possess."

"Oh." She smiled just a little. "No moss."

"No," he said, "no moss," and began to like her very much.

"The car is out in the yard. Through this way."

"Been away, Mr Ashby?" the ticket-collector said, accepting his piece of pasteboard.

"Yes, I've been away."

At the sound of his voice the ticket-collector looked up, puzzled.

"He took you for Simon," Eleanor said, as they got into the car; and smiled properly. Her two front teeth crossed just a little; which gave her face an endearing childishness. It was a cool, determined, small face when she was serious. "You couldn't have come home at a better time of the year," she said as they scrunched over the gravel of the station yard and fled away into the landscape.

"Home," he thought. Her hair was the colour of corn so ripe that it was nearly white. Pale, silky stuff, very fine. It was brushed back into a knot, as if she could not be bothered to do anything else with it.

"The blossom is just beginning. And the first foals are here."

The knees in their worn whipcord were just like a boy's. But the bare arms protruding from the jacket she wore slung over her shoulders were delicately round.

"Honey has a filly foal that is going to make history. Wait till you see it. You won't know Honey, of course. She was after your time. Her real name is Greek Honey. By Hymettus out of a mare called Money For Jam. I hope you will be impressed with our horses."

"I expect to be," he said.

"Aunt Bee says that you're still interested in them. Horses, I mean."

"I haven't done much on the breeding side, of course. Just preparing horses for work."

They came to the village.

So this was Clare. This warm, living, smiling entity was what those little flat squares on the map had stood for. There was the White Hart; there was the Bell. And up there behind, on its knoll, was the church where the Ashby tablets hung.

"The village is looking nice, isn't it," Eleanor said. "Not changed a bit since I can remember. Not changed since the Flood, if it comes to that. The names of the people in the houses come in the same order down the street as they did in the time of Richard the Second. But of course you know that! I keep thinking of you as a visitor."

Beyond the village, he knew, were the great gates of Clare Park. He waited, mildly curious, to see the entrance to what had been Alec Loding's home. It proved to be a sweeping curve of iron lace flanked by two enormous pillars bearing on each a lion passant. Astride the farther lion was a small boy clad in a leopard-skin rug with green baize edging, a seaside pail worn helmet-wise, and nothing else that was visible. A very long brass poker stood up lance-wise from its rest on his bare foot.

71

"It's all right," Eleanor said. "You did see it."

"That comforts me quite a bit."

"Did you know that Clare was a school nowadays?"

He had nearly said yes, when he remembered that this was merely one of the things Loding had told him, not one of the things that he was supposed to know.

"What kind of school?"

"A school for dodgers."

"Dodgers?"

"Yes. Anyone who loathes hard work and has a parent with enough money to pay the fees makes a bee-line for Clare. No one is forced to learn anything at Clare. Not even the multiplication table. The theory is that one day you'll feel the need of the multiplication table and be seized with a mad desire to acquire the nine-times. Of course, it doesn't work out like that at all."

"Doesn't it?"

"Of course not. No one who could get out of the nine-times would ever dream of acquiring it voluntarily."

"And if they don't do lessons what do they do all day?"

"Express their personalities. They draw things; or make things; or whitewash the coach-house; or dress up, like Antony Toselli. That was Tony on the lion. I teach some of them to ride. They like that. Riding, I mean. I think they are so bored with easy things that they find something a little difficult simply fascinating. But of course it has to be something out of the ordinary. The difficult thing, I mean. If it was a difficulty that everyone was supposed to overcome they wouldn't be interested. That would bring them down to the common level of you and me. They wouldn't be 'different' any longer."

"Nice people."

"Very profitable to Latchetts, anyhow. And here is Latchetts."

Brat's heart rose up into his throat. Eleanor turned slowly into the white gateway between the limes.

It was just as well that she was going slowly, for she had no sooner entered the green tunnel than something like a giant blue butterfly shot out from the boles of the trees and danced wildly in front of the car.

Eleanor braked and swore simultaneously.

"Hullo! Hullo!" shouted the butterfly, dancing to Brat's side of the car.

"You little idiot," Eleanor said. "You deserve to be killed. Don't you know that a driver doesn't see well coming into the avenue out of the sunlight?"

"Hullo! Hullo, Patrick! It's me! Ruth. How d'you do. I came to ride up with you. To the house, you know. Can I sit on your knee? There isn't very much room in that awful old car of Eleanor's, and I don't want to crush my dress. I hope you like my dress. It is put on specially for your coming home. You're very good-looking, aren't you? Am I what you expected?"

She waited for an answer to that, so Brat said that he hadn't really thought about it.

"Oh," said Ruth, much dashed. "We thought about you," she said reprovingly. "No one has talked about anything else for days."

"Ah, well," Brat said, "when *you* have run away for years and years people will talk about *you*."

"I shouldn't dream of doing anything so *outré*," Ruth said, unforgiving.

"Where did you get that word?" Eleanor asked.

"It's a very good word. Mrs Peck uses it."

Brat felt that he ought to paint in a little local colour by saying: "How are the Pecks, by the way?" But he had no mind to spare for artifice. He was waiting for the moment when the limes would thin out and he would see Latchetts.

For the moment when he would be face to face with his "twin".

"Simon hasn't come back yet," he heard Ruth say; and saw her sideways glance at Eleanor. The glance, even more than the information, shook him.

So Simon wasn't waiting on the doorstep for him. Simon was "away" somewhere and the family was uneasy about it.

Alec Loding had disabused him of the idea that a feudal staff reception would await him at Latchetts; that there would be a line of servants, headed by the butler and descending in strict order to the latest tweeny, to welcome the Young Master to the ancestral home. That, Loding had said, had gone out with bustles, and Latchetts had never had a butler, anyhow. And he had known, too, that there would be no array of relations. The children's father had been an only son with one sister, Aunt Bee. The children's mother had been an only daughter with

73

two brothers: both of them killed by the Germans before they were twenty. The only near Ashby relation was Great-uncle Charles, reported by Loding to be now nearing Singapore.

But it had not occurred to him that all the available Ashbys might not be there. That there might be dissenters. The ease of his meeting with Eleanor had fooled him. Metaphorically speaking, he picked up the reins that had been lying on his neck.

The car ran out of the thin spring green of the avenue into the wide sweep in front of the house, and there in the too-bright gusty sunlight stood Latchetts; very quiet, very friendly, very sure of itself. The gabled front of the original building had been altered by some eighteenth-century Ashby to conform with the times, so that only the tiled roof showed its age and origin. Built in the last days of Elizabeth, it was now blandly "Queen Anne". It stood there in its grasslands, undecorated and sufficient: needing no garden for its enhancement. The green of the small park flowered at its heart into the house itself, and any other flowering would have been redundant.

As Eleanor swept round towards the house, Brat saw Beatrice Ashby come out on to the doorstep, and a sudden panic seized him; a mad desire to blurt out the truth to her and back out there and then; before he had put foot over the doorstep; before he was definitely "on" in the scene. It was going to be a damnably difficult and awkward scene and he had no idea how to play it.

It was Ruth who saved him from the worst moment of awkwardness. Before the car had come to a halt she was piping her triumph to the world, so that Brat's arrival somehow took second place to her own achievement.

"I met him after all, Aunt Bee! I met him after all. I came up from the gate with them. You don't mind, do you? I just strolled down as far as the gate and when I got there I saw them coming, and they stopped and gave me a lift and here we are and so I met him after all."

She linked her arm through Brat's and tumbled with him out of the car, dragging him behind her as if he were a find of her own. So that it was with a mutual shrug for this display of personality that Brat and Bee greeted each other. They were united for the moment in a rueful amusement, and by the time the amusement had passed so had the moment.

Before awkwardness could come flooding back, there was a second distraction. Jane came riding round the corner of the

74

house on Fourposter on her way to the stables. The instant check of her hands on the reins when she saw the group at the door made it obvious that she had not planned on being one of that group. But it was too late now to back out, even if backing out had been possible. It was never possible to back away from anything that Fourposter might happen to be interested in; he had no mouth and an insatiable curiosity. So forward came the reluctant Jane on a highly interested pony. As Fourposter came to a halt she slid politely to the ground and stood there shy and defensive. When Bee introduced her she laid a small limp hand in Brat's and after a moment withdrew it.

"What is your pony's name?" Brat asked, aware of her antagonism.

"That's Fourposter," Ruth said, appropriating Jane's mount. "The Rector calls him the Equine Omnibus."

Brat put out his hand to the pony, who refused the advance by withdrawing a pace and looking contemptuously down his Roman nose. As a gesture it was pure burlesque; a Victorian gesture of repudiation from a Victorian drama.

"A comedian," remarked Brat; and Bee, delighted with his perception, laughed.

"He doesn't like people," Jane said, half-repressive, half defending her friend.

But Brat kept his hand out, and presently Fourposter's curiosity overcame his stand-offishness and he dropped his head to the waiting hand. Brat made much of him, till Fourposter capitulated entirely and nuzzled him with elephantine playfulness.

"*Well!*" said Ruth, watching. "He never does that to *anyone*!"

Brat looked down into the small tight face by his elbow, at the small grubby hands clutching the reins so tightly.

"I expect he does to Jane when no one is around," he said.

"Jane, it is time you were cleaned up for lunch," Bee said, and turned to lead the way indoors.

And Brat followed her, over the threshold.

12

"I HAVE put you in the old night nursery," Bee said. "I hope you don't mind. Simon has the room that he used to share with—that you used to share with him." Oh, dear, what a gaffe, she thought; shall I ever be able to think of him as Patrick? "And to give you one of the spare rooms was to treat you like a visitor."

Brat said that he would be glad to have the night nursery.

"Will you go up now, or will you have a drink first?"

"I'll go up now," Brat said, and turned to the stairway.

He knew that she had been waiting for this moment; waiting for the moment when he must show knowledge of the house. So he turned from her and led the way upstairs; up to the big first landing and down the narrow corridor to the north wing, and to the children's rooms facing west from it. He opened the third of the four doors and stood in the room that Nora Ashby had arranged for her children when they were small. One window looked west over the paddocks and the other north to the rise of the down. It was on the quiet side of the house, away from the stables and the approach from the road. He stood at the window looking at the soft blue English distances, thinking of the brilliant mountains beyond the whirling dust of the West, and very conscious of Bee Ashby behind him.

There was something else that he must take the initiative about.

"Where is Simon?" he said, and turned to face her.

"He is like Jane," she said. "Late for lunch. But he'll be in at any moment."

It was smoothly done, but he had seen her shy at his unheralded question, as if he had flicked a whip. Simon had not come to meet him; Simon had not been at Latchetts to greet him; Simon, it was to be deduced, was being difficult.

Before he could pursue the subject she took the initiative from him.

"You can have the nursery bathroom all to yourself, but *do* go slow on the hot water, will you? Fuel is a dreadful problem. Now wash and come down at once. The Pecks sent over some of the Rectory sherry."

"Aren't they coming to lunch?"

"No, they're coming to dinner tonight. Lunch is for family only."

She watched him turn to the fourth door, which he knew to be the bathroom of the nursery wing, and went away looking comforted. He knew why she was comforted: because he had known his way about the house. And he felt guilty and ill at ease. Fooling Mr Sandal—with a K.C. sitting opposite you and gimletting holes in you with cynical Irish eyes—had been one thing; fooling Mr Sandal had been fun. But fooling Bee Ashby was another thing altogether.

He washed absentmindedly, turning the soap in his hands with his eyes on the line of the down. There was the turf he had wanted to ride on; the turf he had sold his soul for. Presently he would get a horse and go up there and ride in the quiet, away from human relationships and this fantastic game of human poker, and up there it would once more seem right and worth while.

He went back to his room and found a brassy blonde in tight flowered rayon tweaking the wallflower in the bowl on the window-sill.

"Hullo," said the blonde. "Welcome home, and all that."

"Thanks," Brat said. Was this someone that he should know? Surely not!

"You're very like your brother, aren't you?"

"I suppose so." He took his brushes from his "grip" and put them on the dressing-table; it was a symbolical taking-possession.

"You won't know me, of course. I'm Lana Adams from the village. Adams, the joiner, was my grandfather. I oblige because my boy-friend works in the stables."

So that was what she was: the help. He looked at her and was sorry for the boy-friend.

"You look a lot older than your brother, don't you? I suppose it's knocking about the world that does it. Having to look out for yourself, and all that. Not being spoilt like your brother. You'll excuse me saying it but spoilt he is. That's why he's made all this to-do about you coming back. Silly, I call it. You've only to look at you to know that you're an Ashby. Not much point in saying you're not, I should think.

But you take my tip and stand up to him. He can't stand being stood up to. Been humoured all his life, I should say. Don't let it get you down."

As Brat went silently on with his unpacking, she paused; and before she could resume Eleanor's cool voice said from the doorway:

"Have you everything you want?"

The blonde said hastily: "I was just welcoming Mr Patrick back, and, having flung Brat a radiant smile, made a hip-swinging exit from the room.

Brat wondered how much Eleanor had heard.

"It's a nice room this," Eleanor said, "except that it doesn't get the morning sun. That bed is from Clare Park. Aunt Bee sold the little ones and bought that one at the Clare sale. It's nice, isn't it? It was the one in Alec Ledingham's room. Except for that the room is just the same."

"Yes; the old wallpaper, I notice."

"Robinson Crusoe and Company. Yes. I had a great weakness for Hereward the Wake. He had such an enchanting profile." She pointed to Hereward's place in the pattern of fictional heroes that Nora had chosen for her children's nightly entertainment.

"Is the nursery-rhyme paper still next door?"

"Yes, of course. Come and see."

He went with her, but while she rehearsed the picture tales his mind was busy with the village girl's revelation about Simon and with the ironic fact that he was to sleep in Alec Loding's bed.

So Simon had refused to believe that he was Patrick. "Not much point in saying you're not, I should think." That could only mean that Simon, in the face of all the evidence, refused to accept him.

Why?

He followed Eleanor downstairs, still wondering.

Eleanor led him into a big sunny sitting-room where Bee was pouring sherry, and Ruth was picking out a tune on a piano.

"Would you like to hear me play?" Ruth asked, inevitably.

"No," Eleanor said, "he wouldn't. We've been looking at the old wallpapers," she said to Bee. "I'd forgotten how in love with Hereward I used to be. It's just as well that I was removed from him in time or he might have become a fixation or something."

"*I* never *liked* that baby stuff on the walls," Ruth said.

"*You* never *read*, so you couldn't know anything about them," Eleanor said.

"We gave up using the nursery wing when the twins ceased to have a Nanny," Bee said.   "It was too far away from the rest of the house."

"It was a day's march to call the twins in the morning," Eleanor said, "and as Ruth always needed calling several times we had to move them into the normal family orbit."

"Delicate people need more sleep," Ruth said.

"Since when have you been delicate?" asked Eleanor.

"It's not that I'm delicate but that Jane's more robust, aren't you, Jane?" she said, appealing to Jane, who sidled into the room, the hair at her temples still damp from her hasty ablutions.

But Jane's eyes were on Bee.

"Simon is here," she said in a small voice; and crossed the room to stand near Bee as if for reassurance.

There was an instant of complete silence.   In the moment of suspended animation only Ruth moved.   Ruth sat up and sparkled with anticipation.

Then Bee's hand moved again and went on filling the glasses. "That is very nice," she said.   "We needn't keep luncheon back after all."

It was so beautifully done that Brat, knowing what he knew now, felt like applauding.

"Where is Simon?" Eleanor asked casually.

"He was coming downstairs," Jane said; and her eyes went back to Bee.

The door opened and Simon Ashby came in.

He paused a moment, looking across at Brat, before closing the door behind him.   "So you've come," he said.

There was no emphasis on the words; no apparent emotion in the tone.

He walked slowly across the room until he was standing face to face with Brat by the window.   He had abnormally clear grey eyes with a darker rim to the iris, but they had no expression in them.   Nor had his pale features any expression.   He was so tightly strung, Brat thought, that if you plucked him with a finger he would twang.

And then quite suddenly the tightness went.

He stood for a moment searching Brat's face; and his own was suddenly slack with relief.

"They won't have told you," he said drawling a little, "but I was prepared to deny with my last breath that you were Patrick. Now that I've seen you I take all that back. Of course you are Patrick." He put out his hand. "Welcome home."

The stillness behind them broke in a flurry of movement and competing voices. There was a babble of mutual congratulation, of clinking glasses and laughter. Even Ruth, it seemed, stifled her disappointment at being done out of melodrama, and devoted her talents to wheedling a little more sherry into her glass than the "sip" that was the twins' allowance for health-drinking.

But Brat, drinking the golden liquid and thanking heaven that the moment was over, was puzzled. Why *relief*? he was thinking.

What had Ashby expected? What had he been afraid of?

He had denied the possibility of Brat's being Patrick. Had that been just a defence against hope; an insurance against ultimate disappointment? Had he said to himself: I won't believe that Patrick is alive, and so when it is proved that he isn't I won't have hoped for nothing? And was that overwhelming relief a moment ago due merely to the realisation that he was, after all, Patrick?

It didn't fit.

He watched Simon being the life of the party, and wondered about him. A few moments ago Ashby had been steeled to face something, and now it seemed he had been—let off. That was it. That was what that sudden relief had been. The reaction of someone steeled to face the worst and suddenly reprieved.

Why should he feel reprieved?

He took the small puzzle into luncheon with him, and it lay at the back of his mind while he dealt with the problems of Ashby conversation and answered their crowding questions.

"You're in!" gloated the voice inside him. "You're in! You're sitting as of right at the Ashby table, and they're all tickled to death about it."

Well, perhaps not all. Jane, loyal to Simon, was a small silent oasis in the bright talk. And it was not to be expected that Simon himself, for all his capitulation, was tickled to any great extent. But Bee, entirely uncritical of that capitulation, was radiant; and Eleanor melted moment by moment from conversational politeness to a frank interest.

"But a Comanche bridle is a kind of twitch, isn't it?"

"No; just a gag. The rope goes through the mouth the way a bit does. It's best for a led horse. He'll follow to lessen the pull."

Ruth, having quite forgiven his lack of speculation about her looks, paid assiduous court to him; and she was the only one who called him Patrick.

This became more noticeable as the meal went on, and her continual interjection of "Patrick!" as she claimed his attention contrasted with the others' half-conscious avoidance of the name. Brat wished that his sole "follower" had proved to be Jane and not Ruth. If he had ever had a small sister he would have liked her to be just like Jane. It annoyed him that he had difficulty in meeting Jane's eyes. It cost him the same effort to meet her regard with equanimity as it did to meet the eyes of the portrait behind her. The dining-room was positively papered with portraits, and the one behind Jane was of William Ashby the Seventh, wearing the uniform of the Westover Fencibles, in which he had proposed to resist the invasion of Napoleon the First. Brat had learned those portraits off by heart, sitting under the pagoda in Kew Gardens, and every time he lifted his eyes to those of William Ashby the Seventh he was plagued by the ridiculous notion that William knew all about the pagoda.

One thing helped him enormously, however, in this first difficult meeting with the Ashbys. The tale he had to tell, as Loding had pointed out during that meal at the Green Man, was, except for its beginnings, true; it was the tale of his own life. And since the whole family with one accord avoided any reference to the events which had catapulted him into that life, the conversational ground he moved on was firm. There was need for neither side-stepping nor manœuvre.

Nor was there any need for him to "mind his manners"; and for that too Alec Loding had given loud thanks. It seemed that, short of a first-class and very strict Nanny, there was no more rigorous training in the civilised consumption of food than was to be had at a first-class orphanage. "My God," Loding had said, "if I ever have any change from a round of drinks I'll send it to that caravanserai of yours, as a mark of my gratitude that you were not brought up in some genteel suburb. Gentility is practically ineradicable, my boy. And whatever Pat Ashby might conceivably do, it is quite inconceivable that he should ever stick out his little finger when he drank."

So Brat had no social habits to unlearn. Indeed, his orthodoxy slightly disappointed Ruth, always on the lookout for the flamboyant. "You don't eat with your fork," she said; and when he looked puzzled, added: "The way they do in American pictures; they cut things up with their knives and forks and then they change the fork over to their other hand and eat with it."

"I don't chew gum either," he pointed out.

"I wonder how that very elaborate method of dealing with their food arose," Bee said.

"Perhaps knives were scarce in the early days," Eleanor suggested.

"Knives were far too useful to be scarce in a pioneer society," Simon said. "It's much more likely that they lived so long on hash that when they got things in slices their instinct was to make hash of it as soon as possible."

Brat thought, listening to them, how very English it all was. Here he was, back from the dead, and they were calmly discussing American table manners. There was no back-slapping, congratulatory insistence on the situation as there would be in a transatlantic household. They avoided the do-you-remember theme as determinedly as Americans would have wallowed in it. Remembering his friends of the Lazy Y, he thought what a fine exhibition of Limey snootiness this would be from the point of view of Pete, and Hank, and Lefty.

But perhaps the happiness on Bee's face would have impressed even Lefty.

"Do you smoke?" Bee asked, when she had poured the coffee; and she pushed the cigarette box over to him. But Brat, who liked his own brand, took out his case and offered the contents to her.

"I've given them up," Bee said. "I have a bank balance instead."

So Brat offered the case to Eleanor.

Eleanor paused with her fingers touching the cigarettes, and bent forward to read something engraved on the inside of the case.

"Brat Farrar," she said. "Who is that?"

"Me," said Brat.

"You? Oh, yes; Farrar, of course. But why Brat?"

"I don't know."

"Did they call you that? Brat, I mean?"

"Yes."

"Why Brat?"

"I don't know. Because I was small, I guess."

"Brat!" Ruth said, delighted. "Do you mind if I call you Brat? Do you?"

"No. I haven't been called anything else for a large part of my life."

The door opened and Lana appeared to say that a young man had called to see Miss Ashby and she had put him in the library.

"Oh, what a nuisance," Bee said. "What does he want, do you know?"

"He says he's a reporter," Lana said, "but he doesn't look like a reporter to me. Quite tidy and clean and polite." Lana's experience of the Press, like Brat's knowledge of middle-class life, was derived solely from films.

"Oh, *no*!" Bee said. "Not the Press. Not already."

"The *Westover Times* he says he is."

"Did he say why he had come?"

"Come about Mr Patrick, of course," Lana said, turning her thumb in Patrick's direction.

"Oh, God," Simon groaned, "and the fatted calf not halfway down our gullets. I suppose it had to come sooner or later!"

Bee drank the remains of her coffee. "Come on, Brat!" she said, putting out her hand and pulling him to his feet. "We might as well go and get it over. You too, Simon." She led Brat out of the room, laughing at him, and still hand in hand with him. The warm friendliness of her clasp sent a rush of emotion through him that he could not identify. It was like nothing he had so far experienced in life. And he was too busy with thoughts of the reporter to pause to analyse it.

The library was the dark room at the back of the house where Bee kept her roll-top desk, her accounts, and her reference books. A small young man in a neat blue suit was puzzling over a stud book. At their entrance he dropped the book and said in a rich Glasgow accent: "Miss Ashby? My name is Macallan. I'm working on the *Westover Times*. I'm awfully sorry about barging in like this, but I thought you'd have finished eating this long time."

"Well, we began late, and I'm afraid we lingered over things," Bee said.

"Uh-huh," said Mr Macallan understandingly. "A very special occasion. I've no right to be spoiling it for you, but 'the first with the latest' is my motto, and just this minute you're the latest."

"I suppose you mean my nephew's homecoming."

"Just that."

"And how did you find out about it so soon, Mr Macallan?"

"One of my contacts heard about it in one of the Clare pubs."

"A deplorable word," said Bee.

"Pub?" Mr Macallan said, puzzled.

"No. Contact."

"Och, well, one of my stooges, if you like that better," Mr Macallan said agreeably. "Which of these young gentlemen is the returned prodigal, may I ask?"

Bee introduced Brat and Simon. Some of the cold tightness had come back to Simon's face; but Brat, who had been around when Nat Zuzzo had cut his throat in the kitchen of his ex-wife's eating-house and had witnessed the activities of the American Press on that occasion, was entranced by this glimpse of news-gathering in Britain. He answered the obvious questions put to him by Mr Macallan and wondered if there would be any suggestion of a photograph. If so, he must get out of it somehow.

But it was Bee who saved him from that. No photograph, said Bee. No; positively *no* photograph. All the information he liked to ask for, but no photograph.

Mr Macallan accepted this, but reluctantly. "The story of the missing twin won't be half so good without a photograph," he complained.

"You're not going to call it 'The Missing Twin', are you," Bee said.

"No; he's going to call it 'Back From The Dead'," Simon said, speaking for the first time. His cool drawl fell on the room like a shadow.

Mr Macallan's pale blue eyes went to him, rested a moment on him consideringly, and then came back to Bee. "I *had* thought of 'Sensation at Clare'," he said, "but I doubt the *Westover Times* won't stand for it. A very conservative organ. But I expect the *Daily Clarion* will do better."

"The *Clarion*!" Bee said. "A London paper! But—but I hope there is no question of that. This is an entirely local—an entirely family matter."

"So was that affair in Hilldrop Crescent," Mr Macallan said.

"What affair?"

"Crippen was the name. The world's Press is composed of family affairs, Miss Ashby."

"But this is of no possible interest to anyone but ourselves. When my nephew—disappeared, eight years ago, the *Westover Times* reported it quite—quite incidentally."

"Ay, I know. I looked it up. A small paragraph at the bottom of page three."

"I fail to see why my nephew's return should be of any more interest than his disappearance."

"It's the man-bites-dog affair over again. People go to their deaths every day, but the amount of people who come back from the dead is very small indeed, Miss Ashby. Coming back from the dead, in spite of the advances of modern science, is still a sensation. And that's why the *Daily Clarion* is going to be interested."

"But how should they hear about it?"

"Hear about it!" Mr Macallan said, genuinely horrified. "Miss Ashby, this is my own *scoop*, don't you see."

"You mean you are going to send the story to the *Clarion*?"

"Assuredly."

"Mr Macallan, you mustn't; you really must not."

"Listen, Miss Ashby," Mr Macallan said patiently, "I agreed about the no-photographs prohibition, and I respect the agreement—I won't go sneaking around the countryside trying to snap the young gentlemen unawares, or anything like that—but you can't ask me to give up a scoop like this. Not a scoop of 'London daily' dimensions." And as Bee, caught in the toils of her natural desire to be fair, hesitated, he added: "Even if I didn't send them the story, there's nothing to hinder a sub-editor lifting the story from the *Westover Times* and making it front-page news. You wouldn't be a scrap better off and I'd have lost my chance of doing a bit of good for myself."

"Oh dear," Bee said, tacitly acknowledging that he was right, "I suppose that means swarms of newspaper men from London."

"Och, no. Only the *Clarion*. If it's the *Clarion's* story none of the rest will bother. And whoever they send down you don't have to worry. They're all Balliol men, I understand."

With which flip at the English Press, Mr Macallan looked round for his hat and made motions of departure.

"I'm very grateful to you, and to you, Mr Ashby, for being so accommodating in the matter of information. I won't keep you any longer. May I offer you my congratulations on your happiness"—for a second the pale blue eyes rested in mild benevolence on Simon—"and my thanks for your kindness."

"You're a long way from home, aren't you, Mr Macallan?" Bee said conversationally as she went to the front door with him.

"Home?"

"Scotland."

"Oh, I see. How did you know I was Scots? Oh, my name, of course. Ay, it's a far cry to Glasgow; but this is just the long way round to London, so to speak. If I'm going to work on an English paper it's as well to know something of the—the——"

"Aborigines?" suggested Bee.

"Local conditions, I *was* going to say," Mr Macallan said solemnly.

"Haven't you a car?" Bee said, looking at the empty sweep in front of the door.

"I left it parked at the end of your drive there. I've never got used to sweeping up to strange houses as if I owned them."

With which startling exhibition of modesty the little man bowed, put on his hat, and walked away.

13

IN the library, as the voices of Bee and Mr Macallan faded down the hall and into the out-of-doors, there was silence. Brat, uncertain of the quality of that silence, turned to the shelves and began to consider the books.

"Well," said Simon, lounging in the window," another hazard safely negotiated."

Brat waited, trying to analyse the sound of the words while they still hung in the air.

"Hazard?" he said at length.

"The snags and bunkers in the difficult business of coming back. It must have taken some nerve, all things considered. What moved you to it, Brat—homesickness?"

This was the first frank question he had been asked, and he suddenly liked Ashby the better for it.

"Not exactly. A realisation that my place was here, after all." He felt that that had a self-righteous sound, and added: "I mean, that my place in the world was here."

This was succeeded by another silence. Brat went on looking at books and hoped that he was not going to like young Ashby. That would be an unforeseen complication. It was bad enough not to be able to face the person he was supplanting, now that he was left alone in a room with him; but to find himself liking that person would make the situation intolerable.

It was Bee who broke the silence.

"I think we should have offered the poor little man a drink," she said, coming in. "However, it's too late now. He can get one from his 'contact' at the White Hart."

"The Bell, I suspect," Simon said.

"Why the Bell?"

"Our Lana frequents that in preference to the White Hart."

"Ah, well. The sooner everyone knows the sooner the fuss will be over." She smiled at Brat to take any sting from the words. "Let's go and look at the horses, shall we? Have you any riding clothes with you, Brat?"

"Not any that Latchetts would recognise as riding clothes," Brat said, noticing how thankfully she seized on the excuse not to call him Patrick.

"Come up with me," Simon said, "and I'll find you something."

"Good," said Bee, looking pleased with him. "I'll collect Eleanor."

"Did you like being given the old night nursery?" Simon asked, preceding Brat upstairs.

"Very much."

"Same old paper, I suppose you noticed."

"Yes."

"Do you remember the night we had an Ivanhoe-Hereward battle?"

"No; I don't remember that."

"No. Of course you wouldn't."

Again the words hung on the silence, teasing Brat's ear with an echo of their tone.

He followed young Ashby into the room he had shared with his brother, and noticed that there was no suggestion in the room that it had ever been shared by another person. It was, on the contrary, very much Simon's own room; being furnished with his possessions to an extent that made it as much a sitting-room as a bedroom. Shelves of books, rows of silver cups, framed sketches of horses on the walls, easy chairs, and a small desk with a telephone extension on it.

Brat moved over to the window while Simon rummaged among his clothes for appropriate garments. The window, as he knew, looked over the stables, but a green hedge of lilac and laburnum trees hid the buildings from view. Above them, in the middle distance, rose the tower of Clare church. On Sunday, he supposed, he would be taken to service there. Another hazard. Hazard had been an odd word for young Ashby to choose, surely?

Simon emerged from the cupboard with breeches and a tweed coat.

"I think these ought to do," he said, throwing them on the bed. "I'll find you a shirt." He opened a drawer of the chest which held his dressing mirror and toilet things. The chest stood by the window, and Brat, still uneasy in Ashby's vicinity, moved over to the fireplace and began to look at the silver cups on the mantelpiece. All of them were prizes for horsemanship, and they ranged from a hurdle race at the local point-to-point to Olympia. All of them except one were of a date too late to have concerned Patrick Ashby; the exception being a small and humble chalice that had been awarded to Simon Ashby on "Patience" for being the winner of the juvenile jumping class at the Bures Agricultural Show in the year before Patrick Ashby committed suicide.

Simon, looking round and seeing the small cup in Brat's hand, smiled and said: "I took that from you, if you remember."

"From me?" Brat said, unprepared.

"You would have won on Old Harry if I hadn't done you out of it by doing a perfect second round."

"Oh, yes," Brat said.   And to lay a new scent: "You seem to have done well for yourself since."

"Not badly," Simon said, his attention going back to his shirt drawer. "But I'm going to do a lot better. Ballsbridge and all stops to Olympia." It was said absentmindedly, but with confidence; as if the money to buy good horseflesh would automatically be available. Brat wondered a little, but felt that this was no moment for discussing the financial future.

"Do you remember the object that used to hang at the end of

your bed?" Simon asked casually, pushing the shirt drawer shut.

"The little horse?" Brat said. "Yes, of course. Travesty," he added, giving its name and mock breeding. "By Irish Peasant out of Bog Oak."

He turned from the exhibits on the mantelpiece, meaning to collect the clothes that Ashby had looked out for him; but as he turned he saw Ashby's face in the mirror, and the naked shock on that face stopped him in his tracks. Simon had been in the act of pushing the drawer shut, but the action was arrested half-way. It was, thought Brat, exactly the reaction of some-one who has heard a telephone ring; the involuntary pause and then the resumed movement.

Simon turned to face him, slowly, the shirt hanging over his left forearm. "I think you'll find that all right," he said, taking the shirt in his right hand and holding it out to Brat but keeping his eyes on Brat's face. His expression was no longer shocked; he merely looked blank, as if his mind were elsewhere. As if, Brat thought, he were doing sums in his head.

Brat took the shirt, collected the rest of the clothes, expressed his thanks, and made for the door.

"Come down when you're ready," Simon said, still staring at him in that blank way. "We'll be waiting for you."

And Brat, making his way round the landing to his own room in the opposite wing, was shocked in his turn. Ashby hadn't expected him to know that. Ashby had been so certain, in-deed, that he would not know about the toy horse that he had been rocked back on his heels when it was clear that he did know about it.

And that meant?

It could mean only one thing.

It meant that young Ashby had not believed for a moment that he was Patrick.

Brat shut the door of the peaceful old night nursery behind him and stood leaning against it, the clothes cascading slowly to the ground from his slackened arm.

Simon had not been fooled. That touching little scene over the sherry glasses had been only an act.

It was a staggering thought.

Why had Simon bothered to pretend?

Why had he not said at once, "You are not Patrick and nothing will make me believe that you are!"?

That had been his original line, if Lana's report and the family atmosphere meant anything. Up to the last moment they had been unsure of his reaction to Brat's arrival; and he had gratified them all by a frank and charming capitulation.

Why the gratuitous capitulation?

Was it—was it a trap of some sort? Were the welcome and the charm merely the grass and green leaves laid over a pit he had prepared?

But he could not have known until the actual face-to-face meeting that he, Brat, was not Patrick. And he had apparently known instantly that the person he was facing was not his brother. Why then should he . . .

Brat stooped to pick up the clothes from the floor and straightened himself abruptly. He had remembered something. He had remembered that odd relaxing on Simon's part the moment he had had a good look at himself. That suggestion of relief. Of being "let off".

So that was it!

Simon had been afraid that it *was* Patrick.

When he found that he was faced with a mere impostor he must have had difficulty in refraining from embracing him.

But still that did not explain the capitulation.

Perhaps it was a mere postponement; a setting to partners. It might be that he planned a more dramatic *dénouement*; a more public discrediting.

If that were so, Brat thought, there were a few surprises in store for young Mr Ashby. The more he thought about the surprises the better he began to feel about things. As he changed into riding clothes he recalled with something like pleasure that shocked face in the mirror. Simon had been unaware that he, Brat, had passed any "family" tests. He had not been present when Brat passed the searching test of knowing his way about the house; and he had not had any chance of being told about it. All that he knew was that Brat had satisfied the lawyers of his identity. Having been faced with, to him, an obvious impostor he must have looked forward with a delighted malice to baiting the pretender.

Yes; all ready to pull the wings off flies was young Mr Ashby.

The first tentative pull had been about the Ivanhoe-Hereward battle. Something that only Patrick would know about. But something, too, that he might easily have forgotten.

The little wooden horse was something that only Patrick

would know about and something that Patrick could in no circumstances have forgotten.

And Brat had known about it.

Not much wonder that Ashby had been shocked. Shocked and at sea. Not much wonder that he looked as if he were doing sums in his head.

Brat spared a kind thought for that master tutor, Alec Loding. Loding had missed his vocation; as a coach he was superb. Sometime, somewhere, something was going to turn up that Alec Loding had either forgotten to tell him about or had not himself known; and the moment was going to be a very sticky one; but so far he had known his lines. So far he was word perfect.

Even to the point of Travesty.

A little object of black bog oak, it had been. "Rudimentary and surrealist," Loding had said, "but recognisable as a horse." It had originally been yoked to a jaunting car, the whole turn-out being one of those bog-oak souvenirs that tourists brought back from Ireland in the days before it was more advisable to bring home the bacon. The small car, being made of bits and pieces, soon went the way of all nursery objects; but the little horse, chunky and solid, had survived and had become Patrick's halidom and fetish. It was Alec Loding who had been responsible for its naming; one winter evening over nursery tea. He and Nancy had looked in at Latchetts on their way home from some pony races, hoping for a drink; but finding no one at home except Nora, who was having tea upstairs with her children, they had joined the nursery party. And there, while they made toast, they had sought a name for Patrick's talisman. Patrick, who always referred to the object as "my little Irish horse", and was conscious of no need for a more particular description, rejected all suggestions.

"What would you call it, Alec?" his mother asked Loding, who had been too busy consuming buttered toast to care what a toy was called.

"Travesty," Alec had said, eyeing the thing. "By Irish Peasant out of Bog Oak."

The grown-ups had laughed, but Patrick, who was too young to know the meaning of the word, thought that Travesty was a fine, proud-sounding name. A name filled with the tramplings and prancings and curvettings of war horses, and worthy therefore of the little black object of his love.

"He kept it in a pocket," Loding had said in Queen Adelaide's sitting-room (it was raining that morning), "but when he grew too big for that it hung on a frayed Stewart tartan ribbon off a box of Edinburgh rock at the end of his bed."

Yes: not much wonder that Simon had been shaken to the core. No stranger to the Ashby family could have known about Travesty.

Brat, buttoning himself into Ashby garments and noticing how a well-cut article adapts itself even to an alien figure, wondered what Simon was making of the problem. He had no doubt learned by now that the "impostor" not only knew about the existence of Travesty but had walked about the house with the confidence of long acquaintance. A faint flare of excitement woke in Brat. The same excitement that had made those interviews with old Mr Sandal so enjoyable. For the last couple of hours—ever since his arrival at Guessgate station—he had been received with kindness and welcome, and the result had been a faint queasiness, a sort of spiritual indigestion. What had been a dice game for dangerous stakes had become a mere taking candy from a baby. Now that Simon was his opponent, the thing was once more a contest.

Not dice, thought Brat, considering himself in the mirror. Chequers rather. A matter of cautious moves, of anticipating attack, of blocking an unforeseen thrust. Yes; chequers.

Brat went downstairs buoyed up with a new anticipation. He would not any more have to stand with his back to young Ashby because he was unable to face him. The pieces were laid out on the board and they faced each other across it.

Through the wide-open door of the hall he could see the Ashbys grouped in the sunlight on the steps and went forward to join them. Ruth, with her chronically roving eye, was the first to see him.

"Oh, doesn't he look nice," said Ruth, still paying court.

Brat was aware that he looked "nice" but wished that Ruth had not called attention to his borrowed finery. He wondered if anyone had ever smacked Ruth Ashby.

"You must get some riding clothes from Walters as soon as may be," Bee said. "These are almost a good enough fit to do as a pattern. Which would save you having to go to town for measurements only."

"Those breeches aren't Walters'," Simon said, eyeing the

clothes lazily. "They're Gore and Bowen's. Walters never made a good pair of breeches in his life."

He was draped against the wall by the doorway, relaxed and apparently at peace with the world. His eyes travelled slowly up from Brat's boots to his shirt, and came to rest with the same detached interest on his face.

"Well," he said amiably, pushing himself off the wall, "let's go and look at some horses."

Not chequers, thought Brat. No, not chequers. Poker.

"We'll show you the stables this afternoon," Bee said, "and leave the mares until after tea."

She ran an arm through Brat's and gathered Simon in with her other one, so that they went towards the stables arm-in-arm like old friends; Eleanor and the twins tailing along behind.

"Gregg is all agog to see you," she said. "Not that you'll notice any agogness, of course. His face doesn't permit anything like that. You'll just have to believe me that he is excited inside."

"What happened to old Malpas?" Brat asked, although he had heard all about old Malpas one afternoon outside the Orangery.

"He became very astigmatic," Bee said. "Figuratively speaking. We could never see eye to eye. He didn't really like taking orders from a woman. So he retired about eighteen months after I took over, and we've had Gregg ever since. He's a misanthropist, and a misogynist, and he has his perks, of course; but he doesn't let any of them interfere with the running of the stables. There was a noted drop in the fodder bills after old Malpas left. And the local people like Gregg better because he buys his hay direct from the farmers and not through a contractor. And I think on the whole he's a better horsemaster than Malpas was. Cleverer at getting a poor horse into condition. And a genius at doctoring a sick one."

Why doesn't he relax? she was thinking, feeling the boy's arm rigid under her fingers. The ordeal is over now, surely. Why doesn't he relax?

And Brat for his part was conscious of her fingers clasping his forearm as he had never been conscious before of a woman's hand. He was experiencing again that surge of an unrecognised emotion that had filled him when Bee had taken his hand to lead him to the interview with Mr Macallan.

But his first sight of the stables distracted his attention from both emotional and ethical problems.

His reaction to the stable yard at Latchetts was very much the reaction of a merchant seaman to his first acquaintance with one of His Majesty's ships. A sort of contemptuous but kindly amusement. A wonder that the thing wasn't finished off with ribbons. Only the fact that several horses' heads protruded inquisitively from the loose boxes convinced him that the place was seriously used as a stable at all. It was like nothing so much as one of the toy models he had seen in expensive toy shops. He had always imagined that those gay little affairs with their bright paint and their flowers in tubs had been manufactured to a child's taste. But apparently they had been authentic copies of an actual article. He was looking at one of the articles at this moment, and being very much surprised.

Not even the dude ranch had prepared him for this. There was paint galore at the dude ranch, but there was also a tradition of toughness. The dude ranch would never have thought of mowing the bit of grass in the middle until it looked like a square of green baize, so neat-edged and trim that it looked as if you could roll it up and take it away. At the dude ranch there was still a suggestion of the mud, dung, sweat, and flies which are inseparable from a life alongside horseflesh.

The little building on the left of the yard entrance was the saddle room, and in the saddle-room door was the stud-groom, Gregg. Gregg had in the highest degree that disillusioned air common to those who make their living out of horses. He had also the horseman's quality of agelessness. He was probably fifty, but it would not be surprising to be told that he was thirty-five.

He took two paces forward and waited for them to come up to him. The two paces were his concession to good manners, and the waiting emphasised the fact that he was receiving them on his own ground. His clear blue eyes ran over Brat as Bee introduced them, but his expression remained polite and inscrutable. He gave Brat a conventional welcome and a crushing hand-clasp.

"I hear you've been riding horses in America," he said.

"Only Western ones," Brat said. "Working horses."

"Oh, these work," Gregg said, inclining his head towards the boxes. Don't be in any doubt about it, the tone said. It was as if he had understood Brat's distrust of the spit and polish. His eyes went past Brat to Eleanor standing behind and he said: "Have you seen what's in the saddle room, Miss Eleanor?"

From the gloom of the saddle room there materialised as if in answer to his question the figure of a small boy. He materialised rather reluctantly as if uncertain of his welcome. In spite of a change of costume Brat recognised him as the rider of the stone lion at the gates of Clare. His present apparel, though less startling, was hardly more orthodox than his leopard-skin outfit. He was wearing a striped football jersey that clung to his tadpole body, a pair of jodhpurs so large that they hung in a fold above each skinny knee, a steeplechasing jockey cap with the crash-lining showing at the back, and a pair of grubby red moccasins.

"Tony!" said Eleanor. "Tony, what are you doing here?"

"I've come for my ride," said Tony, his eyes darting to and fro among the group like lizards.

"But this isn't the day for your ride."

"Isn't it, Eleanor? I thought it was."

"You know quite well that you don't ride on a Tuesday."

"I thought this was Wednesday."

"You're a dreadful little liar, Tony," Eleanor said dispassionately. "You knew quite well this wasn't Wednesday. You just saw me in a car with a stranger and so you came along to find out who the stranger was."

"Eleanor," murmured Bee, deprecating.

"You don't know him," Eleanor said, as if the subject of discussion was not present. "His curiosity amounts to a mania. It's almost his only human attribute."

"If you take him today you won't have to take him tomorrow," Simon said, eyeing the Toselli child with distaste.

"He can't come and expect to ride just when he feels like it!" Eleanor said. "Besides, I said I wouldn't take him out again in these things. I told you to get a pair of boots, Tony."

The black eyes stopped being lizards and became two brimming pools of grief. "My father can't afford boots for me," said Tony with a catch in his alto, guaranteed to draw blood from a stone.

"Your father has £12,000 a year free of income tax," Eleanor said briskly.

"If you took him today, Nell," Bee said, "you'd be free to help me tomorrow when half the countryside comes dropping

95

in to have a look at Brat." And, as Eleanor hesitated: "You might as well get it over now that he's here."

"And he'll still be wearing moccasins tomorrow," Simon drawled.

"Indian riders wear moccasins," Tony observed mildly, "and they are very good riders."

"I don't think your destitute father would be very pleased if you turned up with moccasins in the Row. You get a pair of boots. And if I take you this afternoon, Tony, you are not to think that you can make a habit of this."

"Oh, no, Eleanor."

"If you come on the wrong day again you'll just have to go away without a ride."

"Yes, Eleanor." The eyes were lizards again, darting and sliding.

"All right. Go and ask Arthur to saddle Spuds for you."

"Yes, Eleanor."

"No thanks, you'll observe," Eleanor said, watching him go.

"What is the crash helmet for?" Simon asked.

"His skull is as thin as cellophane, he says, and must be protected. I don't know how he got one that size. Out of a circus, I should imagine. What with his Indian longings I suppose I should be thankful that he doesn't turn up in a headband and a single feather."

"He will one day, when it occurs to him," Simon said.

"Oh, well, I suppose I'd better go and saddle Buster. I'm sorry, Brat," she said, smiling a little at him, "but it is really one of those blessings in disguise. The pony he rides will be a lot less fresh with him today than he would be tomorrow, after a day in the stable. And you don't really need three people to show you round. I'll go round the paddocks with you after tea."

14

BRAT's tendency to be patronising about spit and polish died painlessly and permanently somewhere between the fourth and fifth boxes. The pampered darlings that he had been prepared to find in these boxes did not exist. Thorough-bred, half-bred, cob, or pony, the shine on their coats came from condition and grooming and not from coddling in warm stables; Brat had lived long enough with horses to recognise that. The only ribbons that had ever been tied on these animals were rosettes of red or blue or yellow; and the rosettes were quite properly in the saddle room.

Bee did the honours, with Gregg as assistant; but since it is not possible for four horsemen to consider any given horse without entering into a discussion, the occasion soon lost the slight formality of its beginnings and degenerated into a friendly free-for-all. And presently Brat, always a little detached from his surroundings, noticed that Bee was leaving the discussion more and more to Simon. That it was Simon instead of Bee who said: "This is a throw-out from a racing stable that Eleanor is schooling into a hack," or, "Do you remember old Thora? This is a son of hers by Cold Steel." That Bee was quite deliberately edging herself out.

The twins had soon grown tired and evaporated; Ruth because horses bored her, and Jane because she knew all that was to be known about the horses and did not like the thought that they belonged to a person she did not know. And Gregg, congenitally taciturn, fell more and more into the background with Bee. So that in no time at all it was Simon's occasion; Simon's and Brat's.

Simon behaved as if he had not a care in the world. As if this were just another afternoon and Brat just another visitor. A rather privileged and knowledgeable visitor; unquestionably welcome. Brat, coming to the surface every now and then from his beguilement with the horses, would listen to the light drawl discussing pedigree, conformation, character, or prospects; would watch the cool untroubled profile and wonder. "A bit light in front," the cool voice would be saying, and the untroubled eyes would be running over the animal as if no more important matter clouded the sun. "Nice, though, don't you think?" or "This one should really be turned out; he's been hunted all the winter; but I'm going pot-hunting on him this summer. And anyhow Bee's awfully stingy with her pasture."

And Bee would put in her tuppenceworth and fade out again.

It was Bee who "ran" Latchetts, but the various interests involved were divided between the three Ashbys. Eleanor's chief concerns were the hacks and hunters, Simon's were hunters and show jumpers, and Bee's were the mares and the Shetland ponies. During Bill Ashby's lifetime, when Latchetts was purely a breeding establishment, the hacks and hunters in the stables had been there for family use and amusement. Occasionally, when there happened to be an extra-good horse in the stable, Bee, who was a better horsewoman than her brother, would come down from London for a week or two to school it and afterwards show it for him. It was good advertisement for Latchetts; not because Latchetts ever dealt in made horses but because the simple repetition of a name is of value in the commercial world, as the writers of advertisements have discovered. Nowadays the younger Ashbys, under Bee's supervision, had turned the stables into a profitable rival to the brood mares.

"Mr Gates is asking if he can speak to you, sir," said the stableman to Gregg. And Gregg excused himself and went back to the saddle room.

Fourposter came to the door of his box, stared coldly at Brat for a moment, and then nudged him jocosely with his Roman nose.

"Has he always been Jane's?" Brat asked.

"No," Bee said, "he was bought for Simon's fourteenth birthday. But Simon grew so fast that in a year or so he had outgrown him, and Jane at four was already clamouring to ride a 'real' horse instead of a Shetland. So she fell heir to him. If he ever had any manners he has forgotten them, but he and Jane seem to understand each other."

Gregg came back to say that it was Miss Ashby that Gates wanted to see. It was about the fencing.

"All right, I'll come," Bee said. And as Gregg went away: "What he really wants to see is Brat, but he'll just wait till to-morrow like the rest of the countryside. It's so like Gates to try to steal a march. Opportunism is his middle name. If you two go trying out any of the horses, do be back for tea. I want to go round the paddocks with Brat before it gets dark."

"Do you remember Gates?" Simon asked, opening the door of another box.

"No, I don't think so."

"He's the tenant of Wigsell."

"What became of Vidler, then?"

"He died. This man was married to his daughter and had a small farm the other side of Bures."

Well, Simon had dealt him the cards he needed that time. He looked at Simon to see how he had taken it, but Simon's whole interest seemed to be in the horse he was leading out of the box.

98

"These last three boxes are all new acquisitions, bought with an eye on the show ring. But this is the pick of the bunch. He's a four-year-old by High Wood out of a mare called Shout Aloud. His name is Timber."

Timber was a black without a brown hair on him. He had a rudimentary white star, and a ring of white on each coronet; and he was quite the handsomest thing in horseflesh that Brat had ever been at close quarters with. He came out of his box with an air of benevolent condescension, as if aware of his good looks and pleased that they should be the subject of tribute. There was something oddly demure about him, Brat thought, watching him. Perhaps it was just the way he was standing, with his forefeet close together. Whatever it was it didn't go with the self-confident, considering eye.

"Difficult to fault, isn't he," Simon said.

Brat, lost in admiration of his physical conformation, was still puzzled by what he thought of as the butter-wouldn't-melt air.

"He has one of the best-looking heads I've ever seen on a horse," Simon said. "And just look at the bone." He led the horse round. "And a sweet mover, too," he said.

Brat went on looking in silence, admiring and puzzled.

"Well?" Simon said, waiting for Brat's comment.

"Isn't he *conceited*!" said Brat.

Simon laughed.

"Yes, I suppose he is. But not without cause."

"No. He's a good-looker all right."

"He is more than that. He's a lovely ride. And he can jump anything you can see the sky over."

Brat moved forward to the horse and made friendly overtures. Timber accepted the gesture without responding. He looked gratified but faintly bored.

"He should have been a tenor," Brat said.

"A tenor?" Simon said. "Oh, I see. The conceit." He considered the horse afresh. "I suppose he is rather pleased with himself. I hadn't thought about it before. Would you like to try him out, by the way?"

"I certainly would."

"He ought to have some exercise today and he hasn't had it so far." He hailed a stable-man. "Arthur, bring a saddle for Timber."

"Yes, sir. A double bridle, sir?"

"No; a snaffle." And, as the man went, to Brat: "He has a mouth like a glove."

Brat wondered if he was merely reluctant to submit that tender mouth to the ham hands of a Westerner with a cub rein at his disposal.

While Timber was being saddled they inspected the two remaining "acquisitions". They were a long-backed bay mare with a good head and quarters ("Two good ends make up for a middle," as Simon said) who was called Scapa; and Chevron, a bright chestnut of great quality with a nervous eye.

"What are you riding?" Brat asked, as Simon led Chevron back to his box.

Simon bolted the half-door and turned to face him.

"I thought you might like to have a look round by yourself," he said. And as Brat, surprised by this piece of luck, was momentarily wordless: "Don't let him get lit-up too much, will you, or he'll break out again when he has been dried."

"No, I'll bring him back cool," Brat said; and flung his leg across his first English horse.

He took one of the two whips that Arthur was holding out for his choosing, and turned the horse to the inner end of the yard.

"Where are you going?" Simon asked, as if surprised.

"Up to the down, I think," Brat said, as if Simon's question had applied to his choice of a place to ride in.

If that gate at the north-west corner of the yard didn't still lead to the short-cut to the downs, then Simon would have to tell him. If it still did lead there, Simon would have one more item to worry about.

"You haven't chosen a very good whip for shutting gates with," Simon said smoothly. "Or are you going to jump everything you come to?" You rodeo artist, the tone said.

"I'll shut the gates," Brat said equably.

He began to walk Timber to the corner of the yard.

"He has his tricks, so look out for him," Simon said, as an afterthought.

"I'll look out for him," Brat said, and rode away to the inner gate which Arthur was waiting to open for him.

Arthur grinned at him in a friendly fashion and said admiringly: "He's a fly one, that, sir."

As he turned to his right into the little lane he considered the implications of that very English adjective. It was a long time since he had heard anything called fly. "Fly" was "cute"—in the English sense, not in the American. Fly was something on the side. A fly cup. Something sly with a hint of cleverness in it.

A fly one, Timber was.

The fly one walked composedly up the track between the green banks netted with violets, his ears erect in anticipation of the turf ahead of them. As they came in sight of the gate at the far end he danced a little. "No," said Brat's hands, and he desisted at once. Someone had left the gate open, but since there was a notice saying PLEASE SHUT THE GATE neatly painted in the middle of it, Brat manœuvred Timber into the appropriate position for closing it. Timber seemed as well acquainted with gates and their uses as a cow pony was with a rope, but never before had Brat had so delicate and so well-oiled a mechanism under him. Timber obeyed the slightest indication of hand or heel with a lack of questioning and a confidence that was new in Brat's experience. Surprised and delighted, Brat experimented with this new adaptability. And Timber, even with the turf in front of him, with the turf practically under his feet, moved sweetly and obediently under his hands.

"You wonder!" said Brat softly.

The ears flicked at him.

"You perishing marvel," he said, and closed his knees as he turned to face the down. Timber broke into a slow canter, headed for the clumps of gorse and juniper bushes that marked the skyline.

So this was what riding a good English horse was like, he thought. This communion, this being one half of a whole. This effortlessness. This magic.

The close, fine turf slipped by under them, and it was odd to see no little spurt of dust coming up as the shoes struck. England, England, England, said the shoes as they struck. A soft drum on the English turf.

I don't care, he thought, I don't care. I'm a criminal, and a heel, but I've got what I wanted, and it's worth it. By God, it's worth it. If I died tomorrow, it's worth it.

They came to the level top of the down and faced the double row of bushes that made a rough natural avenue, about fifty yards wide, along the crest. This was something that Alec Loding had forgotten to tell him about, and something that had not appeared on a map. Even the Ordnance Survey can hardly

101

take note of juniper growths. He pulled up to consider it. But Timber was in no considering mood. Timber knew all about that level stretch of down between the rows of bushes.

"All right," said Brat, "let's see what you can do," and let him go.

Brat had ridden flyers before. Dozens of them. He had ridden sprinters and won money with them. He had been bolted with at the speed of jet propulsion. Mere speed no longer surprised him. What surprised him was the smoothness of the progress. It was like being carried through the air on a horse suspended to a merry-go-round.

The soft air parted round his face and tickled his ears and fled away behind them, smelling of grass with the sun on it and leather and gorse. Who cares, who cares, who cares! said the galloping feet. Who cares, who cares, who cares! said the blood in Brat's veins.

If he died tomorrow it was all the same to him.

As they came to the end of the stretch Timber began to pull up of his own accord, but it was against Brat's instincts to let a horse make the decisions, so he kept him going, turned him round the south end of the green corridor, and cantered him gently to a walk, and Timber responded without question.

"Brother," said Brat, running his fingers up the dark crest, "are there more like you in England, or do you rate special?"

Timber bent his head to the caress, still with the air of one receiving his due.

But as they walked back on the south side of the irregular green hedge Brat's attention and interest went to the country-side spread below them. Except that he was looking at it up-side down, as it were—from the north, instead of from the south as one looks normally at a map—this was Clare as he had first become acquainted with it. All laid out below his eye in Ordnance Survey clarity and precision.

Down below him, a little to his left, were the crimson roofs of Latchetts, set in the neat squares of paddock. Farther to the left was the church, on its own small rise; and left of it again, the village of Clare, a huddle of roofs in pale green trees. Where the land sloped up from the village to make the south side of the small valley stood Clare Park, a long white house shel-tered from the south-west Channel gales by the slope behind it.

Directly opposite him that slope rose into a smaller and tamer version of the down he was sitting on; a low green hill called Tanbitches. It was an open stretch of grazing, marked half-way up with the green scar of an old quarry, and crowned by the beeches that had given it its name. There were only seven beeches now instead of ten, but the clump made a decorative and satisfying climax to the southern side of the valley.

The other side of the Tanbitches hill, as he knew from the maps, ran away in a gentle slope for a mile and a half to the cliffs. To the cliffs where Patrick Ashby had put an end to his life. Behind the lower rise of the valley, on the reverse slope of Clare Park, were farms that merged imperceptibly in a mile or two into the suburbs of Westover. In the slight hollow that marked the Clare Park slope from Tanbitches hill was a path that led to the coast. The path that Patrick Ashby had taken on that day eight years ago.

It was suddenly more real to him than it had ever been so far: this tragedy which he was using to his advantage. More real even than it had been in the rooms that Patrick had lived in. In the house there had been other associations besides Patrick: associations more present and alive. There had been the dis-tractions of human intercourse and of his own need to be con-stantly wary. Out here in the open and alone it had a reality that it had never had before. Up that straggling path on the other side of the valley a boy had gone, so loaded with misery that this neat green English world had meant nothing to him. He had had horses like Timber, and friends and family, and a belonging-place, and it had all meant nothing to him.

For the first time in his detached existence Brat was per-sonally aware of another's tragedy. When Loding had first told him the story, in that London pub, he had had nothing but contempt for the boy who had had so much and could not do without that little extra. A poor thing, he had thought. Then Loding had brought those photographs to Kew, and had shown him Patrick, and he had had that odd feeling of identi-fication, of partisanship.

"That is Pat Ashby. He was about eleven there," Loding had said, his feet propped comfortably on the railings of the park, and had passed him the piece of paper. It was a snapshot taken with a Brownie 2A, and Brat had accepted it with a curiosity that was active but not urgent.

But Pat Ashby had not been the anonymous "poor thing"

that he had so far held in his mind.   He had been a real person.
A likeable real person.   A person who would have been, Brat
felt, very much his cup of tea.   From being vaguely anti-Patrick
he had become Patrick's champion.

It was not, however, until this moment of quiet above Latchetts that he had been moved to sorrow for him.

Clink—clink! came the faint sound from the valley; and
Brat's eyes travelled down from Tanbitches to the cottage at its
foot.   The blacksmith's, that was.   A quarter of a mile west of
the village.   A tiny black square by the roadside it had been on
the map; now it was a small building with a black chimney and
an occupant who made musical sounds with a hammer.

The whole scene was very like the picture from which he had
acquired his first-year French. *Voilà le forgeron*.   It needed
only a *curé* coming from the church.   And a postman on a
bicycle between the forge and the village.

Brat slid from Timber's back, from long habit loosened the
girths as if he saddled up hours ago, and sat down with his back
to the gorse and juniper to feast his eyes on this primer of the
English countryside.

15

THE great clouds sailed up and past, the sunlight flickered and
ran, the uncertain soft wind edged in and out of the junipers
and made soft scufflings in the grass.   Timber made small
sounds with his bit, and cropped turf in a tentative and superior
fashion.   Brat sank into a daze of pleasure and ceased altogether from conscious thought.

He was roused by the swift fling-up of Timber's head, and
almost at the same moment a female voice behind him said, as
if it were a chant and rhymed:

> "Don't look,
> Don't move,
> Shut your eyes
> And guess who."

It was a slightly Cockney voice, and it dipped with archness.

Like anyone else in the circumstances Brat disobeyed the in-
junction automatically.   He looked round into the face of a
girl of sixteen or so.   She was a large, plumpish girl, with

bright auburn hair and prominent blue eyes. The eyes were remarkable in that they managed to be at once avid and sleepy. As they met Brat's they almost popped out altogether.

"Oh!" said the girl, in a half-shriek. "I thought you were Simon. You're not!"

"No," agreed Brat, beginning to get to his feet.

But before he could move she had dropped to the grass beside him.

"My, you gave me a shock. I bet I know who you are. You're the long-lost brother, aren't you? You must be; you're so like Simon. That's who you are, isn't it?"

Brat said that it was.

"You even wear the same kind of clothes."

Brat said that they were Simon's clothes. "You know Simon?"

"Of course I know Simon. I'm Sheila Parslow. I'm a boarder at Clare Park."

"Oh." The school for dodgers, Eleanor had called it. The place where no one had to learn the nine-times.

"I'm doing my best to have an *affaire* with Simon, but it's uphill work."

Brat did not know the correct rejoinder to this, but she did not need conversational encouragement.

"I have to do something to put some pep into life at Clare Park. You can't imagine the screaming boredom of it. You simply can't imagine. There is nothing, but I mean *nothing*, that you are forbidden to do. I once got so desperate I took off all my clothes and walked into Cedric's office—Cedric is our Leader, he doesn't like being called the Head, but that's what he is, of course—I walked in with nothing on, not a stitch, and all he said was: 'Have you ever thought of going on a diet, Sheila dear?' Just took a look at me and said: 'Have you ever thought of going on a diet?' and then went on with looking up *Who's Who*. He's always looking up *Who's Who*. You don't really stand much of a chance of fetching up at Clare Park unless your father is in *Who's Who*. Or your mother, of course. My father's not in it, but he has millions, my father, and that makes a very good substitute. Millions are a very good introduction, aren't they?"

Brat said that he supposed they were.

"I flapped Father's millions in front of Simon: Simon has a great respect for a good investment and I hoped it would weight my charms, so to speak; but he's a frightful snob, Simon, isn't he?"

"Is he?"

"Don't you *know*?"

"I've only met him today."

"Oh, of course. You've just come back. How exciting for you. I can understand Simon not being overjoyed, of course, but it must be exciting for you to put his nose out of joint."

Brat wondered if she, too, pulled the wings off flies.

"I may have more chance with Simon now that you've taken his fortune from him. I'll have to waylay him somewhere and see. I thought I was waylaying him now, when I saw Timber. He often comes up here because it's his favourite place for exercising the horses. He hates Tanbitches." She jerked her chin at the opposite side of the valley. "And this is a good place for getting him alone. So I came up here on spec, and then I saw that black brute, and I thought I had him cold. But it was only you."

"I'm sorry," Brat said meekly.

She considered him.

"I suppose it's no good my trying to seduce you instead?" she said.

"I'm afraid not."

"Is it that I'm not your type, or is it not your line?"

"Not much in my line, I'm afraid."

"No, I suppose not," she said, agreeing with him. "You have a face like a monk. Funny you should look so like Simon and yet look so different. Simon's no monk; as that Gates girl over at Wigsell could tell you. I make images of that Gates girl and stick pins in them, but it doesn't do any good. She goes on blooming like a blasted peony and fascinating him like fly-paper."

She was rather like a well-blown peony herself, he thought, looking at her wet red mouth and the buttons straining the cloth across her ample bust. A rather drooping and disappointed peony at the moment.

"Does Simon know that you are fond of him?" Brat asked.

"Fond of him? I'm not fond of him. I don't think I like him at all. I just want to have an *affaire* with him to brighten up the term a bit. Until I can leave this boring place."

"If you can do anything you like, why can't you leave now?" Brat asked reasonably.

"Well, I don't want to look too much of a fool, you know. I went to school at Ling Abbey, you see, and I made the place a hell so that my people would take me away and send me here. I thought I was going to have the time of my life here, with no lessons and no timetable and no rules or anything. I had no idea it would be so boring. I could weep with boredom."

"Isn't there anyone at Clare Park you could substitute for Simon? I mean, someone who would be more—accommodating?"

"No, I had a look at them first. Skinny and hairy and intellectual. Have you ever noticed how the intellect runs to hair? Some people get a kick out of disgust, but not me. I like them good-looking. And you have to admit Simon is very good-looking. There was an under-gardener at Ling Abbey that was almost as handsome, but he hadn't that lovely God-damn-you look that Simon has."

"Didn't the under-gardener keep you at the Abbey place?"

"Oh, no, they sacked him. It was easier than expelling me and having a scandal. But they had to expel me in any case, so they might as well have kept poor Albert. He was much better with his lobelias than he was with girls. But of course they couldn't be expected to know that. I suppose you wouldn't put in a good word for me with Simon? It would be such a pity to waste all the agony I've gone through trying to interest him."

"Agony?"

"You don't suppose I endure hours on those horrible quad-rupeds just for *fun*, do you? With that cold stick of a sister of his looking down her nose at me. Oh, I forgot: she's your sister too, isn't she? But perhaps you've been away so long that you don't think of her the way a boy thinks of his sister."

"I certainly don't," Brat said; but she was not listening.

"I suppose you've ridden horses since you could crawl, so you have no idea what it is like to be bumped about on a great shapeless mountain of a thing that's far too high from the ground and has nothing to hold on to. It looks so easy when Simon does it. The horse looks so nice and *narrow* when you're standing on the ground. You think you could ride it the way you ride a bicycle. It's only when you get up you find that its back is simply acres across and you can make no impression on it at all. You just sit there and are bumped about, and your legs slip backwards and forwards instead of staying still like

Simon's, and you get large blisters and can't sit down in the bath for weeks. You don't look quite so like a monk when you smile a bit."

Brat suggested that surely there were better ways of attracting favourable notice than being a tyro at something that the object of one's pursuit already did to perfection.

"Oh, I didn't think that I'd attract him that way. It just gave me an excuse for being round the stables. That sister of—your sister doesn't stand any hanging round if you haven't got business."

"Your sister," he thought, and liked the sound of it.

He had three sisters now, and at least two of them were the kind he would have indented for. Presently he must go down and make their further acquaintance.

"I'm afraid I must go," he said, getting up and putting the reins over Timber's head.

"I wish you didn't have to," she said, watching him tighten the girth. "You are quite the nicest person I have talked to since I came to Clare. It's a pity you aren't interested in women. You might cut Simon out with the Gates girl, and then I'd have more chance. Do you know the Gates girl?"

"No," Brat said, getting up on Timber.

"Well, have a look at her. She's very pretty."

"I'll do that," Brat said.

"Now that you're home, I'll be running across you in the stables, I suppose."

"I expect so."

"You wouldn't like to give me one of my lessons instead of your sister, would you?"

"I'm afraid that's not my department."

"Oh, well." She sounded resigned. "You look very nice on that brute. I suppose *his* back is acres across too. They all are. It's a conspiracy."

"Good-bye," said Brat.

"Do you know, I don't know your name. Someone told me, of course, but I forget. What is it?"

"Patrick."

And as he said the word his mind went back to the path across the valley, and he forgot Miss Parslow almost instantly. He cantered back along the top of the down until he came level with Latchetts, and then began to walk Timber down. Below him, a green ride led through the paddocks to the west of the house and so to the sweep of gravel in front of it. It was by that way that Jane had come this morning, when she had become mixed up with his reception at the front door. The gate to the ride stood open, the gate lying flat against the stout paddock rails that bordered the ride. Brat rode down until the steepness of the down gave way to a gentle slope and then pressed Timber into a canter. The green tunnel of the ride with its soft floor was open before them, and he was not going to spoil it by stopping to shut another gate that someone else had left open.

It was due to no good riding on Brat's part that his left leg was still whole five seconds later. It was due entirely to the years of rough-riding that had made his physical reactions quicker than conscious thought. The swerve was so sudden and so wholehearted that the white rail was scraping along the saddle where his leg should have been before he realised that his leg was not there. That he had taken it away before he had had time to think about it.

As Timber came away from the rails he settled back into the saddle and pulled the horse to a stop. Timber stopped obediently.

"Whew!" said Brat, expelling his pent breath. He looked down at Timber standing innocent and demure in the exact centre of the ride.

"You ornery thing, you," he said, amused.

Timber went on looking demure but the ears listened to him. A trifle apprehensively, Brat thought.

"I know men who'd beat the bejasus out of you for that," Brat said, and turned the horse's nose to the down again. Timber retraced his steps obediently, but was obviously not easy in his mind. When he was far enough away from the gate Brat took him into a canter once more and down to the opening. He had neither spurs nor curb but he was curious to see what Timber would do this time. Timber, as he had expected, swept good-manneredly into the ride, bisecting the distance from either rail with mathematical precision.

"What, me!" he seemed to be saying. "Do a thing like that on purpose? Me, with my perfect manners? Of course not. I just lost my balance for a moment, coming into the ride there. It can happen to the best of us."

"Well, well," thought Brat, pulling him to a walk. "Think you're smart, don't you," he said aloud, walking him down the ride. "Far smarter horses than you have tried to brush me off, take it from me. I've been brushed off horses that would make you look like five cents' worth of candy."

The black ears flickered, listening to him, analysing the sound of his voice, its tone; puzzled.

The mares came to the rails to watch them pass, pleased with this small event in their placid lives; and the foals ran round and round in a self-induced excitement. But Timber took no notice of them. He had lost any active interest in mares at a very early age, and just now his whole interest seemed to be in the fact that he had been outwitted, and that the outwitting one made sounds which he did not understand. His ears, which should have been pricked at the thought of his nearing stable, were restless and inquiring.

Brat rode round the front of the house, as Jane had that morning, but he saw no one. He went on to the stables and found Eleanor just riding in with a led horse, having given Tony his lesson and left him at Clare Park.

"Hullo!" she said, "have you been out on Timber?" She sounded a little surprised. "I hope Simon warned you about him."

"Yes, thank you, he warned me."

"One of my bad buys," she said ruefully, eyeing Timber as they rode side by side towards the yard.

"Yours?" he said.

"Yes. Didn't Simon tell you about that?"

"No."

"That was nice of him. I expect he didn't want you to find out too soon what a fool of a sister you have." She smiled a little at him, as if she were glad to be his sister. "I bought him at the Lerridge Hunt sale. It was Timber who killed old Felix. Old Felix Hunstanton, the Master, you know. Did Simon tell you?"

"No. No, he just told me about his tricks."

"Old Felix had some good horses, and when they were being sold I went over to see what I could pick up. None of the Lerridge Hunt regulars was bidding for Timber, but I thought it was because of sentiment, perhaps. I thought they probably didn't want to own the horse the Master was killed on. As if there was ever any sentiment about horse-dealing! I oughtn't to be let out alone. Even so, I ought to have wondered why I was getting him so cheap: with his looks and his breeding and

110

his performance. It was only afterwards that we found that he had done the same thing to the huntsman a few days later, only the branches were small and broke, instead of braining him or sweeping him off."

"I see," said Brat, who was beginning to.

"Not that anyone needed convincing, apparently. No one who was there when Felix was killed believed it was an accident. It was a Lerridge Castle meet, and they had found in one of the Lerridge woods and gone away over the park. Good open galloping country with the trees isolated. And yet Timber took Felix under an oak, going an awful bat, and he was dead before he hit the ground. But of course we heard about all that later. All I knew when I was bidding for him was that Felix had hit his head on a branch during the hunt. Which is something that has been happening to people ever since William Rufus."

"Did anyone actually see it happen?"

"No, I don't think so. Everyone just knew that with the whole park to choose from Felix wouldn't have ridden under the oak. And when he tried the same thing on Samms, the huntsman, there was no doubt. So he is put into the sale with the rest of the lot and all the Lerridge regulars sit around in silence and watch Eleanor Ashby from over Clare way buying a pup."

"He's a very elegant pup, there's no denying," Brat said, rubbing Timber's neck.

"He's beautiful," Eleanor said. "And a faultless jumper. Did you jump him at all today? No? You must next time. He is safest jumping because his mind is distracted. He hasn't time to think up mischief. It's odd, isn't it: he doesn't *look* untrustworthy," she added, still eyeing her bad bargain with a puzzled eye.

"No."

She caught the tone and said: "You don't sound too sure."

"Well, I must allow he is the most conceited animal I've ever met."

This seemed to be as new an idea to Eleanor as it had been to Simon.

"Vain, is he? Yes, I suppose he is. I expect *I'*d be conceited if I were a horse and I had been clever enough to kill a man. Did he try any tricks today?"

"He swerved at the entrance to the ride, but that was all."

He did not say: He took advantage of the first good stout piece of timber to mash my leg against. That was something between the horse and himself. He and Timber had a long acquaintanceship in front of them, and a lot to say to each other.

"He behaves like an angel most of the time," Eleanor said. "That is what is so lethal about him. We have all ridden him; Simon and Gregg and Arthur and me, and he has only twice played up. Once with Simon and once with Arthur. But of course," she added with a grin, "we have always given trees a wide berth."

"He'd be a great success in the desert. Not a rail or a limb in a day's journey."

Eleanor looked sadly at the black horse as Brat drew up to let her precede him into the yard. "He'd think up something else, I expect."

And Brat, thinking it over, agreed with her. Timber was that rare thing in horses: a deliberate and intelligent rogue. Balked of his normal fun, he would think up something new. There was nothing small-time about Timber.

Nor was Simon exactly small-time. Simon had sent him out on a notorious rogue, with a light remark about the horse "having its tricks". As neat a piece of vicarious manslaughter as anyone ever thought up.

16

BEATRICE ASHBY looked down the dining-table at her nephew Patrick and thought how well he was doing it. The occasion must be an extraordinarily difficult one for him, but he was carrying it off beautifully. He was neither awkward nor exuberant. He brought to the situation the same quiet detachment that he had shown on their first meeting in that Pimlico room. It was a very adult quality, and a little surprising in a boy not yet twenty-one. He had great dignity this Patrick Ashby, she thought, watching him dealing with the Rector. Surely never before can anyone have been so silent by habit without appearing either stiff or stupid.

It was she who had brought Simon up, and she was pleased with the result. But this boy had brought himself up, and the result was even better, it seemed. Perhaps it was a case of "giving the first seven years" and the rest followed automatically. Or perhaps it was that the goodness in Patrick had been so innate that he had needed no other guidance. He had followed his own lights, and the result was this quiet, adult young man with the still face.

It was a mask of a face; a sad mask, on the whole. It was such a contrast to the similar set of features in Simon's mobile countenance that they reminded one of those reversible comedy-tragedy masks that are used to decorate the title-pages of plays.

Simon was being particularly gay tonight, and Bee's heart ached for him. He too was doing it well, and tonight she loved him almost without reservation. Simon was abdicating, and doing it with a grace and spontaneity that she would not have believed possible. She felt a little guilty that she had underrated him. She had not credited for selfish, acquisitive Simon with such a power of renunciation.

They were choosing a name for Honey's filly foal, and the conversation was growing ribald. Nancy was insisting that "honey" was an endearment, and should be translated as "poppet," and Eleanor said that no thoroughbred as good as Honey's present foal should be damned by a name like Poppet. If Eleanor had refused to dress especially for Patrick's arrival, she had now made up for it. It was a long time since Bee had seen her looking so well or so pretty. Eleanor belonged to a type which did not glow easily.

"Brat is in love with Honey," Eleanor said.

"I suppose Bee dragged you round the paddocks before you were well over the doorstep," said Nancy. "Were you impressed, Brat?"

She too had adopted the nickname. Only the Rector called him Patrick.

"I'm in love with the whole bunch," Brat said. "And I found an old friend."

"Oh? Who was that?"

"Regina."

"Oh, yes, of course. Poor old Regina. She must be about twenty!" Nancy said.

"Not so much of the 'poor'," said Simon. "Regina has kept us shod and clothed for a whole generation. We ought to pay her a dividend."

"She takes her dividends out in pasture," Eleanor said. "She was always a greedy eater."

113

"When you drop foals like Regina year after year without a break, you're entitled to an appetite," Simon said.

Simon was drinking a great deal more than usual, but it seemed to be having little effect on him. Bee thought that the Rector looked at him now and then with pity in his eyes.

And Brat, too, at the other end of the table, was watching Simon, but without pity. Pity was not an emotion that Brat indulged in very often: like everyone who despises self-pity he did not readily pity others; but it was not because of his native disinclination to pity that he withheld sympathy from Simon Ashby. It was not even because Simon was his declared enemy; he had admired enemies before now. It was because there was something about Simon Ashby that repelled him. There was something unaccountable about Simon. There he sat, being light-hearted and charming, and there sat his relations and friends silently applauding his nobility and his courage. They were applauding an "act", but they would all be staggered to know what an act Simon was really putting on for their benefit.

Watching him as he displayed his graces, Brat felt that Simon reminded him of someone that he had met quite lately. Someone who had just that air of breeding, and excellent good manners, and good looks, and that—unaccountability. Who could that have been?

He was maddened by that tip-of-the-tongue feeling. In one more second he would remember. Loding? No. Someone on the ship coming over? Not very likely. That lawyer chap: the K.C. chap, Macdermott? No. Then who could it——

"Don't you think so, Patrick?"

It was the Rector again. He must be careful with the old boy. He had been more afraid of meeting George Peck than of anyone but Simon. After a twin brother there is no one who is liable to remember so much about you or to remember that much so well as the man who taught you. There would be a score of small things that George Peck would know about Patrick Ashby that not even Patrick Ashby's mother would know. But the meeting had gone off very well. Nancy Peck had kissed him on both cheeks and said: "Oh, dear, you've got very grown-up and serious, haven't you!"

"Patrick always was," the Rector had said, and had shaken hands.

He had looked consideringly at Brat, but no more consideringly than was normal in a man examining an old pupil met after a decade of absence. And Brat, who had no love for the Cloth, found himself liking the Rector. He was still wary of him, but the wariness was due not to the Rector's calling but to his knowledge of Pat Ashby, and to the intelligence and penetration of the eyes in his simian face.

Considering that intelligence, Brat was glad that he was particularly well primed in the matter of Pat Ashby's schooling. The Rector was Alec Loding's brother-in-law, and Loding had had what he called a front-stall view of the Ashby twins' education.

As for Alec Loding's sister, she was the most beautiful woman that Brat had ever seen. He had never heard of the famous Nancy Ledingham, but her brother had been eloquent about her. "Could have had anyone in the world; any man would have been delighted to keep her just to look at; but she had to choose George Peck." He had been shown Nancy in every kind of garment, from a swimming suit to her court presentation gown, but none of the photographs had done justice to her serene beauty, her gaiety, her general niceness. He felt that George Peck must be all right if Nancy had married him.

"Was that the Toselli child you had out with you?" she was saying to Eleanor. "That object I met you with this afternoon?"

"That was Tony," Eleanor said.

"How he brought back the days of my youth!"

"Tony did? How?"

"You won't remember it, but there used to be things called cavalry regiments. And every regiment had a trick-riding team. And every trick-riding team had a 'comedy' member. And every 'comedy' member of a trick-riding team looked just like Tony."

"So they did!" Bee said, delighted. "That was what he reminded me of this afternoon and I couldn't think of it at the time. That masterly irrelevance. The completely unrelated garments."

"You may wonder why I took him out at all," Eleanor remarked. "But after Sheila Parslow he's a positive holiday. He'll ride quite well some day, Tony."

"To the prospective horseman all things are forgiven, are they?" The Rector said, mocking mildly.

"Doesn't La Parslow get any better?" Simon asked.

"She will never get any better. She skates about in the

saddle like a block of ice on a plate. I could weep for the horse all the time we are out. Luckily Cherrypicker has an indestructible frame and practically no feelings."

The move from the dining-room to the living-room produced an anti-climax. The talk ceased to flow and ran into aimless trickles. Brat was suddenly so tired that he could hardly stand up. He hoped that no one would spring anything on him now; his normally hard head was muzzy with unaccustomed wine, and his thoughts fumbled and stuck. The twins said good night and went upstairs. Bee poured the coffee which had been placed in readiness for them on a low table by the fire, and it was not as hot as it should have been. Bee made despairing grimaces at Nancy.

"Our Lana, is it?" Nancy asked, sympathetic.

"Yes. I suppose she had to meet our Arthur and couldn't wait another ten minutes."

Simon, too, fell silent, as if the effort he had been making seemed suddenly not worth while. Only Eleanor seemed to have brought from the dining-room the warmth and happiness that had made dinner a success. In the moments of silence between the slow spurts of talk the rain fell against the tall windows with a soft shush.

"You were right about the weather, Aunt Bee," Eleanor said. "She said this morning that it was that too-bright kind that would rain before night."

"Bee is perennially right," the Rector said, giving her a look that was half a smile, half a benediction.

"It sounds loathsome," Bee said.

Nancy waited until they had lingered properly over their coffee and then said: "It has been a very full day for Brat, Bee; and I expect you are all tired. We won't stay now, but you'll come over and see us when you can crawl out from under the crush, won't you, Brat?"

Simon fetched her wraps and they all went out to the doorstep to see their guests off. On the doorstep Nancy took off her evening shoes, tucked them under her arm, and stepped into a pair of wellingtons that she had left behind the door. Then she tucked her other arm under her husband's, huddled close to him under their single umbrella, and walked away with him into the night.

"Good old Nancy," Simon said. "You can't keep a Ledingham down." He sounded just a little drunk.

116

"Dear Nan," Bee said softly. She moved into the living-room and surveyed it in an absent fashion.

"I think Nan is right," she said. "It is time we all went to bed. It has been an exciting day for all of us."

"We don't want it to end so soon, do we?" Eleanor said.

"You have La Parslow at nine-thirty tomorrow, Simon reminded her, "I saw it in the book."

"What were *you* doing with the riding book?"

"I like to see that you're not cheating on your income tax."

"Oh, yes, let's go to bed," Eleanor said, with a wide happy yawn. "It's been a wonderful day."

She turned to Brat to say good night, became suddenly shy, gave him her hand and said: "Good night then, Brat. Sleep well," and went away upstairs.

Brat turned to Bee, but she said: "I shall come in to see you on my way up." So he turned back to face Simon.

"Good night, Simon." He met the clear cold eyes levelly.

"Good night to you—Patrick," Simon said, looking faintly amused. He had managed to make the name sound like a provocation.

"Are you coming up now?" Brat heard Bee ask him as he climbed the stairs.

"Not quite yet."

"Will you see that the lights are out, then? And make sure of the locks?"

"Yes, of course I'll do that. Good night, Bee darling."

As Brat turned on to the landing he saw Bee's arms go round Simon. And he was stabbed by a hot despairing jealousy that shocked him. What had it to do with him?

Bee followed him into the old night nursery in a few moments. She looked with a practised eye at the bed and said: "That moron promised to put in a hot-water bottle and she has forgotten to do it."

"Don't worry," Brat said. "I'd only have put it out again. I don't use the things."

"You must think us a crowd of soft-livers," she said.

"I think you're a nice crowd," he said.

She looked at him and smiled.

"Tired?"

"Yes."

"Too tired for breakfast at eight-thirty?"

"That sounds luxuriously late to me."

117

"Did you enjoy it, that hard life—Brat?"

"Sure."

"I think you're nice too," she said, and kissed him lightly. "I wish you hadn't stayed away from us so long, but we are glad to have you back. Good night, my dear." And as she went out: "It's no use ringing a bell, of course, because no one will answer. But if you have a mad desire for fried shrimps, or iced water, or a copy of the *Pilgrim's Progress* or something, come along to my room. It is still the right-hand one in front."

"Good night," he said.

She stood for a moment outside his room, the door-knob still in her hand, and then moved away to Eleanor's door. She knocked and went in. For the last year or so Eleanor had been a great comfort to her. She had been so long alone in her need for judgment and resolution that it was refreshing to have the companionship of her own kind; to have Eleanor's unemotional good sense on tap when she wanted to.

"Hullo, Bee," Eleanor said, looking up through the hair she was brushing. She was beginning to drop the "aunt", as Simon did.

Bee sank into a chair and said: "Well, that's over."

"It turned out to be quite a success, didn't it," Eleanor said, "Simon behaved beautifully. Poor Simon."

"Yes. Poor Simon."

"Perhaps Brat—Patrick—will offer him some kind of partnership. Do you think? After all, Simon helped to make the stable. It wouldn't be fair to walk in and grab the lot after taking no interest for years and years."

"No. I don't know. I hope so."

"You sound tired."

"Aren't we all?"

"D'you know, Bee, I must confess I have the greatest difficulty in connecting the two."

"The two? Simon and Patrick?"

"No. Patrick and Brat."

There was a moment's silence, filled with the soft sound of the rain and the strokes of Eleanor's brush.

"You mean you—don't think he is Patrick?"

Eleanor stopped brushing and looked up, her eyes wide with surprise. "Of course he's Patrick," she said, astonished. "Who else would he be?" She put down the brush and began to tie up her hair in a blue ribbon. "It's just that I have no

118

feeling of ever having met him before. Odd, isn't it? When we spent nearly twelve years of our lives together. I like him: don't you?"

"Yes," Bee said. "I like him." She, too, had no feeling of ever having met him before, and she too did not see "who else he could be".

"Did Patrick not smile very often?"

"No; he was a serious child."

"When Brat smiles I want to cry."

"Good heavens, Eleanor."

"You can 'good heavens' all you like, but I expect you know what I mean."

Bee thought that she did.

"Did he tell you why he didn't write to us all those years?"

"No. There wasn't much opportunity for confidences."

"I thought you might have asked him when you were going round the paddocks with him this evening."

"No. He was too interested in the horses."

"Why do *you* think he didn't take any interest in us after he left?"

"Perhaps he took what old Nannie used to call a 'scunner' to us. It's not so surprising, in a way, as the fact that he ran away in the first place. The urge to put Latchetts behind him must have been overwhelming."

"Yes. I suppose so. But he was such a kind person: Pat. And so fond of us all. He mightn't have wanted to come back, but you would have thought he'd want to let us know that he was safe."

Since this was her own private stumbling-block, Bee had no help to offer.

"It must have been difficult to come back," Eleanor said, running the comb through her brush. "He looked so tired tonight that he looked like a *dead* man. It's not a very lively face at the best of times, is it? If you chopped it off behind the ears and hung it on a wall, no one would know the difference."

Bee knew Eleanor well enough, and agreed with her sufficiently, to translate this successfully.

"You don't think he'll want to sheer off again once the excitement of coming home has worn off?"

"Oh, no, I'm quite sure he won't."

"You think he is here for keeps?"

"Of course I do."

But Brat, standing in the dark before the open window of his room and looking at the curve of the down in the wet starlight, was wondering about that very matter. The thing had succeeded beyond Loding's most extravagant promises, and now?

Where did he go from here? How long would it be before Simon had him cold? And if Simon failed, how long could he go on living a life where at any moment someone might spring a mine?

That is what he had set out to do, of course. But somehow he had not really looked beyond the first stages. In his heart he had been unable to believe that he would succeed. Now that success was his he felt rather like someone who has climbed a pinnacle and can't get down again. Elated but misgiving.

He turned from the window and switched the lamp on. His landlady in Pimlico used to say that she "was so tired that she felt as if she'd been through a mangle"; he knew now how good a description that had been. That was exactly how he felt. Wrung out and empty. So limp that it was an effort to lift a hand to undress. He pulled off his nice new suit—the suit that had made him feel so guilty in that other life way back in London—and made himself hang it up. He peeled off his underclothes and stumbled into his faded old pyjamas. He wondered for a moment whether they would mind if the rain came in and marked the carpet, but decided to risk it. So he left the window wide open and got into bed.

He lay for a long time listening to the quiet sounds of the rain and looking at the room. Now was the time for Pat Ashby's ghost to come and chill that room. He waited for the ghost but it did not come. The room was warm and welcoming. The figures on the wallpaper, the figures that those children had grown up with, looked friendly and alive. He turned his head to look at the groups by the bedside. To look for the one Eleanor had been in love with. The chap with the profile. He wondered if she was in love with anyone now.

His eyes went on to the wood of the bedstead, and he remembered that this was Alec Loding's bed, and was pleased once more by the irony of it all. It was fantastically right that he should come to Latchetts only to sleep in Alec Loding's bed. He must tell him one day. It was the kind of thing that Loding would appreciate.

He wondered whether it was Eleanor or Bee who had put the flowers in the bowl. Flowers to welcome him—home.

Latchetts, he said to himself, looking at the room. This is Latchetts. I'm here. This is Latchetts.

The sound of the word was a soporific; like the swing of a hammock. He put out his hand and switched off the light. In the dark the rain suddenly sounded louder.

This morning he had got up and dressed in that back room under the slates, with the crowding chimney-pots beyond the window. And here he was, going to sleep in Latchetts, with the sweet cold smell of the down blowing in on the damp air from the window.

As sleep drew him under he had an odd feeling of reassurance. A feeling that Pat Ashby didn't mind his being there; that he was on the contrary pleased about it all.

The unlikeness of this roused him a little, and his thoughts, running on approval and disapproval, went to Bee. What was it that he had felt when Bee took his hand to lead him to the interview this afternoon? What was different from any other of the thousand handclasps he had experienced in his time? Why the surge of warmth under his heart, and what kind of emotion was it anyway? He had suffered the same obscure gratification when Bee had thrust her arm through his on the way to the stables. What was so remarkable about a woman putting her hand on your arm? A woman, moreover, that you were not in love with, and were never likely to be in love with.

It *was* because she was a woman, of course, but the thing that made it remarkable was something else again. It had something to do with being taken for granted by her. No one else had taken his hand in just that way. Casual but—no, not possessive. Quite a few had been possessive with him, and he had not been gratified in the least. Casual but—what? Belonging. It had something to do with belonging. The hand had taken him for granted because he belonged. It was the unthinking friendliness of a woman to one of her family. Was it because he had never "belonged" before, that made that commonplace gesture into a benediction?

He went on thinking of Bee as he fell asleep. Her sidelong glance when she was considering something; her courage; the way she had braced herself to meet him that day in the back room in Pimlico; the way she had kissed him before she was sure, just in case he was Patrick; the way she had dealt with the suspense of Simon's absence when he arrived today.

She was a lovely woman, Beatrice Ashby, and he loved her.

He had reached the toppling-over place of sleep when he was yanked of a sudden wide awake.

He had remembered something.

He knew now who it was that Simon Ashby reminded him of.

It was Timber.

17

ON Wednesday morning Bee took him to call on the tenants of the three farms: Frenchland, Upacres, and Wigsell. "Gates last; just to larn him," Bee said. Gates was last also in importance, since Wigsell was the smallest of the three farms. It had originally been the home farm of Latchetts and lay just beyond the Rectory, on the slope north of the village. It was almost too small a farm to be self-supporting, but Gates also ran the butcher's shop in the village (open twice a week) and was not dependent on what he made from Wigsell.

"Do you drive, Brat?" Bee asked, as they prepared to get into the car.

"Yes, but I'd rather you did. You know the"—"road" he had almost said—"the car better."

"Nice of you to call it a car. I expect you're used to a left-hand drive."

"Yes."

"I'm sorry it had to be the bug. It isn't often the car goes wrong on us. Jameson has all its inside out on the garage floor, and is conducting a post-mortem in a silent fury."

"I like the bug. I came from the station in it yesterday."

"So you did. What a very long time ago that seems. Does it seem like that to you?"

"Yes." It seemed years away to him.

"Have you heard that we've been saved from the *Clarion*?" she asked, as they sped down the avenue to the accompaniment of the bug's sewing-machine song.

"No?"

"Are you not a consumer of the Press at breakfast?" asked Bee, who had breakfasted at eight o'clock.

"I never lived where we had papers to read at breakfast. We just switched on the radio."

122

"Oh, lord, yes. I forget that your generation doesn't have to read."

"How have we been saved?"

"We have been rescued by three people we never heard of, and are never likely to meet. The fourth wife of a Manchester dentist, the husband of a principal boy, and the owner of a black leather trunk." She pressed the horn and turned slowly to the right out of the avenue. "The owner of the trunk left it at Charing Cross with someone's arms and legs in it. Or, of course, it may be the owner's arms and legs. That is a question which will occupy the *Clarion* for some time to come, I expect. The husband of the principal boy is suing for alienation of affection, and none of the three people concerned has ever been bothered with an inhibition, which is very nice for the *Clarion*. Since the reports of divorce cases have been pruned the *Clarion* has been suffering from frustration, and a suit of alienation of affection is a gift from heaven. Especially when it is Tattie Thacker's affections." She looked with pleasure at the morning. "I do like a morning after rain."

"You've still one to come?"

"What?"

"The fourth wife of the Manchester dentist."

"Oh. Yes. She, poor wretch, has just been exhumed from a very expensive and elaborate tomb and found to be loaded with arsenic. Her husband is found to be missing."

"And you think that the *Clarion* will be too busy to bother about—us?"

"I'm sure of it. They haven't room as it is for all they want to do with Tattie. She had a whole page to herself this morning. If they ever bothered about the Ashbys they would print the report in a tiny paragraph at the bottom of a page, and five million people would read it and not be able to tell you two minutes later what was in it. I think we are quite safe. The *Westover Times* will have one of their usual discreet paragraphs this morning, and that will be the end of the matter."

Well, that was another snag out of the way. In the meantime he must keep his wits alive for the visits to Frenchland and Upacres. He was supposed to know these people.

Frenchland was farmed by a tall rosy old man and his tall sallow sister. "Everyone was terrified of Miss Hassell," Loding had said. "She had a face like a witch, and a tongue that

123

took the skin off you. She didn't talk; just made one remark and you found that you were raw."

"Well, this is an honour," old Mr Hassell said, coming to the garden gate and seeing whom Bee had with her. "Mr Patrick, I'm glad to see you. I'm tarnation glad to see you." He took Brat's hand in his gnarled old fist and closed on it with his other one. There was no doubt that he was glad to see Patrick Ashby again.

It was difficult to know whether Miss Hassell was glad or not. She eyed Brat while she shook hands with him and said: "This is an unexpected pleasure." Her dry use of the conventional phrase and its wicked appropriateness amused Brat.

"Foreign parts don't seem to have changed you much," she said, as she set out glasses in the crowded little parlour.

"I've changed in one way," Brat said.

"You have?" She wasn't going to gratify him by asking in what way.

"I'm not frightened of you any more."

Old Mr Hassell laughed.

"You beat me there, son. She still puts the fear of God in me. If I'm half an hour late getting home from market I creep up the lane with my tail down like I was a sheep-stealer."

Miss Hassell said nothing, but Brat thought there was a new interest in her glance; almost as if she were pleased with him. And she went away and fetched some shortbread from the kitchen which she had obviously had no intention of producing before.

They drank a liquid called White Port Wine Type, and discussed Rhode Island Reds.

At Upacres there was only plump Mrs Docket, and she was busy making butter in the dairy at the back.

"Come in, whoever you are!" she called, and they went down the cool tiled passage from the open front door, and turned into the chill of the dairy.

"I can't stop this," she said, looking round at them. "The butter is just—Oh, goodness, I didn't know! I just thought it was someone passing. The children are all at school and Carrie is out in the barn and—— Goodness! To think of it!"

Bee automatically took her place at the churn while she shook hands with Brat.

"Well, well," said kind plump Mrs Docket, "a fine, good-looking Ashby you are. You're more like Mr Simon than ever you were."

Brat thought that Bee looked up with interest when she said that.

"It's a happy day for us all, Miss Ashby, isn't it. I could hardly believe it. I just said to Joe, I don't believe it, I said. It's the kind of thing that happens in books. And in pictures and plays. Not the kind of thing that would happen to quiet folk like us in a quiet place like Clare, I said. And yet here you are and it's really happened. My, Mr Patrick, it's nice to see you again, and looking so well and bonny."

"Can I have a shot at that?" Brat asked, indicating the churn. "I've never handled one of those things."

"But of course you have!" Mrs Docket said, looking taken aback. "You used to come in special on Saturday mornings to have a go at it."

Brat's heart missed a beat. "Did I?" he said. "I've forgotten that."

Always say quite frankly that you don't remember, Loding had advised. No one can deny that you don't remember, but they will certainly jump on you if you try to make-believe about anything.

"I thought you did this by electricity now," he heard Bee say as she made way for him at the churn.

"Oh, we do everything else by electricity, of course," Mrs Docket said. "But I can't believe it makes good butter. No more home-made taste to it than you'd get at the International in Westover. Sometimes when I'm rushed I switch on the electricity, but I'm always sorry afterwards. Awful *mechanical*, it is. No artfulness about it."

They drank hot black tea and ate light floury scones and discussed the children's schooling.

"She's a darling, Mrs Docket," Bee said as they drove away. "I think she is still of the opinion in her heart of hearts that electricity is an invention of the devil."

But Brat was thoughtful. He must stop himself from volunteering remarks. It was not important about the churn, but it quite easily might have been something vital. He must be less forthcoming.

"About Friday, Brat," Bee said, as they made their way back to Clare and to Wigsell.

"What is on Friday?" said Brat, out of his absorption.

Bee looked round and smiled at him. "Your birthday," she said.

Of course. He was now the possessor of a birthday.

"Had you forgotten that you are going to be twenty-one on Friday?" she asked.

"I had, almost." He caught her sidelong look at him. After a pause she said: "You came of age a long time ago, didn't you." She said it without smiling and it was not a question.

"About Friday," she went on. "I thought that since we have postponed the celebrations for Uncle Charles's benefit, we wouldn't have a party on Friday. Mr Sandal will be coming down with the papers he wants you to sign, so we shall have him to lunch, and make it just a quiet family party."

Papers to sign. Yes, he had known that there would be papers to sign sooner or later. He had even learned to make his capital letters the way Patrick did, thanks to an old exercise book that Loding had unearthed and filched from the Rectory. And, after all, signing a paper didn't make him any more of a heel than he was being at this moment. It just put him more surely in the Law's reverence, made the thing irrevocable.

"Is that how you would like it?"

"What? Oh, the birthday. Yes, of course. I don't want a party. I don't want a celebration, if it comes to that. Can't we just take this coming-of-age for granted?"

"I don't think the neighbourhood would be very pleased if we did. They are all looking forward to some kind of party. I think we shall have to give them one. Even the invitation cards are all ready. I altered the date to a fortnight after Charles's arrival. He is due in about twenty-three days. So you'll have to 'thole' it, as old Nannie used to say."

Yes, he would have to thole it. Anyhow, he could sit back now and relax for a little. He was not supposed to know the Gates family.

They were coming back to the village now; the white rails of the south paddocks on their left. It was a washed and shining morning, but it had an uneasy glitter. The sky was metallic, and the light had a silver edge to it.

As they passed the entrance to the Rectory Bee said: "Alec Loding came down for the week-end not long ago."

"Oh? What is he doing now?"

"Still playing roué parts in dreadful little comedies and farces.

126

You know: four characters, five doors, and one bed. I didn't see him, but Nancy said he had improved."

"In what way?"

"Oh, more interested in other people. Kindlier. He even made efforts to get on with George. Nancy thought age was beginning to tell. He was quite happy to sit for hours with a book in George's study when George was out. And when George was in they would yarn quite happily. Nancy was delighted. She has always been fond of Alec, but she used to dread his visits. The country bored him and George bored him even more, and he never bothered to hide it. So it was a pleasant change."

Half-way through the village they turned into the lane that led to Wigsell.

"You don't remember Emmy Vidler, do you?" she asked Brat. "She was brought up at Wigsell, and married Gates when he had a farm the other side of Bures. When her father died, Gates put a bailiff into his farm and took over Wigsell. And, of course, the butcher's shop. So they are very comfortably off. The boy couldn't stand his father, and got himself a job in the Midlands somewhere; engineering. But the girl lives at home, and is the apple of her father's eye. She went to an expensive boarding-school, where I understand she was known as Margot. Her name is Peggy."

They swung into the farm entrance and came to rest on the small old cobbles of the yard. Two dogs rushed at them in wild self-importance, yelling their arrival to the world.

"I do wish Gates would train his dogs," said Bee, whose dogs were as well-trained as her horses.

The clamour brought Mrs Gates to the front door. She was a faded and subdued little woman who must once have been very pretty.

"Glen! Joy! Be quiet!" she called, ineffectually, and came forward to greet them. But before she reached them Gates came round the corner of the house, and in a few strides had anticipated her. His pompous welcome drowned her more genuine pleasure, and she stood smiling gently at Brat while her husband trumpeted forth their satisfaction in seeing Patrick Ashby on their doorstep again.

Gates was a large, coarse individual, but Brat supposed that once he had had the youthful vigour and assurance that appealed to pretty, fragile little women like Emmy Vidler.

"They tell me that you've been making money in horses over there," he said to Brat.

"I've earned my living from them," Brat said.

"You come and see what I've got in *my* stable." He began to lead the way to the back of the house.

"But Harry, they must come in and sit down for a little," his wife protested.

"They'll sit down presently. They'd much rather look at a piece of good horseflesh than at your gewgaws. Come along, Mr Patrick. Come along, Miss Ashby. Alfred!" he bellowed as they went down the yard. "Turn out that new horse for Miss Ashby to see."

Mrs Gates, tailing along behind, found herself side by side with Brat. "I am so happy about this," she said quietly. "So happy about your coming back. I remember you when you were little; when I lived here in my father's day. Except for my own son I've never been so fond of a small boy as I was of you."

"Now then, Mr Patrick, have a look at this here, have a look at this! Tell me if that doesn't fill the eye for you."

Gates swept his great limb of an arm at the stable door where Alfred was leading out a brown horse that looked oddly out of place in the small farmyard, even in a region where every small farmer kept a mount that would carry him across country in the winter. There was no denying it, the brown horse was something exceptional.

"There! what do you think of that, eh? What do you think of that?"

Bee, having looked, said: "But that, surely, is the horse that Dick Pope won the jumping on at the Bath Show last year."

"That's the horse," Gates said complacently. "And not only the jumping. The cup for the best riding horse in the show. Cost me a pretty penny, that did, but I can afford it and nothing's too good for my girl. Oh ah! It's for Peggy I bought it. That wouldn't carry me, that wouldn't." He gave an abrupt shout of laughter; at least Brat supposed it was laughter. "But my girl, now, she's a feather in the saddle. I don't have to tell you, Miss Ashby; you've seen her. There's no one in the county deserves a good horse better than my Peggy, and I don't grudge the money for it."

"You've certainly got a good horse, Mr Gates," Bee said, with an enthusiasm in her voice that surprised Brat. He looked

128

across at her and wondered why she was looking so pleased. After all, this brown horse was a potential rival to Timber, and all the other Latchetts animals.

"Got a vet's certificate with it, I need hardly say. I don't buy pigs in pokes."

"Is Peggy going to show it this year?"

"Of course she is, of course she is. What did I buy it for but for her to show?"

Bee's face was positively blissful. "How nice!" she said, and she sounded rapturous.

"Do you like it, Miss Ashby?" Peggy Gates said, appearing at Brat's side.

Peggy was a very pretty creature. Pink and white and gold. Brat thought that if it were possible to cross Miss Parslow and Eleanor the result would probably be Peggy Gates. She accepted her introduction to Brat with composure, but managed to convey the impression that it was personally delightful to her to have Patrick home again. Her small hand lay in his with a soft pressure that was intimate rather than friendly. Brat shook it heartily and resisted a temptation to wipe his palm down his hip.

She accepted Bee's congratulations on her possession of the horse, allowed a decent interval for further contemplation of it, and then, with an admirable display of social dexterity, lifted the whole family from the yard into the drawing-room of the house. It was called the drawing-room, and was furnished as such, but Bee, who remembered it as old Mrs Vidler's parlour, thought the water-colours and wistaria wallpaper a poor exchange for the lustre jugs and framed engravings of Mrs Vidler's day.

They drank very good madeira and talked about the Bures Agricultural Show.

And they drove home with Bee still looking as if someone had left her a fortune. She caught Brat's considering look at her and said: "Well?"

"You look like a cat that has been given cream," he said.

She gave him her sideways, amused glance. "Cream and fish and liver," she said; but did not tell him the translation.

"When all the fuss of Friday is over, Brat," she said, "you must go up to town and get yourself a wardrobe. Walters will take weeks to make your evening things, and you'll need them for the celebration when Uncle Charles comes home."

"What shall I get?" he asked, at a loss for the first time.

"I should leave it to Walters, if I were you."

"Outfit for a young English gentleman," Brat said.

And she looked sideways again, surprised by the twist in his voice.

18

ELEANOR came into the sitting-room as Bee was opening the midday post, and said: "She bumped!"

Bee looked up hazily, her mind still on the contents of her mail.

"She bumped, I tell you. For a whole fifty yards she bumped like a good 'un."

"The Parslow girl? Oh, congratulations, Nell, dear."

"I never thought I'd live to see this day. Is no one having sherry?"

"Brat and I have drunk sufficient strange liquids this morning to last us for the rest of the week."

"How did it go, Brat?" Eleanor asked, pouring herself some sherry.

"Not as badly as I'd been prepared for," Brat said, watching her thin capable hand manipulating the glasses. That hand wouldn't lie soft and confidential and insinuating in one's own.

"Did Docket tell you how he got his wound?"

"Docket was at market," Bee said. "But we had hot buttered scones from Mrs Docket."

"Dear Mrs Docket. What did Miss Hassell give you?"

"Shortbread. She wasn't going to give us that, but she succumbed to Brat's charms." So Bee had noticed that.

"I'm not surprised," Eleanor said, looking at Brat over her glass. "And Wigsell?"

"Do you remember that brown horse of Dick Pope's? The one he swept the board with at Bath last year?"

"Certainly."

"Gates has bought it for Peggy."

Eleanor stopped sipping sherry and thought about this in silence for a moment or two.

"For Peggy to show?"

130

"Yes."

"Well, well!" said Eleanor slowly; and she looked amused and thoughtful. She looked at Bee, met Bee's glance, and looked away again. "Well, well!" she said again, and went on sipping sherry. After an interval broken only by the rip of paper as Bee opened envelopes, she said: "I don't know that that was such a very good move."

"No," said Bee, not looking up.

"I'm going to wash. What is for lunch?"

"Goulash."

"As made by our Mrs Betts, that is just stew."

The twins came in from lessons at the Rectory, and Simon from the stables, and they went in to lunch.

Simon had come down so late to breakfast that Brat's only intercourse with him today had been to wish him good morning. He seemed amiable and relaxed, and inquired with what appeared to be genuine interest about the success of the morning. Bee provided an account, with periodic confirmation from Brat. When she came to Wigsell, Eleanor interrupted her to say:

"Did you know that Gates has bought Peggy a new horse?"

"No," Simon said, looking up with mild interest.

"He has bought her that brown horse of Dick Pope's."

"*Riding Light?*"

"Yes. Riding Light. She is going to show it this year."

For the first time since he had met him Brat saw Simon Ashby flush. He paused for a moment, and then went on with his lunch. The flush slowly died, and the cool pale profile resumed its normal calm. Both Eleanor and Bee had avoided looking at him while he absorbed the news, but Ruth studied him with interest.

And Brat, eating Mrs Betts's goulash, studied him with his mind. Simon Ashby was reputedly crazy about the Gates girl. But was he glad that the girl had been given a good horse? No. He was furious. And what was more, his womenfolk had known that he would be furious. They had known beforehand that he would find Peggy's entry as a rival unforgivable. They had, understandably, not wanted the Gates affair to last or to become serious; and they had recognised instantly, both of them, that Peggy's possession of Riding Light had saved them. What kind of creature was this Simon Ashby, who could not bear to be beaten by the girl he was in love with?

131

He remembered Bee's inordinate pleasure in the brown horse. He saw again Eleanor's slow amusement at the news. They had known at once that that was the end of the Peggy affair. Gates had bought that horse to be "upsides" with Latchetts; to give his daughter a mount as good as any owned by the man he hoped she would marry. And all he had done was to destroy any chance that Peggy ever had of being mistress of Latchetts.

Well, Simon was no longer master of Latchetts, so it would not matter to the Gates family that Simon resented Peggy's possession of the horse. But what kind of heel was Simon that he could not love a rival?

"What is Brat going to ride at the Bures Show?" he heard Eleanor say, and brought his attention back to the lunch table.

"All of them," Simon said. And as Eleanor looked her question: "They are his horses."

This was the kind of thing that the English did not say. Simon must be very angry to desert the habit of a lifetime.

"I'm not going to 'show' any horses, if that is what you mean," Brat said. "That requires technique, and I haven't got it."

"But you used to be very good," Bee said.

"Did I? Oh, well, that is a long time ago. I certainly don't want to show any horses in the ring at Bures."

"The show isn't for nearly three weeks yet," Eleanor said. "Bee could coach you for a day or two, and you'd be as good as ever."

But Brat was not to be moved. It would have been fun to see what he could do against English horsemen; fun especially to jump the Latchetts horses and perhaps win with them; but he was not going to make any public appearance as Patrick Ashby of Latchetts if he could help it.

"Brat could ride in the races," Ruth said. "The races they end up with. He could beat everyone on Timber, couldn't he?"

"Timber is not going to be knocked about in any country bumpkins' race if I still have any say in the matter," Simon said, speaking into his plate. "He is going to Olympia, which is his proper place."

"I agree," Brat said. And the atmosphere ceased to be tense. Jane wanted to know why fractions were vulgar, and Ruth wanted a new bicycle tyre, and the conversation became the normal family conversation of any meal-time in any home.

Before lunch was over the first of the visitors arrived; and the steady stream went on, from after-luncheon coffee, through tea, to six o'clock drinks. They had all come to inspect Brat, but he noticed that those who had known Patrick Ashby came with a genuine pleasure in welcoming him back. Each of them had some small memory of him to recount, and all of them had kept the memory green because they had liked Pat Ashby and grieved for him. And Brat caught himself being gratified in an absurd and proprietorial way, as if some protégé of his own was being praised. The light that had been shed on Simon this morning made him more than ever Patrick's champion. It was all wrong that Latchetts should have been Simon's all those years. It was Patrick's inheritance and it was all wrong that Patrick should not be here to inherit it. Patrick was all right. Patrick would not have gone sick with rage because his best girl had a better horse than he had. Patrick was all right.

So he accepted the small verbal gifts on Patrick's behalf and was pleased and gratified.

About the time when tea-cups were being mixed up with cocktail glasses the local doctor appeared, and Brat ceased to be gratified, and became interested in Eleanor's reactions to the doctor. Eleanor seemed to like the doctor very much, and Brat, knowing nothing whatever about him, was straightway convinced that he was not good enough for her. The only guests left now were Colonel Smollett, the Chief Constable for the county; the two Misses Bryne, who occupied the Jacobean house at the far end of the village and, according to Bee, had their walls hung with "plates and warming-pans, and other kitchen utensils"; and Dr Spence. Dr Spence was young and red-haired and bony, and he had freckles and a friendly manner. He was the successor of the old country doctor who had brought the whole Ashby family up, and he was, so Bee confided in an interval of tea-pouring, "much too brilliant to stay in a country practice." Brat wondered if he stayed for Eleanor's sake; he seemed to like Eleanor very much.

"You caused us a lot of trouble, young man," Colonel Smollett had said, greeting him: and Brat, after the polite evasions he had experienced so far, was glad of his frankness. Just as his notions of English middle-class life had been derived from American films, so his idea of a colonel had been derived

133

from the English Press, and was equally erroneous. Colonel Smollett was a small, thin man, with a beaked nose and a self-effacing manner. What one noticed about him was his extraordinary neatness and his gay blue eyes.

The Colonel gave the Misses Bryne a lift in his car, but the doctor lingered, and it was only when Bee asked him to stay for dinner that he pulled himself together and went.

"Poor Dr Spence," Bee said at dinner. "I'm sorry he wouldn't stay. I'm sure that landlady of his starves him."

"Nonsense," said Simon, who had recovered his good temper and had been very bright all the afternoon; "that lean, red-haired type always look underfed. Besides, he wouldn't have eaten, anyhow. All he wants is to sit and look at Eleanor."

Which confirmed Brat's worst fears.

But all Eleanor said was: "Don't be absurd"; and she said it without heat and without interest.

They were all tired by dinner-time, and it was a quiet meal. The excitement of having Brat there had died into acceptance, and they no longer treated him as a newcomer. Even the unforthcoming Jane had stopped accusing him with her eyes. He was part of the landscape. It was wonderfully restful to be part of the landscape again. For the first time since he came to Latchetts he was hungry.

But as he got ready for bed he puzzled over the problem of Simon. Simon, who was quite sure that he was not Patrick, but had no intention of saying so. (Why? Because he would not be believed, and his protest would be put down to resentment at his brother's return? Because he had plans for a dramatic unveiling? Because he had some better way of dealing with an impostor who would not be unveiled?) Simon, who was so good a dissembler that he could fool his own family about his inmost feelings. Simon, who was so self-centred, so vain, that to come between him and the sun was to insult him. Simon, who had charm enough for ten men, and an appealing air of vulnerability. Simon, who was like Timber.

He stood again at the open window in the dark, looking at the curve of the down against the sky. Perhaps because he was less tired tonight he was no longer so afraid; but the incalculable factor in this life that he was due to lead was still Simon.

If Simon so resented Peggy Gates's owning a better horse than his, what, wondered Brat, could have been his reaction to Patrick's sudden succession to Latchetts?

He considered this a long time, staring into the dark.

And as he turned at last to put the light on, a voice in his mind said: I wonder where Simon was when Patrick went over the cliff.

But he noticed the heinousness of this at once, of course. What was he suggesting? Murder? In Latchetts? In Clare? By a boy of thirteen? He was letting his antipathy to Simon run away with his common sense.

The suicide of Patrick Ashby had been a police affair. An affair of inquest and evidence. The thing had been investigated and the police had been satisfied that it was in truth suicide.

Satisfied? Or just without a case?

Where would that coroner's report be now? In the police records he supposed. And it was not easy for a civilian to persuade the police to satisfy an idle curiosity; they were busy people.

But the thing must have been reported in the local Press. It must have been a local sensation. Somewhere in the files there would be an account of that inquest, and he, Brat Farrar, would unearth it at the first opportunity.

Antipathy or no antipathy, common sense or no common sense, he wanted to know where Simon Ashby was when his twin went over the Westover cliffs.

19

MR SANDAL was to come on Thursday night and stay over till after luncheon on Friday.

On Thursday morning Bee said that she was going into Westover to do some special shopping for Mr Sandal's meals, and what would Brat like to do with his day?

Brat said that he would like to come with her and see West-over again, and Bee looked pleased.

"We can stop on the way through the village," she said, "and let Mrs Gloom run her eye over you. It will be one less for you to meet after church on Sunday."

So they stopped at the newsagent's, and Brat was exhibited,

and Mrs Gloom sucked the last ounce of satisfaction out of the drama of his return, and they laughed together about her as they sped away to the sea.

"People who can't sing are horribly frustrated," Bee said, after a little.

Brat considered this *non sequitur*. "The highest mountain in Britain is Ben Nevis," he said, proffering one in his turn.

Bee laughed at that and said: "No, I just meant that I should like to sing at the top of my voice, but I can only croak. Can you sing?"

"No. I croak too. We could croak together."

"I doubt if it is legal to croak in a built-up area. One never knows nowadays. And anyhow, there is that." She waved her hand at a large sign which read:

MOTORISTS. PLEASE REFRAIN FROM USING YOUR HORN. THIS IS A HOSPITAL.

Brat glanced up at the building, set on the slope above the town, and remarked that it was uncommonly pretty for a hospital.

"Yes; much less terrifying than the normal place. It is a great pity that *that* was allowed to happen." She jerked her chin at the row of cheap shops on the opposite side of the road; some of them not much better than shacks. Dingy cafés, a cobbler's, a bicycle "depot", a seller of wreaths and crosses, a rival seller of flowers, a greengrocer's, and anonymous businesses with windows painted half-way up and odd bills tacked in the window.

They were running down the slope into the town, and this miscellaneous strip of roadside commerce was the last petering-out of the poorer suburbs. Beyond was Westover proper: clean and neat and shining in the reflected light from the sea.

As Bee turned into the car park she said: "You don't want to tail round looking at 'sea-food' for Mr Sandal's consumption. Go away and amuse yourself, and we'll meet for lunch at the Angel about a quarter to one."

He was some distance away when she called him back. "I forgot to ask you if you were short of money. I can lend you some if you——"

"Oh, no, thanks; I still have some of what Cosset, Thring and what-you-may-call-'em advanced me."

He went first to the harbour to see the place that he was supposed to have set out from eight years ago. It was filled with coastwise shipping and fishing boats, very gay in the dancing light. He leaned against the warm stones of the breakwater and contemplated it. It was here that Alec Loding had sat painting his "old scow" on the last day of Pat Ashby's life. It was over those cliffs away to the right that Pat Ashby had fallen to his death.

He pushed himself off the breakwater and went to look for the office of the *Westover Times*. It took him some time to find it because, although every citizen of Westover read the local paper, very few of them had occasion to seek it out in its home. Its home was a stone's-throw from the harbour, in a small old house in a small old street which still had its original cobbles. The entrance was so low that Brat instinctively ducked his head as he went in. Beyond, after the bright sunlight outside, there was blackness. But out of the blackness the unmistakable adolescent voice of an office boy said: "Yes?"

Brat said that he would like to see Mr Macallan.

The voice said that Mr Macallan was out.

"I suppose you couldn't tell me where I could find him?"

"The fourth table on the left upstairs at the Blue Bird."

"That's explicit."

"Can't help it; that's where he is. That's where he always is, this time of day."

The Blue Bird, it seemed, was a coffee-shop round the corner on the harbour front. And Mr Macallan was indeed sitting at the fourth table on the left upstairs, which was the one by the far window. Mr Macallan was sitting with a half-drunk cup of coffee in front of him, glowering down on the bright front. He greeted Brat amiably, however, as one old friend to another, and pulled out a chair for him.

"I'm afraid I haven't been much good to you," Brat said.

"The only way I'll ever get myself on to the front page of the *Clarion* is in a trunk," Mr Macallan said.

"A trunk?"

"In sections. And I can't help feeling that would be a wee bit drastic." He spread out that morning's *Clarion* so that the shrieking black print screamed up from the table. The trunk murder was still front-page news after three days, it having been discovered that the legs in the case belonged to two different persons: a complication which put the present case *hors concours* in the trunk-murder class.

137

"What's horrible about murder," Mr Macallan said reflectively, "is not that it happens, but that it happens to your Aunt Agnes, if you follow me. Hi! *Miss!* A cup of coffee for my friend here. Brother Johnny goes to the war and gets killed and it is all very sad, but no one is shocked—civilisation being what it is. But if someone bumps Aunt Agnes off on her way home one night that *is* a shock. That sort of thing just doesn't happen to people you know."

"It must be worse when someone you know bumps off someone's Aunt Agnes."

"Ay," said Mr Macallan, shooting an extra spoonful of sugar into his half-cold coffee and stirring it vigorously. "I've seen some of that. Families, you know. It's always the same: they just can't believe it. *Their* Johnny. That is the horror in murder. The domesticity of it." He took out his cigarette case and offered it. "And how do you like being Clare's white-headed boy? Are you glad to be back?"

"You can't imagine how glad."

"After that fine free life in Arizona or Texas or wherever it was? You mean you actually prefer this?" Mr Macallan jerked his head at the Westover front filled with placid shoppers. And, as Brat nodded: "Mercy-be-there! I can hardly credit it."

"Why? Don't you like the place?"

Mr Macallan looked down at the southern English walking about in their southern English sunshine, and metaphorically spat. "They're so satisfied with themselves I can't take my eyes off them," he said.

"Satisfied with their lot, you mean? Why not?"

"Nothing in this world came out of satisfaction."

"Except the human race," said Brat.

Mr Macallan grinned. "I'll allow you that." But he went on glowering down at the bright harbour scene. "I look at them and think: 'These people kept Scotland fighting for four hundred years,' and I can't find the answer."

"The answer, of course, is that they didn't."

"No? Let me tell you that my country——"

"They've been much too busy for the last thousand years keeping the shores of England. But for them your Scotland would be part of Spain today."

This was apparently a new idea to Mr Macallan. He decided to let it ride.

"You weren't looking for me, were you? When you came to the Blue Bird?"

"Yes. I went to the office first and they told me you would be here. There's something I want and I thought that you might help me to it."

"Not publicity, I take it," Mr Macallan said dryly.

"No, I want to read my obituary."

"Man, who doesn't! You're a privileged person, Mr Ashby, a very privileged person."

"I suppose the *Westover Times* keeps back numbers."

"Och, yes, back to June the 18th, 1827. Or is it June the 28th? I forget. So you want to look at the files. Well, there's not very much, but you'll find it very interesting of course. One's own death must be a fascinating subject to read about."

"You've read about it, then?"

"Och, yes. Before I went out to Latchetts on Tuesday, I naturally looked you up."

So it was that, when they stumbled down the dark stairs to the cellar of the *Westover Times* offices, Mr Macallan was able to put his hand on the required copy without delay and without raising the dust of a hundred and twenty years about their ears.

"I'll leave you to it," Mr Macallan said, spreading the volume open under the naked light above the old-fashioned sloping desk. "Have a good time. If there is anything else I can do for you, just let me know. And drop in when you feel like it."

He trotted up the stone stairs, and the scuffling sound of his shoes faded upwards into the world of men, and Brat was left alone with the past.

The *Westover Times* appeared twice a week; on Wednesdays and Saturdays. Patrick Ashby's death had occurred on a Saturday, so that a single Wednesday issue carried both the announcement of his death and the report of the inquest. As well as the usual announcement inserted by the family in the list of deaths, there was a short news item on the middle page. The *Westover Times* had been owned and run by a Westover family since its founding, and it still kept the stateliness, the good manners, and the reticence of an early Edwardian doctor's brougham plying between Harley Street and Knightsbridge. The paper announced the sad occurrence and offered its sympathy to the family in this great trial which had come to them so

139

soon after the tragic deaths of Mr and Mrs Ashby in a flying accident. It offered no information beyond the fact that on Saturday afternoon or evening Patrick Ashby had met his death by falling over the cliffs to the west of the town. An account of the inquest would be found on page five.

On page five there was a whole column on the inquest. A column was not enough, of course, to do justice to the inquest in detail, but all the salient facts were there, and now and then a piece of evidence was reported verbatim.

Saturday afternoon was a holiday for the Ashby children and they were accustomed in the summer to take a "piece" with them and pursue their various interests in the countryside until it was time to come home to their evening meal. No alarm had been raised about Patrick's non-appearance in the evening until he had been missing for several hours. It was taken for granted that he had gone farther than he had intended in his latest hobby of bird-watching, and that he was merely late. When darkness closed down and he still had not come home, telephoned inquiries were sent all round the countryside in an effort to find someone who had seen him, so that if an accident had overtaken him rescue might be directed to the proper locality. When these inquiries proved barren, a search-party was organised to beat all the likely places for the missing boy. The search was conducted both on horse and on foot, and along the roads by car, without success.

In the first light of early morning the boy's jacket was found by a coastguard patrolling along the cliffs. Albert Potticary, the coastguard in question, gave evidence that the coat was lying about fifty yards from the cliff-edge, just where the path from Tanbitches began to descend through the gap to the harbour at Westover. It was lying a few yards off the path on the side nearer the cliff, and was weighted in its place by a stone. It was wet with dew when he picked it up, and the pockets were empty except for a note written in thin ink. The note was the one now shown him. He telephoned the news to the police and at once instituted a search for a body on the beach. No body was found. High tide the previous night had been at seven-twenty-nine, and if the boy had fallen into the water, or if he had fallen before high-water so that his body was taken out by the tide, it would not be washed up again at Westover. No one drowned in the Westover district had ever been washed up nearer than Castleton, away to the west; and most of them farther west than that. He was therefore not hopeful of finding any body when he instituted the search. It was merely routine.

The last person to see Patrick Ashby turned out to be Abel Tusk, the shepherd. He had met the boy in the early afternoon, about half-way between Tanbitches and the cliff.

Q. What was he doing?

A. He was lying on his belly in the grass.

Q. Doing what?

A. Waiting for a lark.

Q. What kind of lark?

A. An English lark.

Q. Ah, you mean he was bird-watching. Did he appear his normal self?

Yes, Abel said, as far as he could judge, Pat Ashby had looked much as usual. Never very "gabby" at any time. A quiet boy? Yes, a nice quiet boy. They discussed birds for a little and then parted. He, Abel Tusk, was on his way into Westover by the cliff path, it being also his own half-holiday. He did not get back until late at night and did not hear about the search for the boy until Sunday morning.

Asked if many people used that cliff path he said no. There were buses from the village that got you into Westover in a tenth of the time, but he didn't care for buses. It was rough walking, the cliff part of the path, and not suitable for the kind of shoes that people going to town would be wearing. So no one but someone like himself who was already on the sea side of Tanbitches hill would think of going to Westover that way.

Bee gave evidence that his parents' deaths had been a great shock to the boy, but that he had taken it well and had seemed to be recovering. She had no reason to think that he contemplated taking his own life. The children separated on Saturday afternoons because their interests were different, so that it was not unusual for Patrick to be alone.

Q. His twin did not accompany him?

A. No. Patrick was fascinated by birds, but Simon's tastes are mechanical.

Q. You have seen the note found in the boy's coat, and you recognise it as the handwriting of your nephew Patrick?

A. Oh, yes. Patrick had a very individual way of making his capital letters. And he was the only person I know who wrote with a stylograph.

She explained the nature of a stylograph. The one Patrick

141

owned had been black vulcanite with a thin yellow spiral down the barrel. Yes, it was missing. He carried it always with him; it was one of his pet possessions.

Q. Can you think of any reason why this sudden desire to take his own life should overcome him, when he seemed to his friend, the shepherd, to be normally happy in the afternoon?

A. I can only suggest that he *was* normally happy during the afternoon, but that when it was time to turn homeward the thought of going back to a house empty of so much that had made life fine for him was suddenly too much, and that he was overcome by an impulse born of a moment's despair.

And that was the verdict of the court, too. That the boy had succumbed to a passing impulse at a moment when the balance of his mind had been disturbed.

That was the end of the column and that was the end of Patrick Ashby. Brat turned over the pages of the next issue, filled with the small importances of summer-time Westover: shows, bowling competitions, tennis tournaments, council meetings, trade outings; but there was no mention of Pat Ashby. Pat Ashby already belonged to the past.

Brat sat back in the dead quiet of the cellar and thought about it all. The boy lying in the summer grass waiting for his beloved larks to drop out of the sky. And the night coming. And no boy coming home across Tanbitches hill.

Mechanical interests, Bee had said, describing Simon's way of spending his half-holiday. That meant the internal combustion engine, he supposed. It was about the age of thirteen that one did begin to be interested in cars. Simon had probably been innocently tinkering in the garage at Latchetts. Certainly there was no suggestion at the inquest, as reported in the Press, that his whereabouts had been a matter for question.

When he joined Bee for lunch at the Angel he longed to ask her bluntly where Simon had been that afternoon. But of course one could not say: "Where was Simon the afternoon I ran away from home?" It was an utterly pointless question. He must think up some other way of bringing the subject into the conversation. He was distracted by the old head-waiter at the Angel, who had known all the Ashby children and was shaken to the core, apparently, by Patrick's unexpected return. His old hands trembled as they laid the various dishes in front of him, and each dish was accompanied by a quavered "Mr Patrick, sir," as if he was glad to use the name. But the climax

142

came with the sweet course. The sweet was fruit tart, and he had already served both Bee and Brat, but he returned immediately and with great *empressement* laid a large meringue on a silver dish in front of Brat's place. Brat gazed at it in surprise and then looked up to find the old man waiting for his comment with a proud smile and tears in his eyes. His mind was so full of Simon that he was not quick enough, and it was Bee who saved the situation.

"How wonderful of Daniel to remember that you always had that!" she said, and Brat followed her lead and the old man went away pleased and moved, mopping his eyes on a dazzling white handkerchief that looked as large as a sheet.

"Thanks," Brat said to Bee "I hadn't remembered that."

"Dear old Daniel. I think it is almost like seeing his own son coming back. He had three, you know. They all died in one war, and his grandsons all died in the following one. He was very fond of you children, so I expect it is very wonderful for him to see anyone he has loved come back from the dead. What have you been doing with your morning?"

"Reading my obituary."

"How morbid of you. Or, no, of course, it isn't. It is what we all want to do. Did you see little Mr Macallan?"

"I did. He sent his best respects to you. Aunt Bee——"

"You are too old to begin calling me aunt."

"Bee, what were Simon's 'mechanical interests'?"

"Simon never had any mechanical interests as far as I know."

"You said at the inquest that he had."

"*I* did? I can't imagine what they could have been. What was it apropos of?"

"To explain why we didn't do things together on a Saturday afternoon. What did Simon do when I went bird-watching?" He tried to make it sound like someone trying to remember an old way of life.

"Pottered about, I expect. Simon was always a potterer. His hobbies never lasted longer than a fortnight at the outside."

"So you don't remember what Simon was using for a hobby the day I ran away?"

"It's absurd of me, my dear, but I don't. I don't even remember where he was that day. When something dreadful happens, you know, you push it down in your mind and never bring it up again if you can help it. I do remember that he

143

spent all night out on his pony looking frantically for you. Poor Simon. You did him a bad turn, Brat. I don't know if you realise it. Simon changed after you went. I don't know whether it was the shock of your going or the lack of your sober companionship, but he was a different person afterwards."

Since Brat had no answer to this he ate in silence, and presently she said: "And you did me a bad turn in never writing to me. Why didn't you, Brat?"

This was the weak spot in the whole structure, as Loding had continually pointed out.

"I don't *know*," he said. "Honestly, I don't *know*!"

The exasperation and desperation of his tone had an appropriateness that he had not foreseen.

"All right," she said, "I won't worry you, my dear. I didn't mean to. It is just something that has puzzled me. I was so very fond of you when you were small, and we were such very good friends. It was not like you to live a life of your own without once glancing back."

He raked up an offering from the depths of his own experience. "It's easier than you'd think to drop the past behind you when you are fourteen. If you are continually meeting fresh experience, I mean. The past has no greater reality than something you saw in a cinema. No personal reality, I mean."

"I must try running away one day," she said lightly. "There is a lot of the past I should like to drop behind me."

And Daniel came with the cheese, and they talked about other things.

20

Brat had not been prepared to find birthday presents by his plate on Friday morning. He had not, in fact, reckoned with a birthday at all. "All celebration has been postponed until Mr Charles Ashby comes back to this country," Mr Sandal had said to him in London, and it was not until Bee had drawn his attention to it that he had remembered that, celebration apart, there would inevitably be a day on which he would become twenty-one. He had had so little experience of birthdays that he had taken it for granted that a postponement of celebration meant a simple verbal congratulation from each member of the family, and he was dismayed by the pile of parcels by his breakfast plate. He quailed at the thought of having to open them in public.

The sardonic light in Simon's eye braced him to the task. He had a suspicion that Simon's punctuality at breakfast this morning was due less to the presence of Mr Sandal than to the prospect of enjoying his embarrassment over those presents.

"Happy birthday, Brat!" they said, as they came in. "Happy birthday, Brat!" One after another. So that the light benedictions fell round him like confetti.

He wished he didn't feel so bad about it. He wished that they were really his family, and that these were his presents by his plate, and that it was his birthday. It was a very nice thing, a family birthday.

"Are you an opener-before-breakfast or an opener-after, Brat?" Eleanor asked.

"After," he said promptly, and won a breathing-space.

After several cups of strong coffee he might feel braver.

Simon had, as well as presents, a pile of telegrams from the still large numbers of his acquaintances who had not heard of his twin's return, and he opened them as he ate and shared the contents. Having read each message aloud he added a post-script of comment.

"An exact shilling, the cheeseparing adding-machine! And I gave her a wonderful lunch last time I was in town. . . . What do you imagine Bobby is doing in Skye? He loathes mountains and is a martyr to midges. . . . Gore and Bowen. I suppose that's to remind me to pay my bill. . . . I'm sure I don't know anyone called Bert Burt. Do you think he can be a bookie?"

When eventually Brat could no longer postpone the opening of his parcels, his task was made easier by the fact that his presents were for the most part replicas of those Simon was pulling out of his own pile. Mr Sandal's Georgian sugar-sifter, Bee's silver flask, Eleanor's whip, and the twins' pocket-book, were all duplicated. Only the present from the Rectory was individual. It was a small wooden box that played a tune when the lid was opened. Brat had never seen or heard of such a thing before, and was so delighted with it that he forgot to be self-conscious and became absorbed in it.

"That came from Clare Park," Bee said.

And at that reminder of Loding he came back to reality and shut down the lid on the sweet frail melody.

This morning he was going to sign his soul away. It was no time for tinkling little tunes.

This signing-away was also the subject of surprise. He had imagined in his innocence that various papers would be put in front of him and he would sign them, and that would be that. A matter of twenty minutes at the most. But it proved to be a matter of hours. He and Mr Sandal sat side by side at the big table in the library, and the whole economic history of Latchetts was laid open for his inspection. Cosset, Thring and Noble were accounting to their young client for the years of his minority.

Brat, a little bewildered but interested, toiled after Mr Sandal in his progress through the years, and admired the way the old man handled this legal and mathematical exploration.

"Your dear mother's fortune is not what it was in the prosperous days when she inherited it, of course; but it will be sufficient to ensure that you may live at Latchetts in the future without anxiety. As you have observed, the margin of safety has often been very small during the years of your minority, but it was Miss Ashby's wish that there should be no borrowing on the strength of your inheritance from your mother. She was determined that that should come to you intact when you were twenty-one."

He went on laying statements in front of Brat, and for the first time Brat was aware of the struggle and the insecurity that lay behind the assured contentment that Latchetts presented to the eye.

"What happened that year?" he asked, putting his finger on a particularly black record.

Mr Sandal flipped over some papers. "Ah, yes. I remember. That was a bad year. A very bad year. One of the mares died and two were barren, and a very fine foal broke a leg. A heart-breaking year. It is a precarious way of making a living. That year, for instance," his thin dry finger pointed out another unsatisfactory report, "everything went swimmingly at Latchetts but it happened to be a year when no one was buying and none of the yearlings made their reserve price at the sales. A matter of luck. Merely luck. You will observe that some of the years were exceedingly lucky ones, so that the losses were overtaken."

He left the stables and went on to the farms: the conditions of lease, the improvements, the standing of the tenants, the nature of the crops. Eventually he came to the matter of personal income.

"Your father made a very good income in his profession of consulting engineer, and there seemed, of course, nothing to prevent him making that large yearly sum for a lifetime to come. He therefore spent generously on Latchetts and on the horses that were his hobby. Bought expensive and finely-bred mares, and so on, so that when he died his investments were not very extensive, and death duties had of course to be paid, so the investments had to go."

He slipped another sheet in front of Brat's eye, showing how the duty had been paid without mortgaging Latchetts.

"Miss Ashby has her own income and has never taken an allowance from the Latchetts estate. Except a house-keeping one, that is. The two elder children have had increasing allowances as they grew up. With the exception of some personal possessions—the children's ponies, for instance—the horses in the stable belong to the estate. When the children went to sales to buy for re-selling they were given money by Miss Ashby, and any profit on the improved horses went towards the expenses of Latchetts. I understand, however, that Simon has lately bought one or two with the results of profitable bets, and Eleanor with the results of her efforts as an instructress in the art of riding. Miss Ashby will no doubt tell you which these are. They do not appear in the relevant papers. The Shetland ponies were Miss Ashby's own venture, and are her own property. I hope that is all clear?"

Brat said that it was.

"Now about the future. It is the bank's advice that the money left you by your mother should stay invested as it is now. Have you any objection to that?"

"I don't want any lump sum," Loding had said. "I should only blue it, in the first place. And in the second place, it would cause a shocking amount of heart-searching at the bank. We don't want any heart-searching once you're in the saddle. All I want is a cosy little weekly allowance for the rest of my life, so that I can thumb my nose at Equity, and managements, and producers who say that I'm always late for rehearsal. *And* landladies. Riches, my boy, don't consist in having things, but in not having to do something you don't want to do. And

147

don't you forget it. Riches is being able to thumb your nose."

"What income would that bring me, as it is?" Brat asked Mr. Sandal, and Mr Sandal told him.

That was all right. He could peel Loding's cut off that and still have enough to meet his obligations at Latchetts.

"There are the children's present allowances. The twins, of course, will be going away to school presently, and that will be a charge on the estate for a few years."

He was surprised by the smallness of the allowances. Why, he thought, I made more than that in three months at the dude ranch. It subtly altered his attitude to Simon that Simon in the matter of spending money should have been so much his inferior.

"They're not very big, are they?" he said to Mr Sandal, and the old man looked taken aback.

"They are in accordance with the size of the estate," he said dryly.

"Well, I think they ought to be stepped up a bit now."

"Yes; that would be quite in order. But you cannot expect to carry two adults as passengers on the estate. It would not be just to the estate. They are both capable of earning their own living."

"What do you suggest, then?"

"I would suggest that Eleanor be given a slightly increased allowance while she lives at Latchetts, or until she marries."

"Is she thinking of getting married?"

"My dear boy, all young ladies think of getting married, especially when they are as pleasant to look upon as your sister. I am not aware, however, that she has so far exhibited any specific interest in the matter."

"Oh. And Simon?"

"Simon's case is difficult. Until a few weeks ago he looked upon Latchetts as his. He is not likely to remain long at Latchetts now, but the slightly increased allowance you suggest could be paid to him while he gives you his services here."

"I don't think that is good enough," said Brat, who was surprised by Mr Sandal's assumption that Simon would go. Simon showed no signs of going. "I think a bit of the estate is owing to him."

"Morally owing, you mean?"

"Yes, I suppose so."

148

"No doubt you are right, but it is a dangerous assumption which you cannot expect me to countenance. One cannot hand out bits of a financial estate and still keep the said estate in good heart. An allowance is one thing: it comes out of income. But the giving away of the fabric of the thing is to damage its whole structure."

"Well, I suggest that if Simon wants to go away and begin somewhere on his own that the money to start should be lent to him out of the estate at a nominal rate of interest. I suppose if I say without interest you'll jump down my throat."

The old man smiled on him, quite kindly. "I think there is nothing against that. I am looking forward to a period of great prosperity for Latchetts now that the lean years are over. I don't suppose a loan to Simon would greatly incommode the estate. There would be the saving of the allowance to balance it. Now, about the increase in the present allowances——"

They settled the amounts of that.

"Lastly," said Mr Sandal, "the pensioners."

"Pensioners?"

"Yes. The various dependants of the family who have become too old to work."

For the fourth time that morning Brat was surprised. He looked at the long list and wondered if all established English families had this drain on their income. Mr Sandal seemed to take it as a matter of course; as much a commonplace of honourable practice as paying one's income tax. Mr Sandal had frowned on any extravagance where the family was concerned: able-bodied Ashbys must earn their own living. The obligation to support the aged and infirm retainers of the family he took for granted. There was Nannie, who was now ninety-two and lived in a place called New Deer in Scotland; there was an old groom of eighty-nine who lived in the village, and another at Guessgate; there was a cook who had cooked for them until she was sixty-eight and now lived with a daughter of sixty-nine in Horsham; and so on.

He thought of the brassy blonde in the flowered rayon who had bade him welcome to Latchetts. Who would pension her? The country, he supposed. For long and honourable service?

Brat agreed to the continuance of the pensions, and then Simon was called in to do his share of signing. It pleased Brat, who had found it a depressing morning, to notice the sudden widening of Simon's eye as it lighted on his own signature.

It was nearly a decade since Simon had set eyes on those capital letters of Patrick's, and here they were blandly confronting him on the library table. That would "larn" him to be sardonic over Brat's efforts to carry off a birthday that was not his.

Then Bee came in, and Mr Sandal explained the increased provisions in the matter of allowances and the plan for providing for Simon's future. When Simon heard of the plan he eyed Brat thoughtfully; and Brat could read quite plainly what the look said. "Bribery, is that it? Well, it won't work. I'm damned well staying here and you will damned well pay me that allowance." Whatever plans Simon had, they centred round Latchetts.

Bee seemed pleased, however. She put her arm through his to lead him to lunch, and squeezed it. "Dear Brat!" she said.

"I congratulated you both and gave you my good wishes at breakfast," Mr Sandal said, picking up his glass of claret, "but I should like now to drink a toast." He lifted his glass to Brat. "To Patrick, who has not only succeeded to his inheritance but has accepted its obligations."

"To Patrick!" they said. "To Patrick!"

"To Patrick!" said Jane, last.

He looked at her and found that she was smiling at him.

21

SIMON took Mr Sandal to the station in the afternoon, and when they had gone Bee said: "If you want to avoid the social life this afternoon I'll hold the fort for you. I have the books to do, anyhow. Perhaps you would like to take out one of the horses with Eleanor. She has gone back to the stables, I think."

There were few things in life that Brat would have liked so much as to go riding with Eleanor, but there was one thing that he wanted to do more. He wanted, on this day when Pat Ashby should have come into his inheritance, to walk over Tanbitches hill by the path that Pat had taken on the last day of his life.

"I want to go with Brat," Ruth said; and he noticed that Jane lingered to hear the result of this proposition, as if she too might have come. But Bee quashed the suggestion. Brat had had enough of his family for a little, she said.

"But he is going with Eleanor!" protested Ruth.

But Brat said no. He was going walking by himself.

He avoided the avenue, in case that he might meet visitors bound for the house, and went down through the paddocks to the road. In one of the paddocks that bordered the avenue Eleanor was lunging a bay colt. He stood under the trees and watched her; her unruffled patience, her mastery of the puzzled and resentful youngster; the way she managed, even at the end of a long rein, to reassure him. He wondered if that doctor fellow knew anything about horses.

The turf on Tanbitches delighted him. He had not had turf like that underfoot since he was a child. He walked slowly upward, smelling the grassy smell and watching the great cloud shadows flying before the wind. He bore away from the path towards the crown of beeches on the hill-top. If he went up there he would be able to see the whole slope of the countryside to the cliff edge; the countryside that Pat Ashby had shared with the larks.

As he came level with the green clump of bushes and young trees that marked the old quarry, he found an old man sitting in its shelter eating solid slabs of bread and jam, and gave him a greeting as he passed.

"Proud, a'nt yu!" said the old man tartly.

Brat swung on his heel and stared.

"Wonderful dentical and Frenchy furrin parts makes folks, surely."

He took another large bite and surveyed Brat from under the battered felt of his hat.

"Dunnamany nestes you'd never seen but fur me."

"Abel!" said Brat.

"Well, that's summat," said the old man grudgingly.

"Abel!" said Brat, and sat down beside him. "Am I glad to see you!"

"Adone do!" Abel said to his dog, who came out from under the spread of his coat to sniff at the newcomer.

"Abel!" He could hardly believe that yesterday's occupant of a newspaper morgue was here in the flesh.

Abel began to exhibit signs of gratification at this undoubted enthusiasm for his society, and allowed that he had recognised him afar off. "Lame, are yu?"

"Just a bit."

"Bruck?"

"Yes."

"Weren't never one to make a pucker," Abel said, approving his laconic acceptance of bad luck.

Brat propped his back against the stout wooden fencing that kept the sheep from the quarry face, took out his cigarette case, and settled down for the afternoon.

In the hour that followed he learned a great deal about Pat Ashby, but nothing that helped to explain his suicide. Like everyone else, old Abel had been shocked and surprised by the boy's death, and now felt that his disbelief in a suicidal Patrick had been vindicated.

Patrick "weren't never one to make a pucker", no matter how "tedious bad" things were.

The old shepherd walked with him to the beeches, and Brat stayed there and watched man and dog grow small in the distance. Long after they were indistinguishable he stayed there, soothed by the loneliness and the great "hush" of the wind in the beech trees. Then he followed them down into the green plain until he came to the path, and let it lead him back over the hill to Clare.

As he came down the north slope to the road, a familiar "clink-clink" came up to him on the wind. For a moment he was back on the Wilson ranch, with the forge glowing in the thin mountain air and—what was her name?—Cora waiting for him beyond the barn when he was tidied up after supper. Then he remembered where the forge was: in that cottage at the foot of the hill. It was early yet. He would go and see what an English smithy looked like.

It looked very like the Wilson one, when at last he stood in the doorway, except that the roof was a good deal lower. The smith was alone, his mate being no doubt an employee and subject to a rationing of labour, and he was fashioning horse-shoes. He looked up as Brat darkened the doorway, and gave him a greeting without pausing in his work. Brat watched him for a little in a companionable quiet, and then moved over to work the bellows for him. The man looked up and smiled. He finished what he was doing at the moment and then said: "I didn't know you against the light. I'm unaccountable glad to see you in my place again, Mr Patrick."

"Thanks, Mr Pilbeam."

"You're a deal handier with that thing than you used to be."

"I've earned my living at it since I saw you last."

"You have? Well, I'll be——!" He took a half-made shoe red-hot from the furnace and was about to resume work when he changed his mind and held it out with a grin to Brat. Brat accepted the challenge and made a good job of it, Mr Pilbeam acting as mate with critical approval.

"Funny," he said, as Brat plunged the shoe into the water, "if any Ashby was to earn his living at this job it ought to have been your brother."

"Why?"

"You never showed much interest."

"And did Simon?"

"There was a time when I couldn't keep him out of this place. There wasn't anything he wasn't going to make from a candlestick to gates for the avenue at Latchetts. Far as I remember, all he ever made was a sheep-crook, and that not over-well. But he was always round the place. It was a craze of his for the whole of a summer."

"Which summer was that?"

"Summer you left us, it was. I'd misremember about it, only he was here seeing us put an iron on a cartwheel the day you ran away. I had to shoo him home for his supper."

Brat considered the shoe he had made, while Mr Pilbeam made ready to call it a day.

"I ought to hang that up," Mr Pilbeam said, nodding at Brat's handiwork, "and label it: Made by Patrick Ashby of Latchetts. And I couldn't make a better one myself," he added handsomely.

"Give it to old Abel to nail on his door."

"Bless you, old Abel wouldn't have cold iron on his threshold. Keep his visitors away."

"Oh. Friendly with 'them', is he?"

"Do all his washing up and keep his house clean, if you'd believe all you hear."

"I wouldn't put it past him," Brat said. And set out for Latchetts.

So Simon had an alibi. Simon had been nowhere near the cliffs that afternoon. He had never been out of the Clare valley.

And so that was that.

On his way home up the ride between the paddocks he met

153

Jane. Jane had every appearance of "hanging around", and he wondered if it was to intercept him that she lingered there. She was talking to Honey and her foal, and made no effort to efface herself as she had done hitherto at his approach.

"Hullo, Jane," he said, and joined in the intercourse with Honey to give her time. Her small pale face had flushed, and she was evidently struggling with a quite unusual emotion.

"It's about time we were going home to wash up," he suggested at last, as she seemed no nearer speech.

She dropped her hand from Honey's head and turned to face him, braced for effort.

"I wanted to say something to you. Do you mind?"

"Something you want me to do for you?"

"Oh, no. Nothing like that. It's just that I wasn't very nice to you when you came home from America, and I want to apologise."

"Oh, Jane," he said, wanting to take the small brave figure in his arms.

"It wasn't because I *wanted* to be horrid to you," she said, anxious that he should understand. "It was because—it was because——"

"I know why it was."

"Do you?"

"Yes, of course. It was a very natural thing to feel."

"Was it?"

"In fact, all things considered, it does you credit."

"Then you'll accept my apology?"

"I accept your apology," Brat said gravely, and they shook hands.

She did not immediately put her arm through his as Ruth would have done. She walked beside him in a grown-up fashion, talking politely about the chances of Honey's foal in the market, and what it should be called. The matter of the name was such an absorbing and exciting one that presently she forgot her self-consciousness, so that by the time they reached the house she was chattering unreservedly.

As they crossed the wide gravel sweep, Bee came to the door and stood there watching them come.

"You are going to be late for dinner, you two," she said.

22

So Brat took possession of Latchetts and of everyone in it, with
the exception of Simon.

He went to church on Sunday and submitted to being stared
at for an hour and a half with time off for prayers. The only
people not in Clare church that morning were the Nonconformists and three children who had measles. Indeed, there
were, as Bee pointed out, several members of the congregation
whose normal place of Sunday worship was the blue brick barn
at the other end of the village, and who had decided to put up
with ritual and prelacy this once in order to share in the sensation of his appearance. As for the orthodox flock, there were
individuals there, Bee said, who had not entered a church since
their last child was christened. There was even Lana Adams
who, as far as anyone knew, had not been in any church since
her own baptism in the blue brick barn some twenty years ago.

Brat sat between Bee and Eleanor, and Simon on the other
side of Bee. The twins were beyond Eleanor; Ruth wallowing
in the drama and singing hymns loudly with a rapt expression,
and Jane looking at the congregation with stony disapproval.
Brat read the Ashby tablets over and over again, and listened to
the Rector's unemphatic voice providing the inhabitants of
Clare with their weekly ration of the abstract. The Rector did
not preach, in the accepted meaning of the term. He sounded
as if he were arguing the matter out for himself; so that, if you
shut your eyes, you could be in a chair at the other side of the
Rectory fireplace listening to him talk. Brat thought of the
fine variety of preachers who had come to take Sunday service
at the orphanage: the shouters, the between-you-and-me-ers,
the drama merchants who varied their tones and dropped their
voices like amateur reciters, the hearties, the mincing aesthetes;
and he thought that George Peck came very well out of the
comparison. George Peck really did look as if he were not
thinking about himself at all; as if he might conceivably have
become a clergyman even if there had been no such inducement
as public appearances in a pulpit.

After service Brat went to Sunday lunch at the Rectory, but

not until he had run the gamut of village good wishes. Bee had come out of church at his side ready to pilot him through the ordeal, but she was accosted by Mrs Gloom, and he was left defenceless. He looked in panic at the first of these unknowns bearing down on him: a big apple-cheeked woman with pink roses in a crinoline hat. How was he going to pretend to remember her? Or all the others who were obviously lingering?

"You remember Sarah Godwin, who used to come on washing days," a voice said, and there was Eleanor at his elbow. She moved him on from one group to another as expertly as a social secretary, briefing him quickly in a muttered phrase as each new face loomed up. "Harry Watts. Used to mend our bicycles." "Miss Marchant. Village school." "Mrs Stapley. Midwife." "Tommy Fitt. Used to be the gardener's boy." "Mrs Stack. Rural industries."

She saw him safely to the little iron gate that led into the Rectory garden, opened it, pushed him through, and said: "Now you're safe. That's 'coolee'."

"That's what?"

"Don't tell me you have forgotten that. In our hide-and-seek games a safe hide was always a 'coolee'."

Some day, Brat Farrar, he thought as he walked down the path to the Rectory, you are going to be faced with something that you *couldn't possibly* have forgotten.

At luncheon he and his host sat in relaxed silence while Nancy entertained them, and afterwards he walked in the garden with the Rector and answered his questions about the life he had been leading these last eight years. One of George Peck's charms was that he listened to what was said to him.

On Monday he went to London and sat in a chair while rolls of cloth were exhibited several yards away from him, and were then brought forward to touching distance so that he might guage the weight, texture, and wearing qualities of the cloth. He was fitted by Gore and Bowen, and measured by Walters, and assured by both that in record time he would have an outfit that no Englishman would blush to own. It was a revelation to him that shirts were made to measure. He had been pleased that he could present himself to the Ashby tailors in a suit as respectworthy as that made for him by Mr Sandal's tailor, and it was a shock to him to be sympathised with about the nice clean blue American shirt he was wearing under it. How-

156

ever, when in Rome . . . So he was measured for shirts too.

He lunched with Mr Sandal, who took him to meet the manager of his bank. He cashed a cheque at the bank, bought a registered envelope, and sent a fat wad of notes to Alec Loding. That had been the arrangement; "notes and no note", Loding had said. No telephones either. There must never be any communication between them again beyond the anonymous notes in the registered envelope.

This first payment to his partner in crime left a taste in his mouth that was not entirely due to the gum on the envelope that he had licked. He went and had a beer to wash it away, but it was still there. So he got on a 24 bus and went to have a look at his late lodgings in Pimlico, and immediately felt better.

He caught the 4.10 down, and Eleanor was waiting in the bug at Guessgate to meet him. His heart was no longer in his mouth, and Eleanor was no longer an abstraction and an enemy.

"It seemed a shame to let you wait for the bus when I was free to come to meet you," she said, and he got in beside her and she drove him home.

"Now you won't have to go away again for a long time," she said.

"No. Except for a fitting, and to the dentist."

"Yes; just up for the day. And perhaps Uncle Charles will expect someone to go up to meet him. But until then we can settle down and be quiet."

So he settled down.

He exercised the horses in the mornings, or schooled them over the jumps in the paddock. He rode out with Eleanor and the children from Clare Park; and so satisfied Antony Toselli's romantic soul that he arrived for his lesson one morning in a complete "child's riding outfit", to obtain which he had sent telegrams of a length and fluency that made history in the life of the Clare post office. He lunged the yearling for Eleanor, and watched while she taught a young thoroughbred from a racing stable to walk collected and carry his head like a gentleman. Nearly all his days were spent with Eleanor, and when they came in in the evenings it was to plan for tomorrow's task.

Bee watched this companionship with pleasure, but wished that Simon had more share in it. Simon found more and more excuses to be away from home from breakfast to dinner. He would school Timber or Scapa in the morning, and then find some excuse for going into Westover for lunch. Occasionally when he came home for dinner after being out all day Bee wondered whether he was quite sober. But except for the fact that he now took two drinks where once he would have taken one, he drank little at home, and so she decided that she must be mistaken. His alternate fits of moodiness and gaiety were nothing new: Simon had always been mercurial. She took it that his absence was his way of reducing the strain of a difficult situation, and hoped that presently he would make a third in the partnership that was blossoming so happily between Eleanor and Patrick.

"You'll have to do *something* at the Bures Show," Eleanor said one day as they came in tired from the stables. "Otherwise people will think it very odd."

"I could ride in a race, as Ruth suggested."

"But that is just fun. I mean, no one takes that seriously. You ought to show one of the horses. Your own riding things will be here in time, so there's no reason why you shouldn't."

"No."

"I'm getting to know that monosyllable of yours."

"It's no monopoly of mine."

"No. Just your speciality."

"What could I ride in the races?"

"Well, after Timber, Chevron is the fastest we have."

"But Chevron is Simon's."

"Oh, no. Chevron was bought by Bee with stable money. Have you ridden races at all?"

"Oh, yes. Often. Local ones, of course. For small stakes."

"Well, I think Bee plans to show Chevron as a hack, but that's no reason she shouldn't be entered for the races at the end of the day. She's very nervous and excitable, but she jumps clean and she's very fast."

They put the proposition to Bee at dinner, and Bee agreed to it. "What do you ride at, Brat?"

"Nine stone thirteen."

Bee looked at him reflectively as he ate his dinner. He was too fine-drawn. None of the Ashbys of the last two generations had run to weight, but there was a used-up look about the boy; especially at the end of the day. Presently, when the business of the celebration was all over, they must do something about his leg. Perhaps that accounted for the stung look that marked his spareness. Both physically and psychologically it must be a drag on him. She must ask Peter Spence about a good surgeon to consult.

Bee had been delighted to find that Brat had what Simon so conspicuously lacked: an interest in the genus horse in the abstract. Simon was knowledgeable about breeding in so far as it concerned his own particular interests, but his theoretical study of the matter was confined to *Racing Up to Date*. Brat, on the other hand, took to stud books as some people take to detection. She had gone in one evening to turn off a light that someone had evidently left on in the library, and found Brat poring over a stud book. He was trying to work back on Honey's pedigree, he said.

"You've got the wrong book," she said, and provided him with the right one. She was busy with some W.R.I. matter and so she left him to it and forgot him. But nearly two hours later she noticed the light still there and went in to find Brat surrounded by tomes of all kinds and so dead to the world that he did not hear her come in.

"It's fascinating, Bee," he said. He was mooning over a photograph of Bend Or, and had propped various other volumes, open at photographs that gave him particular pleasure, so that the big table looked like some second-hand bookstall with the plates exhibited to entice the purchaser.

"You haven't got my favourite in your collection," she said, having examined his choice, and brought another tome from the shelves. And then, finding that he was totally ignorant, she took him back to the beginning and showed him the foundations —Arab, Barb, and Turk—of the finished product. By midnight there were more books on the floor than there were on the shelves but they had both had a marvellous time.

After that if Brat was missing from the normal orbit, one could always find him in the library, either working out something in a stud book or going slowly through the photographs of remarkable horses.

He sat openly at Gregg's feet, with the result that in a week Gregg was according him a respect that he had never paid to Simon. Bee noticed that where he addressed Simon as "Mr Simon", Brat was "Mr Patrick, sir". There was never any trace of the defensive attitude of a stud-groom faced with a new-comer who was also his master. Gregg recognised an enthusiast who did not think that he already knew it all, and so Brat

159

was "Mr Patrick, sir". Bee would smile as she passed the saddle room and heard the long monotone of Gregg's speech punctuated by Brat's monosyllables.

"Shoot him, I said, I'll do nothing of the kind, that horse'll walk out of here like a Christian inside a month, your blasted hounds can starve, I said, before they get their jaws on as good a piece of horseflesh as ever looked through a bridle, so what do you think I did?"

"What?"

Bee was humbly grateful to fate not only for her nephew's return but for the form in which he had returned. Rehearsing in her mind all the shapes that Patrick might have reappeared in, she was filled with wonder that the actual one should be so cut-to-measure, so according to her own prescription. Brat was what she would have indented for if she could have chosen. He was too silent, of course; too reticent. One felt at peace in his company without having any feeling of knowing him. But his unchanging front was surely easier to deal with than Simon's fluidity.

She wrote a long letter to Uncle Charles, to meet him at Marseilles, describing this new nephew to him, and saying all that could not be said in the initial cables. It would not impress Charles, of course, that Brat was useful with horses, since Charles loathed horses; which he held to be animals of an invincible stupidity, uncontrolled imagination, and faulty deduction. Indeed, Charles claimed that a three-months-old child not actually suffering from encephalitis or other congenital incapacity was more capable of drawing a correct deduction than the most intelligent and most impeccably bred thorough-bred. Charles liked cats; and if ever against his better judgment he was lured within smell of a stable, he made friends with the stable cat and retired with it to some quiet corner until the process of horse exhibition was finished. He was rather like a cat himself; a large soft man with a soft round face that creased only sufficiently to hold an eyeglass; in either eye, according to which hand Charles had free at the moment. And although he was over six feet tall, he padded as lightly on his large feet as though he were partly filled with air.

Charles was devoted to his old home and to his family, but was fond of declaring himself a throw-back to a more virile age when a horse was simply a means of transport, capable of carrying a respectable weight, and it was not necessary for a

160

man to develop bones that would disgrace a chicken so that brittle thoroughbreds should be induced to surmount unnecessary and unwarrantable obstacles.

A half-starved cat could out-jump any horse anyhow; and no one had to teach it to, either.

But his brother's grandchildren were the apple of his eye, and he loved every brittle bone of them. And it was to this Charles that Bee commended his new nephew.

"In the short two weeks that he has been here, he has passed from being a complete stranger to being so much part of Latchetts that one doesn't notice him. He has a peculiar trick of being part of the landscape, of course, but it is not just that he is self-effacing. It is that he has dropped into place. I notice that even the country people, to whom he ought still to be strange and a matter for sideways-looking, treat him as if he had been here all along. He is very silent, and rarely volunteers a remark, but his mind is extraordinarily alive, and his comment when he makes one would be blistering sometimes if it were not uttered so gently. He speaks very correct American —which, dear Uncle Charles, is very correct English with a flat A—and drawls a little. It is quite a different drawl from Simon's. I mean, from the drawl Simon uses when he drawls. It is not a comment; just a method of production.

"His greatest conquest was Jane, who resented his coming bitterly, on Simon's behalf. She made a wide sweep round him for days, and then capitulated. Ruth made a tremendous fuss of him, but got little encouragement—I think he felt her disloyalty to Simon—and she is now a little 'off' him.

"George Peck seems pleased with him, but I think finds it hard to forgive his silence all those years. I do too, of course. I find it inexplicable. One can only try to understand the immensity of the upheaval that sent him away from us.

"Simon has been beyond praise. He has taken his relegation to second place with a fortitude and a grace that is touching. I think he is very unhappy, and finds it difficult to join up this new Patrick with the old one. The greatest wrong Pat did in keeping silence was the wrong to Simon. I can only suppose that he intended never to come back at all. I have tried to sound him about it, but he is not an easy person to talk to. He was a reserved child and he is even more reserved today. Perhaps he will talk to you when you come.

"We are busy preparing for the Bures show—which, you will

be glad to hear, occurs at least three days before you are even due to arrive in England—and have hopes of a little successful publicity for Latchetts. We have three new horses that are well above average, and we are hoping that at least two of them are of Olympia standard. We shall see what their ring manners are like when we take them to Bures. Patrick has refused to take any part in this year's showings, leaving all the kudos to Simon and Eleanor—to whom, of course, it belongs. I think that, more than anything, describes this Patrick who has come home to us."

23

BECAUSE it was Simon who would show Timber and jump him, Brat left his schooling entirely to him, and shared his attentions between the other horses. But there were days, especially now that Simon absented himself more and more, when someone else had to exercise Timber, and Brat looked forward to those days more than he acknowledged even to himself. He liked most of the Latchetts horses, despised a few, and had an affection for the lively Chevron, the kind, sensible Scapa, and Eleanor's aged hack, Buster: a disillusioned but lovable old gentleman. But Timber was something else again. Timber was challenge, and excitement, and satisfaction; Timber was question and glory.

He planned to cure Timber of brushing people off his back, but he would do nothing yet awhile. It was important, if he was going to be jumped at Bures, that nothing should be done to damage his self-confidence. Some day, if Brat had anything to do with it, Timber was going to feel very small indeed, but meanwhile let Simon have at his command every jot of that lordly assurance. So Brat exercised him mildly, and as he rode round the countryside kept his eyes open for a likely curing-place for Timber when the time came. The beeches on Tanbitches had no branches low enough for his purpose, and there was no room on that hill-top to get up the necessary speed. He wanted some open country with isolated or bunched trees with their lowest branches the right height from the ground to tempt Timber to his undoing. He remembered that Timber's most spectacular exploit had been in Lerridge Park and over

162

there was Clare Park, with its surrounding stretch of turf and trees.

"Do the Clare Park people mind if we ride through the park?" he asked Eleanor one day when there was still seven days before the Bures show.

Eleanor said no, provided they kept away from the playing fields. "They don't play anything because organised games are dreadful unless they are organised by Russians in Russia, but they keep the playing fields because they look well in the prospectus."

So Brat took Timber to the other side of the valley, and cantered him gently on the centuries-old turf of Clare Park, keeping well away from the trees. Then he walked him round the various clumps, gauging the height of the lowest limbs from the ground. This manœuvre was received by Timber with a puzzled but passionate interest. One could almost see him trying to work it out. What was this for? What did the man come and look at large trees for? With a horse's abnormal memory, he was well aware that large trees were associated with private delights of his own, but, being a horse, he was also incapable of drawing any reasonable deduction from his rider's interest in the same kind of trees.

He walked up to each clump with a mannerly grace, until they approached the large oak which had been for five hundred years the pride of Clare Park. As they came within its flung shadow Timber propped himself suddenly on his forelegs and snorted with fright. Brat was puzzled. What did he remember about the oak that would cause a reaction as strong as that? He looked at the ears that were sticking up as stiff as horns. Perhaps it wasn't a memory. Perhaps there was something in the grass.

"Do you always sneak up on girls under trees?" said a voice from the shadows, and from the grass there emerged the seal-like form of Miss Parslow. She propped herself on an elbow and surveyed the pair. Brat was a little surprised that she was alone. "Don't you ever ride anything but that black brute?"

Brat said that he did, quite often.

"I suppose it would be too much to expect that you were looking for me when you came over to the park to ride?"

Brat said that he was looking for a place to teach Timber manners.

"What's the matter with his manners?"

"He has a habit of diving suddenly under a tree so that he scrapes his rider off."

Miss Parslow propped herself a little farther up and looked with new interest at the horse. "You don't say! I never thought the brutes had that much sense. How are you going to stop him?"

"I'm going to make riding under trees a painful experience for him."

"You mean you'll beat him when he tries to do it?"

"Oh, no. That wouldn't do much good."

"After he has actually done it, then?"

"No. He mightn't associate the beating with a tree at all." He rubbed his whip up Timber's dark crest, and Timber bowed. "You'd be surprised at the odd things they associate."

"Nothing would surprise me to any extent about horses. How are you going to do it then?"

"Let him go full bat near a nice tempting tree, and when he swerves under it give him a cut on the belly that he'll remember all his life."

"Oh, no, that's too bad. The poor brute."

"It will be just too bad if I don't time my slip sideways on the saddle properly," Brat said dryly.

"And will that cure him?"

"I hope so. Next time he sees a likely tree he'll remember that it hurt like blazes last time he tried it."

"But he'll hate you."

Brat smiled. "I'd be very surprised if he associated me with the business at all. I'd be surprised if he even associated it with the whip. Horses don't think like humans."

"What will he think hurt him, then?"

"The tree, more than likely."

"I always *thought* they were awfully silly animals."

It occurred to Brat that she had not made one of those riding parties on which he had accompanied Eleanor. Nor had he seen her about the stables lately. He asked how her riding was getting on.

"I've given it up."

"Altogether?"

"Uh-huh."

"But you were getting on well, weren't you? Eleanor said you had learned to bump."

"It was a very slithery bump, and it hurt me far more than it

164

hurt the horse." She pulled a long grass and began to chew it, eyeing him with a sly amusement. "I don't have to hang around the stables any more. If I want to see Simon I know where to find him nowadays."

"Where?" said Brat before he could stop himself.

"The upstairs bar at the Angel."

"In Westover? But are you allowed to go to Westover when you like?"

"I'm attending a Westover dentist." She giggled. "Or rather, I was. The school made the first appointment for me, of course, but after that I just told them when I had to go next. I've reckoned that I have about thirty teeth, which should last me till the end of term quite nicely." She opened her red mouth wide and laughed. They were excellent teeth. "That's what I'm doing at the moment. Putting off time till the Westover bus is due. I could have gone with the earlier one but there is a very good-looking conductor on this one. He's got the length of asking me to the pictures one night next week. If Simon was going on the way he has been all those months, not knowing I'm alive, I'd maybe have done something about the conductor boy—he has lashes about an inch long—but now that Simon has stopped looking down his nose I think I'll give the conductor boy a miss." She chewed the stalk provocatively. "Got quite matey, Simon has."

"Oh."

"Have you been seducing the Gates girl from him, like I suggested?"

"I have not."

"That's funny. He's distinctly off her. And he's not awfully enamoured of you, if it comes to that. So I thought you'd been cutting him out with that Peggy woman. But I suppose it's just that you cut him out at Latchetts."

"You're going to miss your bus, aren't you?"

"You can be just as squashing as Simon, in your own way."

"I was only pointing out that the bus is almost at the smithy. It will be at the Park gates in——"

"What!" she shrieked, exploding to her feet in one enormous convulsion, so that Timber whirled in alarm from the wild eruption. "Oh, great heavens! Oh, for the love of . . .! Oh! Oh!"

She fled down the park to the avenue gates, screaming her distress as she went. Brat watched the green bus skim along the road past the white gates of Latchetts and slow down as it came to the gates of Clare Park. She was going to catch it after all, and her day would not be wasted. She would find Simon. At the Angel. In the upstairs bar.

That Simon should spend his time in Westover in the Angel bar was distressing but not, in the circumstances, surprising. What was surprising was the emergence of a Simon who was "matey" with Sheila Parslow. In Simon's eyes the Parslow girl had always been something beneath contempt; a lower form of life. He dismissed her with a gibe when her name was mentioned and in her presence was, as she had said herself, unaware that she was alive. What had happened to Simon that he was not only resigned to her companionship, but was "matey"? The girl was not lying about it. If her glowing self-satisfaction was not sufficient evidence, there was the obvious fact that Simon could avoid her by changing his drinking place. There was no lack of pubs in Westover; most of them more exclusively masculine haunts than the very social and female-ridden Angel.

Brat tried to imagine Simon with Sheila Parslow and failed.

What had come over Simon—the fastidious, critical Simon— that he found it possible to endure her? To spend hours in her company?

Was it a sort of "larning" his family for the disappointment he had been caused? A sort of you-don't-like-me-therefore-I'll-take-up-with-Sheila-Parslow? A sorry-when-I'm-dead reaction? There was a very childish side to Simon.

There was also, Brat thought from all he had heard, a very practical side, and Sheila Parslow had money, and Simon needed it. But somehow Brat could not believe that Simon, even in his most deplorable moments, would ever consider pawning his life to a nymphomaniacal moron.

As he walked Timber home he considered yet once more the general oddity of Simon, but as usual came to no conclusion.

He handed Timber over to Arthur to be rubbed down, and went down with Eleanor to inspect Regina's new foal.

"She's an old marvel, isn't she," Eleanor said, watching the new arrival stagger about on its out-of-proportion legs. "It's another good one. Not much wonder that she looks complacent. People have been coming to admire her foals for practically a lifetime, the old duchess. I think foals to her are just a means of achieving this annual homage. She doesn't care a rap about the foal."

"It's not any better than Honey's," Brat said, looking at the foal without enthusiasm.

"You and your Honey!"

"And you wait and see what Honey will produce next year with this new mating. A foal that will make history."

"Your enthusiasm for Honey borders on the indecent."

"You heard Bee say that."

"How do you know?"

"I heard her too."

They laughed a little, and she said: "It's so nice to have you here, Brat." He noticed that she did not say: It is so nice to have you back, Patrick; but he realised that she herself was unaware of any oddity in the form she used.

"Is that doctor chap going over to Bures for the show?"

"I shouldn't think so. He's much too busy. What made you think of him?"

Brat did not know.

They pottered round the paddocks for so long that they came in for tea very late, and had it by themselves. Jane was pounding her way through a Chopin valse with conscientious accuracy, and stopped with undisguised relief when they came in.

"Could I say twenty-five minutes was half an hour, Eleanor?" she asked. "It's twenty-five-and-a-half minutes, really."

"You can say anything you like as long as we don't have to listen to that valse while we eat."

So Jane slid off the piano-stool, removed the glasses that gave her such an owl-like look, pushed them into her breeches pocket, and disappeared thankfully into the out-of-doors.

"Ruth puts in all the tiddley bits and the expression and doesn't mind how many wrong notes she strikes, but with Jane it is accuracy or nothing. I don't know which Chopin would have hated more," Eleanor said, folding bread and butter into a thickness that would match her appetite.

Brat watched her pour the tea with a delight in her clean un-hurried movements. Some day the foundation of the life he was living here would give way; Simon would achieve the plan he was devising to undo him, or some incautious word of his own would bring the whole structure crashing down; and then there would be no more Eleanor.

It was not the least of his fears for the future.

They ate in a friendly silence, dropping unrelated remarks into the quiet as they happened to occur to them.

Presently Eleanor said: "Did you ask Bee about colours for the race next week?"

Brat said that he had forgotten.

"Let's go and look them out now. They are in that locker in the saddle room."

So they went back to the stables. The saddle room was empty; Gregg had gone home to his supper; but Eleanor knew where the key was.

"They are practically in ribbons, they are so old," she said as she spread the colours on the table. "They were actually made for Father, and then they were taken in a bit for Simon to wear at point-to-points when he was narrower than he is now. And then let out again when he grew. So they are just hanging together. Perhaps now we'll be able to afford——". She pulled herself up.

"Yes. We'll have a new set."

"I think violet and primrose are nice colours, don't you; but they do fade an unattractive shade. Simon goes blue with cold in the winter, and he says the colours were designed to tone with his face."

They rummaged in the chest, turning up souvenirs of old races. They moved round the saddle room studying the long row of ribbon rosettes, each with its tab under it telling where and how it had been won.

At last Eleanor shut the chest, saying: "It is time we got ready for dinner." She locked the chest and hung up the key. "We'll take the colours with us. I expect they'll fit you all right, since Simon was the last to wear them. But they'll have to be pressed."

She took the colours in her arms, and together they walked out of the saddle-room door and came face to face with Simon.

"Oh, you're back, Simon," Eleanor was beginning, when she caught sight of his face.

"*Who had Timber out?*" he said, furious.

"I had," Brat said.

"Timber is my business and you have no right to have him out when my back is turned."

"Someone had to exercise him today," Brat said mildly.

"*No one* exercises Timber but me. *No one.* If I'm going to be responsible for jumping him, then I say when he is to be exercised, and *I* do the exercising."

"But, Simon," Eleanor said, "that is absurd. There are——"

"Shut up!" he said, through his teeth.

"I will *not* shut up! The horses are Brat's, and if anyone says who does what, and when, then it is——"

"Shut up, I tell you. I won't have a ham-handed lout from the backwoods ruining a good piece of horseflesh like Timber."

"Simon! *Really!*"

"Coming from nowhere and interfering in the stables as if he had lived here all his life!"

"You must be drunk, Simon, to talk like that about your own brother."

"My brother! *That!* Why, you poor little fool, he isn't even an Ashby. God knows what he is. Somebody's groom, I have no doubt. And that is what he should be doing. Sweeping our stables. Not lording it round the countryside on my best horses. After this, you damned little upstart, you leave the horses I intend to ride in their stable unless I say they are to be taken out, and if I say they are to be taken out it is not you who will ride them. We have plenty of other stablemen."

His chin was sticking out about two feet from Brat's face, and Brat could have brought one from the ground that would have lifted him half over the saddle room. He longed to do it, but not with Eleanor there. And not now, perhaps. Better not do anything that he could not foresee the consequences of.

"Well? Did you hear me?" shouted Simon, maddened by his silence.

"I heard you," Brat said.

"Well, see that you remember what I said. Timber is my business, and you don't put a leg across him again until I say so."

And he flung away from them towards the house.

Eleanor looked stricken.

"Oh, Brat, I'm sorry. I'm so sorry. He had that mad notion about your not being Patrick before he ever saw you, and now that he has been drinking I suppose it came from the back of his mind and he said it because he was angry. He always did say a lot of things he didn't mean when he was in a temper, you know."

It was Brat's experience that, on the contrary, it was only when a person was in a temper that they said exactly what they did mean. But he refrained from telling Eleanor that.

"He *has* been drinking, you know," she went on. "I know he doesn't look as if he has, but I can tell from his eyes. And

169

he would never have behaved like that when he was sober, even in a temper. I do apologise for him."

Brat said that everyone made a fool of themselves sometime or other when they had "drink taken", and she was not to bother about it.

They followed Simon to the house soberly, the happiness of their long afternoon together vanished as if it had not been.

As he changed into what he still thought of as "his good suit" Brat thought that if the cracks that were showing in Simon widened sufficiently he might one day show his hand, and he would find out what Simon's plans for him were. He wondered if Simon would be sober enough to behave normally at dinner.

But there was no Simon at dinner, and when Eleanor asked where he was, Bee said that he had gone over to the pub at Guessgate to meet a friend who was staying there. Someone had telephoned just before dinner, it appeared.

Bee looked equable, and Brat decided that Simon had seemed normal to her and that she had believed his story of the friend staying the night at the Guessgate inn.

And in the morning Simon came down to breakfast his usual sunny self.

"I'm afraid I was tight last night," he said. "And very objectionable, I'm afraid. I apologise unreservedly."

He regarded Brat and Eleanor, the only other people at the table, with friendly confidence. "I ought never to drink gin," he said. "It obscures the judgment and destroys the soul."

"You were quite horrible," Eleanor said coldly.

But the atmosphere cleared, and the day was just another day. Bee came in from out-of-doors for her second cup of coffee; Jane arrived clutching to her stomach the bowl of porridge which she had fetched from the kitchen for herself, according to Latchetts routine; Ruth came flying in very late with a "diamond" clasp in her hair and was sent back to take the thing off.

"Where did she get that loathsome object?" Bee said, when Ruth had disappeared with wild cries that Bee was going to make her late for lessons.

"She bought it at Woolworth's last time we were in Westover," Jane said. "They're not real diamonds, you know, but it seemed a bargain for one-and-sixpence."

"Why didn't you buy one then, Jane?" Bee asked, looking at the aged kirby-grip that kept Jane's hair off her face.

"Oh, I don't think I'm the diamond type," Jane said.

So the Ashby household settled back to its normal placidity, and to its preparations for that day at Bures that was to alter all their lives.

24

BURES was a little market town, set north of Westover and almost in the middle of the county. It was like almost every other little town in the south of England, except perhaps that it stood in slightly richer and more unspoiled country than most. For which reason the Bures Agricultural Show, although a small country affair, had a standing and reputation considerably greater than its size alone would warrant. Every year animals would appear at the Bures Show on their way to more mature triumphs elsewhere, and it was common for someone, watching an exhibit at one of the great shows, to say: "I remember that when it was a novice at Bures three years ago."

It was a pleasant, civilised little town, with a minster, some fine old inns, a High Street both broad and gay, and no self-consciousness whatsoever. The farmers who brought their wares to its markets would have annoyed Mr Macallan exceedingly by their content with their lot, and their evident unawareness that there were other worlds to conquer. An air of well-being came off the Bures pavements like reflected sunlight. Bad years there might be, for both tradespeople and farmers, but that was a risk that was incidental in a life that was satisfying and good.

The annual show, in the early summer, was a social reunion as well as a business affair, and the day ended with a "ball" in the assembly room of the Chequers, at which farmers' wives who hadn't seen each other since New Year swopped gossip, and young blades who had not met since the Combined Hunts Ball swopped horses. The combined hunts, between them, embraced the town; the Lerridge to the south and the Kenley Vale to the north; and did much to ensure that the horses exhibited at Bures should be worth more than a passing glance. And since almost every farmer well enough off to own both a horse and a tractor belonged to one or other of the hunts, there was never any lack of competition.

In the early days of the show, when transport was still by

171

horse and slow, it was the custom to stay overnight at Bures; and the Chequers, the Rose and Crown, the Wellington, and the Kenley Arms packed them in three to a bed. But with the coming of the motor all that changed. It was more fun to go home nine-to-a-car in the summer dawn than to sleep three-to-a-bed in the Wellington. It was not always a successful method of getting home, of course, and more than one young farmer had spent his summer months in hospital after the Bures Show, but to the younger generation it was inconceivable that they should sleep in an inn when their home was less than forty miles away. So only the older exhibitors, who clung to tradition, or those who lived at an inconvenient distance from Bures, or could not, owing to difficult communications, get their animals away on the evening of the show, still stayed overnight at Bures. And of these most stayed at the Chequers.

The Ashbys had had the same bedrooms at the Chequers for the night of the Bures Show since the days of William Ashby the Seventh: he who had joined the Westover Fencibles to resist the expected invasion of Napoleon the First. They were not the best bedrooms, because in those days the best bedrooms went to the Ledinghams of Clare, who also, of course, had a yearly reservation for the night of the show. What the Ledinghams left went to the Shirleys of Penbury and the Hallands of Hallands House. The Hallands, on whose lands on the outskirts of the town the show was held, had used the bedrooms only for their overflow of guests, but a Hallands guest rated a great deal higher, of course, than any Ashby in the flesh.

Penbury was now the possession of the nation in the shape of the National Trust; a shillingsworth of uplift for coachloads who didn't know Gibbons from Adam and wanted their tea. Hallands House was also the possession of the nation, in the shape of a Government department. No one quite knew what this alien community did. Mrs Thrale, who ran the Singing Kettle tea-rooms out on the Westover road, once boldly asked a young Government employee who was drinking her coffee what her task was at the moment, and was told that it was "arranging the translation of *Tom Jones* into Turkish"; but this was held to be merely a misunderstanding on Mrs Thrale's part, and no one had the heart to question the aliens further. They kept themselves to themselves very determinedly, and it was no longer possible for the people of Bures to walk through Hallands Park.

It would have been possible long ago for the Ashbys on their annual visit to have some of the finer bedrooms at the Chequers, but no such idea ever crossed an Ashby mind. The difference between Number 3 and Number 17 was not that one was a fine room with a pleasant outlook and good furniture and the other a back room looking on to the roof of the assembly room, but that one wasn't "their" room and the other was. So they still had the three little rooms in the older wing, which, since the bathroom had been added at the end of the passage, made it practically an Ashby apartment.

Gregg took the horses over to Bures on Tuesday evening. Arthur followed on Wednesday morning with the ponies and Eleanor's hack, Buster, who hated any box but his own, and was liable to kick a strange stable to pieces. Simon and the twins went in the car with Bee; and Brat shared the bug with Eleanor and Tony Toselli, who had insisted on being allowed to compete in the Best Child Rider class. ("My father will commit suicide if I am not allowed to try.")

Brat wished that this tadpole creature was not sitting between himself and Eleanor. The feeling that his time with Eleanor was short was constantly with him, making each indifferent moment a matter of consequence. But Eleanor seemed happy enough to feel charitable even to Tony Toselli.

"It's going to be perfect weather," she said, looking at the high arch of the sky with no cloud in it. "I can remember only one real soaker at Bures and that's years ago. They've always been awfully lucky. Did I put my string gloves in the locker?"

"Yes."

"What are you going to do all the morning? Look at Mrs Godwin's jam exhibit?"

"I'm going to walk the course."

"Canny Brat," she said, approving. "How right you are."

"The other fellows probably know every inch of it."

"Oh, yes. For most of them it is an annual. In fact, if you started the horses off they'd probably go round by themselves, they are so used to it. Did Bee remember to give you your stand ticket?"

"Yes."

"And have you got it with you?"

"I have."

"I sound a fusser this morning, don't I? You are a nice reassuring person to be with. Do you never get excited, Brat?"

173

"Oh, yes."

"Inside-churning excited?"

"Inside turning over and over."

"That's interesting. It just doesn't show, I suppose."

"I suppose not."

"It's an extraordinarily useful sort of face to have. Mine goes a dull unhealthy pink, as you can see."

He thought the warm childish flush on her normally cool features touching and endearing.

"I hear that Peggy Gates has a new outfit for the occasion. Have you ever seen her on a horse? I can't remember."

"No."

"She looks nice," Eleanor said approvingly. "She rides very well. I think she will do justice to that horse of Dick Pope's."

It was typical of Eleanor that her judgment was independent of her emotions.

The High Street of Bures glittered in the low morning sunlight. Large Motoring Association signs encouraged the traveller, and fluttering advertisements cajoled him. "Carr's Meal for Calves," said a banner. "Saffo, the Safe Disinfectant!" screamed a chimney-to-chimney pendant. "Pett's Dip," said a placard quietly, taking it for granted that the Dip was sufficiently famous to explain itself.

In the dim hall of the Chequers Bee was waiting for them. Simon had gone round to the stables, she said.

"The rooms are Numbers 17, 18 and 19, Brat. You are sharing 17 with Simon, Nell and I have 18, and the twins are in the connecting one, 19."

Sharing a room with Simon was something he had not reckoned with, but there was nothing he could do about it. He picked up Eleanor's bag and his own and went upstairs with them, since the hall was a flurry of arriving guests. Eleanor came with him and showed him where the rooms were.

"The first time I came here and was allowed to stay the night I thought life had nothing left to offer," she said. "Put it down there, Brat, thank you, and I'll unpack it at once or my frock will be ruined."

In Number 17 Simon's things were already strewn all over the room, including the second bed. It was odd how these inanimate belongings of Simon's had, even in his absence, a kind of arrogance.

Brat cleared his own bed and unpacked, hanging his new

evening things carefully in the still empty wardrobe.   Tonight for the first time in his life he would wear evening clothes.

"In case you get lost, Brat," Bee said to him when he came down, "lunch is at twelve-thirty in the luncheon tent.   The last table to your left as you come in.   What do you plan to do this morning?   Poke the pigs?"

"No, he is going to walk the course," Eleanor said.

"All right.   Don't stray off it into any Government holy-of-holies and get yourself arrested, will you?"

Tony was handed over to Mrs Stack, who, being interested solely in rural industries, represented a Fixed Point in the flux of an agricultural show.

"If he tells you that his father is dying and he is urgently wanted at home, don't believe him," Eleanor said.

"Is his father ill, then?"

"No, but Tony may grow bored before half-past twelve. I'll come and fetch him for lunch."

Brat walked into the High Street of Bures with a feeling of escape.   For the first time for nearly a month he was his own master, free to be himself.   He had forgotten what it was like to walk about without care.   For nearly three hours he could go where he liked, ask what he wanted, and answer without a curb on his tongue.

"Hallands Park," said the direction sign on a bus, so he got on the bus and went there.   He had never been to a country show before, and he went round the exhibits with an interest that was at once fresh and critical, comparing all he saw with similar things seen elsewhere.   Homespuns in Arizona, farm implements in Normandy, rams in Zacatecas, Herefords after American air, pottery in New Mexico.   Occasionally some-one looked at him curiously, and more than one hand was half lifted in salutation only to fall again.   He was too like an Ashby ever to be completely free in Bures.   But, speaking generally, people were too absorbed in the exhibits and in their own cares at that hour of the morning to take much interest in the passer-by.

Having exhausted the exhibition, he walked out into the park, where the red flags marked out the temporary racecourse. It was a straight, fast-galloping course over hurdles for the first half-mile through the park, then it went out into the country in a wide curve of a mile or more, came back to the park about half a mile from the stands, and from then on was another series of hurdles up to the finish in front of the stands.

Except for the sharp turns and a few very blind fences in the country, it was not a difficult course. The hurdles in the park stretches were regulation racing ones, and the turf was wonderful. Brat's heart lifted.

It was very peaceful out there in the country, and he came back to the show with a sense of reluctance. But he was surprised to find how glad he was to see the familiar faces round the table in the luncheon tent when he got there; how glad he was to sink into the place kept for him, and be part of this family again.

People came up to their table to welcome him back to Bures Show, to England. People who had known Bill and Nora Ashby, and Bill's father before him. None of them expected him to remember them, and he had merely to be polite.

25

"I THINK I'm going to be sick," Ruth said, when she and Brat were left alone in the stand.

"I don't wonder," said Brat.

"Why?" she was surprised into saying, this being not at all the reaction she expected.

"Three ices on top of dressed crab."

"It is not anything I *ate*," she said, repressive. "It's that I have a delicate nervous system. Excitement makes me feel ill. I get sick with it."

"I should go and get it over," Brat advised.

"Be sick, you mean?"

"Yes. It's a wonderful feeling."

"If I sit very still I may feel better," Ruth said, giving up.

Ruth was feeling her lack of importance today. She avoided horses too consistently for the rest of the year to claim any right to exhibit any on this one day at Bures, so she sat in the stand in her neat grey flannel and looked on. It was to her credit that she did not grudge her twin her well-earned place in the sun, and was passionately anxious that Jane should come first in her class.

"There's Roger Clint with Eleanor."

Brat looked for the couple and found them.

"Who is Roger Clint?"

"He has a big farm near here."

Roger Clint was a black-browed young man, and he was being old-friendly with Eleanor.

"He's in love with Eleanor," said Ruth, having failed with one try for drama.

"A very good person to be in love with," Brat said, but his heart contracted.

"It would be a very good thing if she married him. He has lots of money and a lovely big house and simply scads of horses."

Against his will Brat asked if Eleanor were thinking of it.

Ruth considered the pros and cons of this as they fitted into her dramatic framework.

"She is making him serve his seven years for her. You know: like Jacob. He is simply frantic about it, poor Roger, but she is La Belle Dame Sans Merci."

La Belle Dame Sans Merci bade Mr Clint a temporary farewell and came up to join them in the stand as the Novices under Ten filed into the ring.

"Do you know that Tony scraped into this by the skin of his teeth," she said, sitting down by Brat. "He is going to be ten the day after tomorrow."

There were eleven novices, the youngest being a fat child of four in a black velvet jockey cap, who bounced about on a solid pony of which she had no control whatever.

"Well, at least Tony never looked as awful as that, even in his bad days," Eleanor said.

"Tony looks wonderful," Ruth said, and Tony did indeed look wonderful. As Eleanor had said on an earlier occasion, Tony had the root of the matter in him.

The novices walked, and trotted, and cantered, under the lenient eye of the judges, and presently the seeding began. Even from the stand the fanatic determination in Tony's snail-black eyes was plain to see. He was going to be in the money or die in the attempt. From being six possibles they were narrowed down to four, but these four kept the judges puzzled. Again and again they were sent out to canter and brought back for inspection, and sent out to canter again. There were only three prizes and one must go.

It was at this stage that Tony played what he evidently considered his ace. As he cantered along in front of the stand he got to his knees in the saddle and with a slight scramble stood up in it, straight and proud.

"Oh, God," said Eleanor reverently and with feeling.

A ripple of laughter went through the stand. But Tony had another shot in his locker. He slipped to his knees, grabbed the front edge of the saddle, and stood on his head, his thin spider-legs waving rather uncertainly in the air.

At that a gale of laughter and applause broke out, and Tony, much gratified, resumed his seat and urged his astonished pony, who had slowed to a trot, into a canter again.

That of course settled the matter very nicely for the judges, and Tony had the mortification of seeing the three rosettes handed to his rivals. But his mortification was nothing to the mortification he had already inflicted on his preceptress.

"I hope I don't see that child until I cool off," she said, "or I am liable to take an axe to him."

But Tony, having handed his pony over to Arthur, came blithely to the stands to find her.

"Tony, you little *idiot*," she said, "what made you do a thing like that?"

"I wanted to show how I could ride, Eleanor."

"And where did you learn to do those circus tricks?"

"I practised on the pony that mows the lawn. At school, you know. He has a much broader back than Muffet, and that's why I wasn't so steady today. I don't think these people appreciate good riding," he added, nodding his head at the offending judges.

Eleanor was speechless.

Brat presented him with a coin and told him to go and buy himself an ice.

"If I didn't want to see Jane ride," Eleanor said, "I would go and bury my shame in the ladies' room. I'm *curdled* with humiliation."

Jane, on Rajah, in her best riding things, was a pleasant sight. Brat had never seen her in anything but the shabby jodhpurs and shapeless jersey that she wore at home, and was surprised by this trim little figure.

"Jane has the best seat of all the Ashbys," Eleanor said affectionately, watching the serious and efficient Jane making Rajah change his leg to order. "That is her only rival: that tall girl on the grey."

The tall girl was fifteen and the grey very handsome, but the judges preferred Jane and Rajah. Jane might have lost for all the emotion she showed, but Ruth was rapturous.

"Good old Jane," said Simon, appearing beside them. "A veteran at nine."

"Oh, Simon, did you *see*!" Eleanor said, in agony again as she remembered.

"Cheer up, Nell," he said, dropping a commiserating hand on her shoulder. "It might have been worse."

"How *could* it be worse?"

"He didn't yodel," Simon said.

At that she began to laugh, and went on laughing. "Oh, I suppose it is very funny," she said, wiping her eyes, "and I expect I shall laugh over it for years, but at the moment I just wish I could be in Australia for the rest of the afternoon."

"Come on, Nell," he said. "It's time to collect the horses," and they went away together as Jane came to sit in the stand.

"This is the exciting class coming now. It isn't very much to win a Fifteen and Under," was her answer to Brat's congratulations. "Some day I'll be down there with *them*. With Aunt Bee, and Eleanor, and Simon, and Peggy, and Roger Clint, and all of them."

Yes, there was Roger Clint. Eleanor was riding the long-backed bay mare Scapa, and Roger Clint was standing next to her on a chestnut with four of the longest and whitest stockings Brat had ever seen. While the judges walked down the row he and Eleanor talked quietly together.

"Who do you think will be first?" Jane asked.

Brat took his eyes from Eleanor and Clint and forced himself to consider the entry. The judge had sent Bee out to canter Chevron, the chestnut he was going to race this afternoon, and she was coming down in front of the stands now. He had never seen Bee in formal riding clothes, and was surprised again, as he had been with Jane. It was a new, serious, rather intimidating Bee.

"Who do you think, Brat?" Jane said again.

"Timber, of course."

"Not Peggy's horse? The one Dick Pope had?"

"Riding Light? No. He may win the jumping, but not this."

And he was right. This was the judges' first sight of Timber and they were too much impressed to be seduced even by the looks and reputation of Riding Light.

And it was a popular verdict. As Simon cantered Timber down in front of the stands after accepting the rosette the applause broke into cheering.

"Isn't that the brute that killed old Felix?" a voice behind said. "They ought to shoot it instead of giving it prizes."

Second was Peggy on Riding Light, looking flushed and pleased; her father's extravagance had been justified. Third, rather unexpectedly, was Bee on Chevron.

"The Ashbys cleaning up as usual," the voice said, and was instantly shushed, and the proximity of the Ashbys presumably indicated.

It was when the Open Jumping Class began that the real excitement of the day was reached, and Bee came to sit in the stand and share it with them.

"Number One, please," said the loud-speaker, and Eleanor came into the ring on Scapa. Scapa was a careful and unemotional jumper, but could never be persuaded into standing away from her fences. By dint of patient schooling with a guard rail, Eleanor hoped that she had now persuaded her into better ways. And for half a round it worked, until Scapa noticed that there was no plaguey obstruction to beware of at the foot of these jumps, and began to go close in again, with the inevitable result. Nothing Eleanor could do would make her take off in time. She jumped "fit to hit the moon," but came down in the wrong place, and the little battens of white-painted wood came down with her.

"Poor Nell," said Bee. "After all her schooling."

Number Two and Number Three did not appear to have been schooled at all.

"Number Four, please," said the loud-speaker, and Riding Light appeared. Peggy's "new outfit" consisted of a dark snuff-coloured coat a little too tight in the waist, and a pair of buff breeches a little too pale in the buff, but she looked well on the brown horse and handled him beautifully. Or rather, she sat still and let Riding Light do his stuff. He was a finished jumper who took the obstacles in his stride, propelling himself into the air in a long effortless curve and tucking his hind feet after him like a cat. He went out having done a perfect round.

"Number Five, please," said the loud-speaker.

Number Five was Roger Clint's mount with the long white stockings. "Do you know what he calls it?" Bee said. "Operation Stockings."

"It's very ugly," Brat said. "Looks as if he had walked through a trough of whitewash.

"He can jump, though."

180

He could certainly jump, but he had a phobia about water.

"Poor Roger," laughed Bee, watching Stockings refuse the water. "He has been jumping him backwards and forwards across the duck pond at home in the hope of curing him, and now he does this!"

Stockings continued to refuse, and Clint had to take him out, in a burst of sympathetic applause.

Numbers Six and Seven had one fault each.

Number Eight was Simon on Timber.

The black horse came into the ring exactly as he had come out of his box on the day Brat first saw him, pleased with himself and ready for homage. His excited, flickering ears pricked into attention as he caught sight of the jumps. Simon took him into a canter and moved down to the first one. Even from where he was sitting, Brat could feel the smoothness of that action. The smoothness that had astonished him that first day at Latchetts when he had ridden on the top of the down. Smoothly the black horse rose into the air and came down on the far side of the jump, and a murmur of admiration came from the crowd at the almost feline beauty of it. Brat, with the most wholehearted respect, watched Simon's body swing with the black horse's rise and fall as though he were part of it. It was right that Simon should ride it. He would never attain that perfection if he lived to be a hundred. A great silence settled on the crowd as one by one the jumps fled away behind Timber. It would be monstrous if this beauty were to fail or be faulted. It was so quiet when he faced the water jump that the voice of a paper-seller far away at the main gate was the only sound to be heard. And when he landed smoothly and neatly on the far bank, a great sigh went up from them. They had seen a perfect thing. They had not been cheated of it after all.

So moved were they that Simon was almost out of the ring before the applause broke out.

The last three entries had been scratched, and Simon was the final performer, so the second round began as soon as he had left.

Eleanor came back on Scapa, and by dint of voice and spur managed to make the unwilling mare take off at the proper place, and so did something to retrieve her self-respect. The crowd, appreciating what had been wrong in the first place and what she had now succeeded in doing, gave her credit for it.

Number Two did a wild but lucky round, and Number Three

a wild and unlucky one; and then came Peggy again, still flushed from the pleasure of her perfect round.

Again she had the sense to sit still while Riding Light heaved her into the air with the thrust of his tremendous quarters, sailed over the jump, and made for the next one with his ears erect and confident. It seemed that there was nothing to hinder the brown horse doing this all day. There was an air of routine about the business that somehow detracted from his performance; he made it look too easy. There seemed little doubt that he would do another perfect round. His judgment of distance was faultless. He never had to stop and put in a short one to bring him to the proper taking-off point; he arrived at the taking-off point by some computing of his own, taking the jumps in his stride as if they were hurdles. He was coming up to the wall now, and they waited to see if he would treat that, too, like a hurdle.

"Thump! Thump! Thump!" said the drum of the Bures Silver Band, as the preliminary to *Colonel Bogey* and their entry into the front gate of the show for their afternoon performance. Riding Light's ears flickered in question, in doubt. His mind was distracted from that rapidly nearing wall. His ears shot forward again in alarm as he saw it almost upon him. He shortened his stride, trying to fit it into the remaining space, but he had misjudged it. He rose at it with determination and landed on the other side, flinging his quarters upwards in a successful effort to avoid hitting the fence that was now too close under him. But the shoe of his near fore had touched the wall as he rose to it, and a billet slid out of place, wavered a moment on the edge, and then dropped to the ground.

"A-a-ah!" said the crowd in quick sympathy, and Peggy looked back to see what had happened. She saw the little gap in the top of the wall, but it did not rattle her. She collected Riding Light, patted him encouragingly on the neck, and headed him for the next.

"Good girl, Peggy!" murmured Bee.

The distant band was now playing *Colonel Bogey*, and Riding Light took no further notice of them; he knew all about bands. Bands had been the accompaniment to some of his best performances. He settled down again to his routine, and finished by taking the water jump with a margin that made the crowd gasp.

"Simon will never beat that," Bee said. "That perfect round of Timber's was a miracle in the first place."

182

The four long stockings of Roger Clint's mount flashed round the ring in a brisk and willing fashion until they came to the water. Faced with the long distance to the last jump, Stockings stopped and pondered. Clint argued amiably with him, but Stockings would have none of it. "I know what is behind that hedge quite well, and I *don't like* it!" he seemed to be saying. And then, with that perennial unreasonableness of horses, he decided to have a go at it. Of his own accord he turned towards the jump and began to canter. Roger sat down and drove him at it, and Stockings went flying down to it with purpose in every line of him. In the last half-second he changed his mind just as suddenly as he had made it up, stuck both toes in hard, and skidded to a stop up against the fence.

The crowd laughed, and so did Roger Clint. He hauled himself back into the saddle from his position round his mount's neck. He took Stockings round to the other side of the fence and showed him the water. He took him up to it and let him inspect it at close quarters. He walked him round it and let him look at the other edge. And then he took him back to the far end of the ring and turned him to the jump. With an air of "Oh, well, let's get this thing over with" Stockings jumped off his haunches, tore down the ring, and fled over the water with a yard or two to spare.

The crowd laughed delightedly, and the white teeth showed in Clint's brown face. He lifted his hat to the applause without looking at them, as a cricketer lifts his cap, and rode out of the ring, well satisfied to have ignored the judge's disqualifying eye long enough to have induced Stockings to cross the hated obstacle.

Number Six had two faults. Number Seven two-and-a-half.

"Number Eight, please," said the loud-speaker, and Jane shivered and put her hand in Bee's. For once Ruth did not have to manufacture drama to suit her; her mouth was open with suspense and she was entirely oblivious of Ruth Ashby.

Timber had neither the experience nor the machine-like power of Riding Light. He had to be ridden. It rested as much on Simon's judgment as on Timber's powers whether they could beat the almost faultless performance of Peggy Gates's horse. Brat thought that Simon looked very white about the mouth. There was more in this for Simon than winning a cup at a small country show. He had to take that prize from the girl who had tried to be upsides with him by introducing a made winner to beat his own untried horses.

Timber came in looking puzzled. It was as if he said: "I've *done* this." His ears pricked at the sight of the jumps and then flickered in question. There was no eagerness to go at them as there had been when it was a new experience. But he went good-manneredly down to the first and cleared it in his effortless fluid fashion. Brat thought that he could hear the Ashby hearts thumping alongside him. He could certainly hear his own; it was making a noise like the Bures Silver Band's drum. Simon was half-way round. Ruth had shut her mouth and her eyes and looked as if she were praying. She opened her eyes in time to see Timber clear the gate; a smooth river of black pouring over the white barrier. "Oh, thank you, God," said Ruth. There was only the wall and the water left.

As Timber turned at the far end of the ring to come back to the wall a gust of wind lifted Simon's hat from his head and sent it bowling along the ground behind him. Brat was of the opinion that Simon was not even aware of it. Not even Tony Toselli had shown a concentration like Simon's. For Simon there quite patently existed nothing in this world but himself, the black horse, and the jumps. No one, *no one*, was going to come between Simon Ashby and the sun and get away with it.

Everything that Simon knew of riding, everything he had learned since he first sat on a pony at the age of two, was devoted to getting Timber safely over the wall. Timber did not like hard bare obstacles.

He had started his canter to the wall when a shrieking white terrier shot out from the stand in pursuit of the distant hat, streaking across in front of the advancing Timber like a hard-kicked ball, and yelling its excitement as only a terrier can.

Timber swerved from this terror and broke into a sweat.

Ruth shut her eyes again and resorted to further prayer. Simon soothed Timber patiently, cantering him round and making much of him while someone retrieved the dog and brought it back to its owner. (Who said: "Poor darling Scottie, he might have been killed!") Patiently, while the unforgiving seconds ticked on, Simon worked to reassure Timber. He must know that time was running out, that the dog incident was now officially over and each additional second's delay piling up against him.

Brat had marvelled often at Simon's power of self-control, but he had never seen a more remarkable sample of it. The temptation to take Timber to the jump as he was must be

normous. But Simon was taking no chances with Timber.
He was pawning time to gain a little better odds for Timber.

And then, having apparently calculated his time to the nearest
possible margin, he brought Timber, still sweating but collected,
to the wall again. Just before he came to the fence Timber
hesitated a little.

And Simon sat still.

If it had been possible for Brat to like Simon Ashby he would
have liked him at that moment.

The horse, undistracted from the task in front of him, gathered himself together and catapulted himself over the hated
obstacle. And then, relieved to have it behind him, he raced
on delightedly to the water and rocketed across it like a blackbird.

Simon had done it.

Jane took her hand out of Bee's, and wiped her palms on a
screwed-up ball of handkerchief.

Bee slipped her arm through Brat's and squeezed it.

The great burst of cheering made speech inaudible.

In the quiet that succeeded it Ruth said, as one remembering
an awkward engagement: "Oh, dear! I've pawned my
month's allowance."

"To whom?" asked her aunt.

"God," said Ruth.

26

BRAT surveyed himself in the small cracked mirror of the
Gents' Temporary Dressing-room and decided that primrose
and violet did not become him any better than they became
Simon. It would take Roger Clint's dark face to do justice to
those springtime glories. Roger Clint would probably look
dashing in them. He was in no mood to look favourably on
Roger Clint. Whenever he had caught sight of Eleanor this
afternoon it seemed that she was in the company of Mr Clint,
and what is more, seemed to be enjoying the company.

Brat tugged the yellow visor a little farther over his eyes.
A sick misery burned in him; a spiritual heartburn.

"What's it got to do with you?" said a voice in him. "You're
her brother: remember?"

"Shut up!"

"Can't have your cake and eat it, you know."

"*Shut up!*"

He walked out of the almost deserted dressing-room and went to find Chevron. The serious business of the day was over and there was an air of relaxation. In the shade of the trees competitors who had taken part in the sober events were now walking ponies and coffee-housing while they waited for the bending race. Alone for the moment, on a solid dun pony, was Peggy Gates, her eyes roving over the crowd in search of someone She looked tired and discouraged. As Brat came level with her he paused and said:

"That was very bad luck."

"Oh, hullo, Mr Ashby! What was?"

"The big drum."

"Oh, that!" she said, and smiled at him. "Oh, that was just one of those things."

She sounded quite philosophical about it, and yet Brat could have sworn that when he came up she had tears in her eyes.

"Good luck to the race," she said.

Brat thanked her and was moving away when she said: "Mr Ashby, have I done anything to offend Simon, do you know?"

Brat said no, not that he knew.

"Oh. It's just that he seems to be avoiding me lately, and I'm not aware of having done anything—anything that he wouldn't——"

There were undoubted tears in her eyes now.

"Oh, you *know*," she said, tried a smile, didn't manage it very well, and moved away with a wave of her hand.

So it had not been a desire to be mistress of Latchetts that had moved pretty Peggy; it was devotion to Simon. Poor Peggy. Simon would never forgive her for Riding Light.

Eleanor was waiting under the trees on Buster, but stirrup to stirrup with her was Roger Clint, who had also found a pony for the bending race. Roger was pouring out a long story and Eleanor was nodding sympathetically; Brat gave them a wide berth and betook himself to the stables. In the stables he found Bee and Gregg. Gregg saw him weighed out and saddled Chevron, who was nervous and unhappy.

"It's the sound of the crowd that worries her," Gregg said. "Something she hears and can't understand. If I were you, Mr Patrick, sir, I'd take her out and walk her. Take her out and show her the crowds and she'll be so interested she'll forget her nerves."

So Brat took the dithering chestnut out into the park, and she became gradually quieter, as Gregg had known she would. Presently Simon found him and suggested that it was time to be going down to the start.

"Did you remember to sign the book?" he asked.

"Book?" said Brat. "Sign for what?"

"To show that you consent to your horse running."

"I never heard of anyone signing a book. The horse was entered, wasn't it?"

"Yes, but in previous years they had trouble with gate-crashers. Some bright sparks who took out horses that didn't belong to them, when their owners didn't intend to run them. Had a free jaunt on them, and in at least one case broke the already tired horse down."

"All right. Where is the book?"

"In the weighing-room place. I'll look after Chevron till you come back. No need to take her into that mêlée."

In the little office, sitting behind the desk, was Colonel Smollett.

"Well, young Ashby, your family has been doing very well to-day, eh? Three firsts, no less. Are you going to add a fourth? Book? What book? Oh, the paper. Yes, yes. Here it is."

Brat, signing the single sheet of paper that was presented to him, said that he had never heard of this procedure.

"Probably not. Never heard of it myself. But it does insure the Show against loss to a certain extent. That fellow whose horse was ridden unbeknownst to him last year, he sued the Show for damages. Very nearly got them, too. So your brother suggested this method of insurance."

"My brother? Simon suggested it?"

"Yes. Got a head on him, Simon. Now no one can say that his horse was pulled out without his permission."

"I see."

He went back and retrieved Chevron from Arthur's custody.

"Mr Simon said he couldn't wait, Mr Patrick, but he said to wish you luck. He's gone back to the stands with the rest of the family to watch the finish."

"All right, Arthur; thanks."

"Would you like me to come to the start with you, sir?"

"Oh, no, thanks."

"In that case, I'll go and see about getting myself a place to see from. Good luck, sir. We're betting on you."

And he hurried off through the crowd.

Brat put the reins over Chevron's head and was just about to mount when he thought that he would take one more look at the girth. He had already tightened it, but perhaps he had made it too tight.

But someone had loosened the girth.

Brat stood holding up the flap with his hand and stared. Someone had loosened it since he left the mare with Simon. He put his hand under the girth and tested its degree of slackness. He reckoned that it would have got him out of the park into the country and would have lasted perhaps another two fences. After that, the saddle would have slipped round on the highly excitable Chevron and she would have gone crazy.

Arthur? No, not Arthur. Simon almost certainly.

He tightened the girth and made for the start. As he arrived he was overtaken by Roger Clint in white and scarlet of Operation Stockings.

"You're Patrick Ashby, aren't you?" he said. "My name is Roger Clint." He leaned over and shook hands. "Very nice to have you at Bures again."

"Who won the bending race?" Brat asked.

"I did. By a short head from Nell."

"Nell" indeed!

"She won it last year on Buster, so it is just as well that the thing should go round. And I wanted a silver cup, anyway."

Brat had no time to ask why he had this longing for a silver cup. They were lining up, and he was Number Five, and Roger Clint was away on the outside. There were fourteen runners and a considerable amount of jostling. There was no gate, of course, the start being by flag.

Brat was in no hurry at the start. He let the others lead him so that he could gauge the opposition. At least five, he decided, were horses that had been ridden so much today that they were of no consequence and were merely cluttering up the course and spoiling things for their betters. Three more he had seen jumped in a junior competition, and had no belief that they would ever get round the course. That left five possibles, and of these three were dangerous: a bay charger ridden by his officer owner; a great raking brown youngster ridden by young farmer; and Roger Clint's mount.

They took the hurdles at a tearing pace, and two of the over worked lot, fighting for position, struck into each other and rolled into a third. One of the "junior" jumpers came a frightful purler over the first fence going into the country, and brought down the other two over-tired animals. Which cleared the field very happily.

Chevron liked seeing her horses in front of her, and was patently enjoying herself. She loved jumping and was taking her fences with an off-handed confidence. One could almost hear her humming. She watched the other two "junior" jumpers fail to get over a blind fence and flicked her heels in their faces.

The field was thinning out very nicely.

Brat began to move up.

He passed the fifth of the possibles without effort. The fourth was making a noise like a pipe band but seemed good for a little yet. In front of him at the farthest point of the course were the soldier on the bay charger, the farmer on the big young brown horse, and Roger Clint on the chestnut with the white stockings. Apart from his own Chevron, Clint's was probably the best quality horse in the race, but the soldier was riding like a veteran, and the farmer like someone who has no respect for his neck.

It was a right-handed course, and the farmer's young horse jumped consistently to the right, so that no one could with any safety come up on the inside of him as long as he hugged the turns tightly. And since no one wanted to go wider than they need at the turns they dallied a little behind the big brown until they could come into the straight and pass him without disadvantage. It was going to be a race when they came back to that last half-mile of park.

Gradually the pipe band that had been so long at his left ear faded backwards into the distance, and when they came back to the park there were only four of them in it: the soldier, the farmer, Clint, and himself. He didn't mind about the other two, but he wanted very much to beat Roger Clint.

Clint had a look round as they left the country behind, and flashed a friendly smile to him. After that there was no time for courtesies. The pace was turned on with the suddenness of a tap, and the four of them pounded down the green avenue between the fluttering red flags as if classic honours were waiting for them at the other end. The big young brown horse began to sprawl; and the charger, though steady as a rock and apparently tireless, seemed to have no turn of speed to finish with.

Brat decided to keep Chevron's nose level with the chestnut's quarters and see what transpired. Together they forged ahead of the bay and the brown. The farmer was using his whip and his horse sprawled more at every lift of it. The soldier was sitting still on the bay and evidently hoping that stamina would tell in the end.

Brat had a good look at Stockings and decided that he was tiring rapidly and that Clint, from the careful way he was riding him, knew it. There were two hurdles to go. He had no idea how much speed or stamina Chevron might have left, so he decided that the safest method was to try to trick Clint out of it. He shook Chevron up and took her up level with Stockings as if he were making his effort. Clint increased his speed to match, and together they crossed the last two obstacles, Brat still by his own choice a little in the rear, and therefore out of Clint's vision. Then Brat eased the pressure momentarily, and Clint, taking it for granted that a falling back so near the post argued failing stamina, was glad that he would not have to ask his mount for the last ounce and relaxed a little. Brat gathered Chevron together with all his strength and came like a rocket from behind him. Clint looked up, startled, and set Stockings alight again, but it was too late. They were far too near the post for that, as Brat had reckoned. He had stolen the race.

"Of all the 'old soldier' tricks to fall for!" laughed Clint, as they walked their horses together to the weighing-room. "I ought to have my head examined."

And Brat felt that whether Eleanor was going to marry him or not he really did like Roger Clint quite a lot.

27

BRAT had expected that Simon's success would have shored up his disintegrating spiritual structure and that the cracks would have disappeared. But it seemed that the very opposite had happened. The strain of the afternoon followed by the triumph of having beaten a performer like Riding Light had eaten away a little more of the foundation and shaken his equilibrium still further.

"I've never seen Simon so cock-a-hoop," Eleanor said, watching Simon over Brat's shoulder as they danced together that night. She said it as one making an apology. "He is usually so off-hand about his triumphs."

Brat said that it was probably the champagne, and turned her away from her view of Simon.

He had looked forward all day to dancing with Eleanor, but it was with Bee that he had danced first. Just as he had given up his first chance of a ride with Eleanor to walk on Tanbitches with the ghost of Pat Ashby, so when faced with the moment of his first dance with Eleanor he had found something else that he wanted more. He had crossed the room to Bee and said: "Will you dance with me?" They had danced together in a happy quiet, her only remark being: "Who taught you to cheat someone out of a race like that?"

"I didn't have to be taught. It's original sin."

She laughed a little and patted him with the hand that was lying on his shoulder. She was a lovely woman, Bee Ashby, and he loved her. The only other person he had ever loved was a horse called Smoky.

"I haven't seen much of you this afternoon since that awful exhibition of Tony's," Eleanor said.

Brat said that he had wanted to talk to her before the race but that she was in deep conversation with Roger Clint.

"Oh, yes. I remember. His uncle wants him to give up the farm and go and live in Ulster. His uncle is Tim Connell, you know, who has the Kilbarty stud. Tim wants to retire, and would lease the place to Roger, but Roger doesn't want to leave England."

Understandable, Brat thought. England and Eleanor together was heaven enough. "I don't see him here tonight?"

"No, he didn't stay for the dance."

"No?" said Brat, surprised.

"He just came to get a silver cup to take home to his wife."

"His *wife*!"

"Yes, she had their first baby last week, and she sent him to the show to get a christening mug for it. What is the matter?" she asked.

"Remind me sometime to break Ruth's neck," he said, beginning to dance again.

She looked amused and said: "Has Ruth been romancing?"

"She said he wanted to marry you."

"Oh, well, he did have an idea like that but it's a long time ago. And of course he wasn't married last year, so Ruth probably didn't know about it. Are you going to be all patriarchal and supervise my marriage plans?"

"Have you any?"

"None at all."

As the night wore on and he danced more and more with Eleanor, she said: "You really must dance with someone else, Brat."

"I have."

"Only with Peggy Gates."

"So you've been keeping track of me. Am I keeping you from dancing with someone you want to dance with?"

"No. I love dancing with you."

"All right then."

This was perhaps the first and the last night he would ever dance with Eleanor. A little before midnight they went up together to the buffet, filled their plates, and took them to one of the little tables in the balcony. The buffet was part of the actual hotel building, and the balcony, a piece of Regency ironwork, looked down on the little garden at the side of the hotel. Chinese lanterns hung in the garden and above the tables in the balcony.

"I'm too happy to eat," Eleanor said, and drank her champagne in a dreamy silence. "You look very nice in your evening things, Brat."

"Thank you."

"Do you like my frock?"

"It's the most beautiful frock I ever saw."

"I did hope you would like it."

"Have you had supper already tonight?"

"No. Only some drinks and a sandwich."

"Better eat, then."

She ate in an uninterested fashion that was new in Eleanor.

"It has been an Ashby occasion, hasn't it, the Seventy-fourth Annual Show of the Bures Agricultural . . . Stay still for a moment, you have a gnat crawling down your collar."

She leant over and struck the back of his neck lightly. "Oh, it's going down!" In a rough sisterly fashion she bent his head aside with one hand while she retrieved the insect with the other.

"Got it?" he said.

But she was silent, and he looked up at her.

"You're *not* my brother!" she said. "I couldn't feel the way I——" She stopped, horrified.

192

In the silence the beat of the distant drums came up from the assembly room.

"Oh, Brat, I'm sorry! I didn't mean that! I think I must have drunk too much." She began to sob. "Oh, Brat, I'm sorry!" She gathered up her bag from the table and stumbled from the dim balcony into the buffet room. "I'll go and lie down and get sober."

Brat let her go and sought counsel in the bar. There was some sort of stunt in the assembly room at midnight, and the bar was deserted except for Simon, all by himself with a bottle of champagne at a table in the far corner.

"Ah! My big brother," said Simon. "Are you not interested in the lottery drawing? Have a drink."

"Thanks. I'll buy my own."

He bought a drink at the bar and carried it down the long room to Simon's table.

"I suppose lottery odds are too long for you," Simon said. "You want the table rigged before you bet."

Brat ignored that. "I haven't had a chance of congratulating you on your win with Timber."

"I don't need praise from you."

Simon was certainly drunk.

"That was very rude of me, wasn't it?" he said like a pleased child. "But I enjoy being rude. I'm behaving very badly tonight, aren't I? I seem to be slipping. Have a drink."

"I've got one."

"You don't like me, do you?" He looked pleased by Brat's dislike.

"Not much."

"Why not?"

"I suppose because you are the only one who doesn't believe that I am Patrick."

"You mean, don't you, that I'm the only one who *knows* you're not?"

There was a long silence while Brat searched the shining eyes with their odd dark rim.

"You killed him," he said, suddenly sure of it.

"Of course I did." He leaned forward and looked delightedly at Brat. "But you'll never be able to say so, will you? Because of course Patrick isn't dead at all. He's alive, and I'm talking to him."

"How did you do it?"

"You'd like to know, wouldn't you? Well, I'll tell you It's very simple." He leaned still closer and said in a mock-confidential undertone: "You see, I'm a witch. I can be in two places at once."

He sat back and enjoyed Brat's discomfiture.

"You must think that I'm a lot drunker than I am, my friend," he said. "I've told you about Patrick, because you are my posthumous accomplice. A wonderful epithet, that, and I managed it very well. But if you think that I am going to make you free of the details, you are mistaken."

"Then, why did you do it?"

"He was a very stupid little boy," he said in his airy "Simon' tone, "and not worthy of Latchetts." Then he added, without façade: "I hated him, if you want to know."

He poured himself another glass of the Ayala, and drank it He laughed under his breath, and said: "It's a wonderful spiritual twinship, isn't it? I can't tell about you and you can't tell about me!"

"You have the advantage of me, though."

"I have? How?"

"You have no scruples."

"Yes; I suppose it is an advantage."

"I have to put up with you, but you have no intention of putting up with me, have you? You did your best to kill me this afternoon."

"Not my best."

"You'll improve on it, I take it?"

"I'll improve."

"I expect you will. A person who can be in two places at once can do better than a loosened girth."

"Oh, much better. But one has to accept the means to hand."

"I see."

"I suppose you wouldn't like, in return for my confidences, to tell *me* something?"

"Tell you what?"

"Who you are?"

Brat sat looking at him for a long time.

"Don't you recognise me?" he said.

"No. Who are you?"

"Retribution," said Brat, and finished his drink.

He walked out of the bar and hung for a little over the

banisters until his inside settled down and his breath came more easily. He tried to think of some place where he could be alone to think this thing out. There was nowhere in the hotel; even in his bedroom Simon might join him at any moment: he would have to go out.

He went to get his coat from Number 17, and on the way back again he met Bee.

"Has everyone gone crazy?" Bee said angrily. "Eleanor is upstairs crying, Simon is getting drunk in the bar, and now you look as if you had seen a ghost. What is the matter with everyone? Have you had a quarrel?"

"A quarrel? No. Eleanor and Simon have had a wearing day, I expect."

"And what makes *you* so white about the gills?"

"Ballroom air. I'm from the wide open spaces: remember?"

"I've always understood that the wide open spaces were just seething with dance halls."

"Do you mind if I take the car, Bee?"

"Take it where?"

"I want to see the sun rise over Kenley Vale."

"Alone?"

"Definitely alone."

"Put on your coat," she said. "It's cold out."

At the top of the rise looking over Kenley Vale he stopped the car and shut off the engine. It was still dark and would be dark for some time yet. He got out and stood on the grass verge, leaning against the bonnet, and listened to the silence. The earth and grass smelt strong in the cool damp after the sun of yesterday. The air was motionless. Far away across the Vale a train whistled.

He had a cigarette, and his stomach felt better. But the turmoil had merely moved up. The turmoil was now in his head.

He had been right about Simon. He had been right in seeing the resemblance to Timber: the well-bred creature with the beautiful manners who was also a rogue. Simon had told the truth, back there in the bar. He had been glad to tell him the truth. They said all killers wanted to boast about their killings; Simon must have longed often to tell someone how clever he had been. But he could never tell until now; when he had a "safe" listener.

He, Brat Farrar, was the "safe" listener.

195

He, Brat Farrar, owned Latchetts, and Simon took it for granted that he would keep what he had taken. That he would keep it as Simon's accessory.

But that, of course, was not possible. The unholy alliance with Loding was one thing; but the alliance that Simon took so mockingly for granted was not possible. It was monstrous. Unthinkable.

And that being that, what was he going to do about it?

Go to the police and say: Look, I'm not Patrick Ashby at all. Patrick Ashby was killed by his brother eight years ago. I know, because he told me so when he was a little drunk.

And then they would point out that in the course of their investigations into the death of Patrick Ashby it was proved that Simon Ashby had spent the relevant hours in the smith's company in Clare.

He could tell them the truth about himself, but nothing would be changed except his own life. Patrick Ashby would remain a suicide.

How had Simon done it?

"One has to accept the means at hand," he had said, about his slackening of the girth.

What "means at hand" had there been that day eight years ago?

The slackening of the girth had been a combination of planning and improvisation. The "signing the book" suggestion had been a long shot. If it worked successfully to get him out of the way, then Simon was free to complete the rest of his plan. If it did not work, then no harm was done. The set-up was innocent to the observer's eye.

That was the way Simon's mind had worked about the girth, and that was the way it had worked eight years ago, undoubtedly. The set-up that was innocent and unquestionable. The using of the means at hand.

How, eight years ago, had Simon used an innocent set of circumstances to provide him with the chance he wanted?

Brat's mind was still toiling round and round the problem when the first sigh of the stirring air told him that the dawn was coming. Presently the wind came again, lifting the leaves this time and ruffling the grass, and the east was grey. He watched the light come. The first bird notes dropped into the quiet.

He had been there for hours and he was no nearer a solution of the problem that faced him.

A policeman came along at leisure, pushing a bicycle, and paused to ask if he were in trouble. Brat said that he was getting some fresh air after a dance.

The policeman looked at his starched linen and accepted his explanation without remark. He looked at the interior of the car and said: "First time I ever saw a young gentleman getting fresh air alone after a dance. You haven't made away with her, by any chance, have you, sir?"

Brat wondered what he would say if he said: "No, but I'm accessory after the fact to another murder."

"She turned me down," he said.

"Ah. I see. Nursing your grief. Take it from me, sir, a week from now you'll be so thankful you'll feel like dancing in the street."

And he pushed his bicycle away along the ridge.

Brat began to shiver.

He got into the car and headed after the policeman. Where could he get something hot, he asked?

There was an all-night café at the main crossroads two miles ahead, the policeman said.

At the café, warm and bright and mundane after the grey spaces of the dawn, he drank scalding coffee. A buxom woman was frying sausages for two lorry-drivers, and a third was trying his luck at a penny-in-the-slot game in the corner. They glanced incuriously at his dance clothes, but beyond exchanging greetings with him they left him alone.

He came back to Bures at breakfast time, and put the car in the garage. The Chequers vestibule had a littered look; it was still only half past seven, and Show people notoriously made a night of it. He went up to Number 17 and found Simon fast asleep, with all his clothes in one single heap on the floor just as he had peeled them off. He changed into his day clothes, quietly at first and then less carefully as he realised that only long shaking would awaken Simon in his present condition. He looked down at Simon and marvelled. He slept quietly, like a child. Had he grown so used to the thing after eight years that it no longer troubled him, or was it that it never had been a monstrous thing in his estimation?

It was a charming face, except perhaps for the pettish mouth. A delightful face; delicately made and proportioned. There was no more suggestion of wrong-doing about it than there was in the beauty that was Timber.

He went downstairs and washed, wishing that he had thought in time of having a bath. He had been too obsessed by the desire to change clothes without having to talk to Simon.

When he came into the dining-room he found Bee and the twins having breakfast, and joined them.

"Nell and Simon are still asleep," Bee said. "You'd better come back with me and the twins in the car, and let Eleanor take Simon when they waken."

"What about Tony?"

"Oh, he went back yesterday with Mrs Stack."

It was a relief to know that he could go back to Latchetts with Bee in peace.

The twins began to talk about Tony's exploit, which was patently going to be part of Latchetts history, and he did not have to make conversation. Bee asked if the dawn had come up to expectation, and remarked that he was looking the better for it.

Through the green early-morning countryside they drove home to Clare, and Brat caught himself looking at it with the emotions of someone who has only a short time to live. He looked at things with a that-will-still-be-there attitude.

He would never come to Bures again. He might never even drive with Bee again.

Whatever else Simon's confession meant, it meant the end of his life at Latchetts.

28

It was Thursday morning and on Sunday Charles Ashby would come sailing up Southampton Water, and nothing would stop the subsequent celebrations. He followed Bee into the hall at Latchetts feeling desperate.

"Do you mind if I desert you and go into Westover?" he asked Bee.

"No, I think you are due a little rest from the family. Simon is for ever running away."

So he took the bus into Westover and waited until it was time for Mr Macallan to be having his mid-morning coffee. He went to the *Westover Times* office and asked to see the files. The office boy, who showed no sign of ever having seen him before, took him to the cellar and showed him where they were.

Brat read the report of the inquest all over again, but could find no help there.

Perhaps in the full report there would be something?

He went out and looked up Colonel Smollett in the telephone book. Where, he asked the Colonel, would the report of the inquest on himself be now? With the police? Well, would he make it easy for him to see it?

The Colonel would, but he considered it a most morbid and undesirable ambition, and implored young Ashby to think again.

So armed with the Colonel's telephoned introduction, he went to see a highly amused police force, who sat him down in a leather armchair and offered him cigarettes, and set before him the coroner's report of eight years ago with the *empressement* of a conjurer who has produced the rabbit from the hat.

He read it all through several times. It was merely the *Westover Times*'s report in greater detail.

He thanked the police, offered them cigarettes in his turn, and went away as empty of suggestion as he had come. He went down to the harbour and hung over the wall, staring westward at the cliffs.

He had a fixed point, anyhow. A fixed point that could not be altered. Simon Ashby was in Clare that day. That was held to by a man who had no reason for lying, and no suspicion that the fact was of any importance. Simon had never been long enough away from Mr Pilbeam's vicinity to make his absence felt.

Pat Ashby must have been killed between the time that old Abel met him in the early afternoon and the moment when Mr Pilbeam had to chase Simon home for six o'clock supper.

Well, there was that old saying about Mahomet and the mountain.

He thought the Mahomet theory over, but was stumped by the coat on the cliff-top. It was Simon who had written that note, but Simon was never out of Clare.

It was two o'clock when he came to himself, and he went to have lunch at a small pub in the harbour. They had nothing much left, but it did not matter because he sat staring at his plate until they put the bill in front of him.

He went back to Latchetts and, without going to the house, went to the stables and took out one of the horses that had not been at Bures. There was no one about but Arthur, who

199

reported that all the horses were safely back and all well except that Buster had an overreach.

"Taking him out like that, sir?" Arthur asked, nodding at Brat's tweed suit. And Brat said that he was.

He turned up to the down as he had that first morning when he took out Timber, and did again what he had done on Timber's back. But all the glory was gone. The whole world looked sick. Life itself tasted bad.

He dismounted and sat down where he had sat that morning a month ago, looking out over the small green valley. It had seemed paradise to him then. Even that silly girl who had come and talked to him had not sufficed to spoil it for him. He remembered how her eyes had popped when she found he was not Simon. She had come there sure of seeing Simon because it was his favourite place for exercising the horses. Because he . . .

The horse by his side threw up his head as Brat's sudden movement jerked the bit in his mouth.

Because he . . .?

He listened to the girl's voice in his mind. Then he got slowly to his feet and stood a long time staring across the valley.

He knew now how Simon had done it. And he also knew the answer to something that had puzzled him. He knew why Simon had been afraid that, by some miracle, it was the real Patrick who had come back.

He got on the horse and went back to the stables. The great clouds were racing up from the south-west and it was beginning to rain. In the saddle room he took a sheet of writing paper from the desk and wrote on it: "Out for dinner. Leave the front door on the latch for me, and don't worry if I am late." He put it in an envelope, addressed it to Bee, and asked Arthur to hand it in at the house when he was passing. He took his burberry from the back of the saddle-room door, and went out into the rain, away from Latchetts. He had the knowledge now. What was he going to do with it?

He walked without conscious purpose, unaware of anything but the dreadful question to be answered. He came to the smithy where Mr Pilbeam was still working, and greeted him, and exchanged opinions on the work in hand and on the weather to come, without having for a moment ceased to battle with the thing in his mind.

He walked up the path to Tanbitches and up the hill over the wet grass to the crown of beeches, and walked there to and fro among the great boles of the trees, distracted and stricken.

How could he bring this thing on Bee?

On Eleanor? On Latchetts?

Had he not already done Latchetts sufficient harm?

Would it matter so much if Simon were left in possession as he had been for eight years?

Who had been harmed by that? Only one person: Patrick.

If Simon was to be brought to justice for Patrick's death, it would mean horror beyond horror for Bee and the rest.

He didn't have to do it at all. He could go away; stage a suicide. After all, Simon had staged Patrick's suicide, and it had passed a police investigation. If a boy of thirteen could do that he could do it. He could just drop out, and things would be as they were a month ago.

And—Pat Ashby?

But Pat, if he could choose, would not want justice on Simon at the cost of his family's ruin. Not Pat, who had been kind and always thought first of others.

And Simon?

Was he to make good Simon's monstrous supposition that he would do nothing? Was Simon to spend a long life as the owner of Latchetts? Were Simon's children to inherit Latchetts?

But they would still be Ashbys. If Simon were brought to justice there would be no more Ashbys at Latchetts.

And how would it advantage Latchetts to have its inheritance made safe by the condoning of murder?

Was it not, perhaps, to uncover that murder that he had come by such strange ways to Latchetts?

He had come half across a world to that meeting with Loding in the street, and he had said to himself that so strange a chance must be destiny. But he had not imagined it to be an important destiny. Now, it would seem, it was an all-important one.

What was he to do? Who could advise him? Decide for him? It was not fair that this should be put on his shoulders. He had not the wisdom, the experience, to deal with a thing of this magnitude.

"I am retribution," he had said to Simon, and meant it. But that was before he had the weapon of retribution in his hand.

What was he to do?

Go to the police tonight? Tomorrow?

Do nothing, and let the celebrations begin when Charles Ashby came home?

What was he to do?

It was late that night that George Peck, sitting in his study and conscious every now and then even from his distant vantage point in Thebes of the lashing rain on the window of the Rectory in Clare, heard a tapping at that window, and came back from Thebes and went to the front door. It was by no means the first time that people had tapped on that window late at night.

In the light from the hall he saw one of the Ashbys, he could not tell which because the soaked hat almost obscured the face.

"Rector, may I come in and talk to you?"

"Of course, Patrick. Come in."

Brat stood on the step, the rain sluicing from his coat.

"I'm afraid I'm very wet," he said vaguely.

The Rector looked down and saw that the grey tweed of his trousers was black, and his shoes an oozing pulp. His eyes went sharply to the boy's face. Brat had taken off his limp hat and the rain-water from his soaked hair was running down his face.

"Take off your coat and leave it here," the Rector said. "I'll give you another one when you are ready to go." He went to the hall cloakroom and came back with a towel. "Rub your head with that."

Brat did as he was told, with the obedient air and fumbling movements of a child. The Rector went through to the empty kitchen and brought a kettle of water.

"Come in," he said. "Just drop the towel where your wet coat is." He led the way into his study and put the kettle on an electric ring. "That will be hot in no time. I often make tea for myself when I sit up late. What was it you wanted to talk to me about?"

"A pit in Dothan."

"What?"

"I'm sorry. My mind has stopped working. Have you a drink of any kind?"

The Rector had meant to put the whisky in the tea, as a toddy, but he poured a stiff one now and Brat drank it.

"Thank you. I am sorry to come and worry you like this but I had to talk to you. I hope you don't mind."

"I am here to be talked to. Some more whisky?"

"No, thanks."

"Then let me give you some dry shoes."

"Oh, no, thank you. I'm used to being wet, you know. Rector, I want your advice about something very important, but can I talk to you as if—as if it were confessional? I mean, without your feeling that you must do something about it."

"Whatever you say I shall treat as confession, certainly."

"Well, first I have to tell you something. I am not Patrick Ashby."

"No," agreed the Rector. And Brat stared.

"You mean—you mean, you *knew* I wasn't Patrick?"

"I rather thought you weren't."

"Why?"

"There is more to any person than a physical presence; there is an aura, a personality, a being. And I was almost sure the first time I met you that I had never met you before. There was nothing in you that I recognised, although you have many things in common with Patrick as well as your appearance."

"And you did nothing about it!"

"What do you suggest that I should have done? Your lawyer, your family, and your friends had all accepted and welcomed you. I had no evidence to show that you were not Patrick. Nothing but my own belief that you weren't. What good would it have done to express my disbelief? It did not seem to me that it would be long before the situation resolved itself without my interference."

"You mean: that I should be found out."

"No. I mean that you did not seem to me someone who would be happy in the life you had chosen. Judging by your visit tonight, I was right."

"But I didn't come here tonight just to confess to not being Patrick."

"No?"

"No, that is only—— I had to tell you that because it was the only way you could understand what has—— I wish my mind was clearer. I've been walking about trying to get things straight."

"Perhaps if you told me first how you came to Latchetts at all, it would at least clear *my* mind."

"I—I met someone in America who had lived in Clare. They—she thought I looked like an Ashby, and suggested that I should pretend to be Patrick."

203

"And you were to pay her a share of the proceeds of the deception."

"Yes."

"I can only say that she earned her percentage whatever it was. As a tutor she must be remarkable. I have never seen a better piece of coaching. Are you American, then?"

"No," said Brat, and the Rector smiled faintly at the emphasis. "I was brought up in an orphanage. I was left on its doorstep."

And he sketched for the Rector the story of his life.

"I have heard of your orphanage," the Rector said, when he had finished. "It explains one thing that puzzled me: your good upbringing." He poured tea, and added whisky. "Would you like something more substantial than biscuits, by the way? No? Then have the oatmeal ones; they are very filling."

"I had to tell you all this because of something I found out. Patrick didn't commit suicide. He was murdered."

The Rector set down the cup he was holding. For the first time he looked startled.

"Murdered? By whom?"

"His brother."

"*Simon?*"

"Yes."

"But, Patrick! That—— What is your name, by the way?"

"You forget. I haven't got one. I've always been called Brat. It was a corruption of Bartholomew."

"But my dear fellow, that is absurd. What evidence have you of anything so incredible?"

"I have Simon's word for it."

"*Simon* told you?"

"He boasted about it. He said that I could never do anything about it because it would mean giving myself away. He knew as soon as he saw me that I wasn't Patrick, you see."

"When did this extraordinary conversation take place?"

"Last night, at the Bures ball. It wasn't as sudden as it sounds. I began to wonder about Simon long before that, and I challenged him about it because of something he said about *knowing* I wasn't Patrick, and he laughed and boasted about it."

"I think that the setting of this scene does a lot to explain it."

204

"You mean you think we were drunk?"

"Not exactly. Elated, shall we say. And you challenged Simon on the subject, and Simon with his perverted sense of mischief provided you with what you expected from him."

"Do you really believe I have as little intelligence as that?" Brat asked quietly.

"It surprises me, I must admit. I have always considered you to be highly intelligent."

"Then believe me, I am not here because of a piece of fooling on Simon's part. Patrick didn't commit suicide. Simon killed him. Deliberately. And what is more, I know how he did it."

And he told him.

"But Brat, you have no evidence even now. That is theory, what you have just told me. An ingenious and likely theory, I admit. It has the merit of simplicity. But you have no evidence whatsoever."

"We can get the evidence, if the police once know the truth. But that isn't what I want to know. What I want advice about is—well, whether to let sleeping dogs lie."

And he explained his dilemma.

But the Rector, rather surprisingly in view of his silence about his doubts of Brat's identity, had no doubts on the subject at all. If murder had been done, then the law must be invoked. Anything else was anarchy.

His point was that Brat had no case against Simon. His mind had run on murder, he had taunted Simon with it, Simon had one of his well-known impish moments and confessed, and Brat after long thought had found a theory to fit the alleged confession.

"And you think that I've been walking about in the rain since four o'clock because of a little joke of Simon's? You think that I came here tonight and confessed to not being Patrick because of a little joke of Simon's?" The Rector was silent. "Tell me, Rector, were you surprised when Pat committed suicide?"

"Exceedingly."

"Do you know anyone who wasn't surprised?"

"No. But suicide *is* a surprising thing."

"I give up," Brat said.

In the contemplative silence that followed, the Rector said: "I see what you meant by the pit in Dothan. That was an excellent upbringing at the orphanage."

"It was a very thoroughly Biblical one, if that is what you mean. Simon knows that story, too, by the way."

"I expect so, but how do you happen to know?"

"When he heard that Patrick had come back he couldn't help, in spite of his denials, a fear that it might be true. There had been that other case, you see. That time the victim had survived by a miracle. He was afraid that by some miracle Patrick had survived. I know, because he came into that room, the first day I was there, strung up to face something dreadful. And his relief when he saw me was almost funny."

He drank down the rest of his tea and looked quizzically at the Rector. In spite of himself he was beginning to feel better.

"Another of Simon's little jokes was to send me out that first day on Timber, without telling me he was a rogue. But I suppose that was just his 'perverted sense of mischief'. And still another of his little jokes was to loosen my girth yesterday before I started a race on Chevron. But I suppose that was just one of his 'well-known impish moments'."

The Rector's deep eyes considered Brat.

"I am not defending Simon—he has never been an admirable character—but tricks played on an interloper, a pretender—even dangerous tricks, are one thing, and the murder of a well-beloved brother is quite another. Why, by the way, did Simon not denounce you at once if he did not believe you were his brother?"

"For the same reason that you didn't."

"I see. He would merely be held to be—difficult."

"And of course, having got rid of one Patrick with impunity, he looked forward with confidence to getting rid of another."

"Brat, I wish I could convince you that this is a figment of your imagination."

"You must have a great respect for my imaginative powers."

"If you look back, critically and honestly, you must see how the thing grew in your mind from quite small beginnings. An edifice of your own making."

And that, when Brat took his leave towards two o'clock in the morning, was still the Rector's opinion.

He offered Brat a bed, but Brat compromised on the loan of a waterproof and a torch, and found his way back to Latchetts by the soaking field-path with the rain still pouring hopelessly down.

"Come and see me again before you decide anything," the

Rector had said; but he had at least been helpful in one direction. He had answered Brat's main question. If it was a choice between love and justice, the choice had to be justice.

He found the front door of Latchetts unlocked, a note from Bee on the hall table, saying: "Soup on the ring in the pantry," and a silver cup on an ebony stand bearing a card in Eleanor's writing which said: "You forgot this, you blasé rodeo hound!"

He put out the lights and crept up through the silent house to his bed in the old night nursery. Someone had put a hot-water bottle in his bed. He was asleep almost before his head touched the pillow.

29

On Friday morning Simon came bright and cheerful to breakfast and greeted Brat with pleasure. He commented on the progress of the "trunk" murder investigations, the character of Tattie Thacker (whose value had been estimated by the court at one halfpenny) and the iniquity of poisoning as a means of ridding oneself of a human encumbrance. Except for an occasional gleam in his eye he showed no awareness of their changed relationship. He was taking their "spiritual twinship" for granted.

Eleanor too seemed to be back on the old footing, although she seemed shy, like someone who has made a social gaffe. She suggested that in the afternoon they should take the four silver cups into Westover and give instructions for their engraving.

"It will be nice to have 'Patrick Ashby' on a cup again," she said.

"Yes, won't it!" Simon said.

Simon evidently looked forward to years of baiting his spiritual twin. But when Brat said, in answer to Bee, that he had talked late with the Rector, Simon's head came up as if he had heard a warning. And after that Brat caught Simon's glance at him every now and then.

When Eleanor and Brat were setting off for Westover in the afternoon, he appeared and insisted on making a third in the bug's scanty space. One of the cups was his own unaided work, he said, and he had a right to say what was to go on it, and whether it should be in Roman, Arabic, Hebrew, Greek or Cyrillic script, or mere shorthand.

So powerful was Simon's indifferent charm that even Brat found himself on the verge of wondering whether the Rector had been right and he had built his story out of whole cloth. But he remembered the horse that Farmer Gates had bought for his daughter Peggy, and concluded that that was a more reliable guide to Simon than anything Simon himself might provide.

When they had decided on the lettering for the names on the cups, Simon and Eleanor went to tea, but Brat said that he had some shopping to do. Brat had decided what he had to do in the present impasse. He could not go to the police with his story in its present form with any more hope of being believed than he had been by the Rector. If the Rector, who knew Simon's weaknesses, refused to believe without concrete evidence, how much more would the police refuse to believe, when Simon to them was not a wayward boy but Mr Ashby of Latchetts?

Brat therefore proposed to provide them with the evidence.

He went down to the harbour and sought a chandler's, and there, after some consultation and a deal of choosing, bought two hundred feet of rope. The rope was so thin that it was not much thicker than stout string, but its breaking-point under tension was very much that of steel. He asked them to pack it in a cardboard box and deliver it to the Angel garage, where the bug was. He received it at the garage and packed it away in the luggage compartment.

When the others arrived to go home he was waiting innocently in the car with an evening paper.

They had packed themselves into the bug and were preparing to go when Simon said: "Whoa! We've forgotten to leave that old tyre with them," and he got out and opened the rear compartment to get the tyre.

"What is in the box, Nell?"

"I didn't put any box there," Eleanor said, not moving. "It can't be for us."

"It's mine," Brat said.

"What is it?"

"Secret."

"James Fryer and Son, Ship Chandlers," said Simon's voice.

Oh, God! There was a label on the box that he had not noticed.

Simon shut the luggage compartment with a bang and came

208

back to his seat. "What have you been buying, Brat? One of those ships in a bottle? No, it is a little too large for that. One of those ships not in a bottle. One of those full-sailed galleons that sit on suburban sideboards to delight the heart of our Island Race and comfort it for being sick on the trip to Margate."

"Don't be a fool, Simon. What is it, Brat? Is it really a secret?"

If Simon wanted to find out what was in the box he most certainly would, by one method or another. And to make a mystery of it was to call attention to it. Far better to be apparently frank about it.

"If you must know, I'm afraid I'll lose the knack of spinning a rope, so I've bought some to practise on."

Eleanor was delighted. Brat must show them some spinning that very evening.

"No. Not till I've tried it out *in camera* first."

"You'll teach me how, won't you?"

Yes, he would teach her how to throw a rope. She was going to hate him one day soon, if that rope did what it was bought for.

When they arrived back at Latchetts he took the rope out and left it openly in the hall. Bee asked about it, and accepted the explanation of its presence, and no one took any more notice of it. He wished that his last short time at Latchetts did not have to be spent in lying. It was odd that, having spent his whole time at Latchetts lying like a Levantine, he should mind so much about this smaller deception.

There was still time to do nothing about it. To leave the rope there, and not ask it to answer any question. It was the wrong kind of rope for throwing, but he could change it for the right kind.

But when night came, and he was alone in his room, he knew that he had no choice. This was what he had come half across a world to do, and he was going to do it.

The household went early to bed, still tired from their excitements at Bures, and he gave them till half past twelve, and then prospected. There seemed to be no light anywhere. There was certainly no sound. He went downstairs and took the rope from its corner. He unlatched the dining-room window, stepped over the sill into the night, and drew it gently down again behind him. He waited for any reaction, but there was none.

209

He made his way softly over the gravel to the grass, sat down in the shelter of the first paddock trees, out of the range of the windows, and without need of any light, deftly knotted foot-holds at intervals down the length of rope. It was a pleasant reassuring thing to feel the familiar touch of rope after so long. It was a well-bred rope and answered sweetly to his demands. He felt grateful to James Fryer and Son.

He wound the rope and put the coil of it over his shoulder. In half an hour the moon would be up. It was a young moon, and not much of a lamp, but he had two good torches in his pocket and he did not very much desire a full moon's frankness tonight.

Every five minutes he stopped and waited to see if he had been followed. But nothing at all moved in the night. Not even a cat.

The grey light of the coming moon greeted him as he came towards the foot of Tanbitches, and he found the path to Westover without having to flick a torch. He followed it up a little and then, when he could see the beech-crown of the hill against the sky, he struck off it until he reached the thicket on the upper side of the old quarry. There he sat down and waited. But again there was no sound in all the sleeping countryside except the sudden cry of a sheep on the hill.

He tied the rope round the bole of the largest of the young beeches that had seeded themselves there, and let it uncoil itself until it fell over the edge of the quarry into the green thickness below. This was the steep side of the quarry. The lower side had had a narrow entrance, but it had long ago fallen together and become overgrown with an impenetrable denseness of briars. Old Abel had told him all about it the day they had sat there and talked of Patrick. Abel knew all about the quarry because he had once rescued a sheep from it. It was much easier to go down the sheer face, Abel said, than in at the lower side. In fact, to go in at the lower side, or any other side, was plumb impossible. No, there was no water in it; at least there wasn't any twenty years ago, which was when last he went down after a sheep; the water all drained away under the hill to the sea.

Brat tested the rope several times, and felt for it fraying. But the bole of the tree was smooth, and where it went over the lip of the quarry he had padded it. He slid over the edge and felt for his first toe-hold. Now that he was level with the ground he was more aware of the brightness of the sky. He could see the dark shape of the low thicket against it, and the larger darkness of the tree above him.

He had found his first foothold in the rope now, but his hands were still on the rope where it lay taut on the turf.

"I should hate," said Simon's voice in its most "Simon" drawl, "to let you go without an appropriate farewell. I mean, I could just cut the rope and let you think, if you had time to think at all, that it had broken. But that wouldn't be any fun, would it?"

Brat could see his bulk against the sky. From the shape of it, he was half-kneeling on the edge, by the rope. Brat could touch him by putting out a hand.

Fool that he had been to underrate Simon. Simon had taken no chances. He hadn't even taken the chance of following him. He had come first and waited.

"Cutting the rope won't do much good," he said. "I'll only land in the branches of some tree farther down, and yell my head off until someone comes."

"I know better than that. A personal acquaintance of mine, this quarry is. Almost a relation, one might say." He expelled his breath in a whispered laugh. "A sheer drop to the ground, half a hillside away."

Brat wondered if he had time to slide down the rope in one swift rush before Simon cut it. The footholds had been for coming up again. He could just ignore them and slide. Would he be near enough the bottom before Simon realised what he had done?

Or would it be better——? Yes. His hand tightened on the rope and he pressed on his toe-hold and lifted himself until he had almost got one knee on the turf again. But Simon must have his hand on the rope somewhere. He had felt the movement.

"Oh, no, you don't!" he said, and brought his heel down on Brat's hand. Brat grabbed the foot with his other hand and hung on, his fingers in the opening of the shoe. Simon brought his knife down on Brat's wrist and Brat yelled, but continued to hang on. He dragged his right hand from under Simon's shoe and caught him round the back of the ankle. He was covering with his body the rope in front of Simon and as long as he held on Simon could not turn to cut the rope behind him. It is very upsetting to have one's foot grasped from below when one is standing on the very edge of a precipice.

211

"Let go!" said Simon, stabbing frantically.

"If you don't stop that," panted Brat, "I'll drag you over with me."

"Let go! Let go!" Simon said, hitting wildly in blind panic and not listening.

Brat removed the hand that was holding on to the edge of the shoe and caught the knife-hand as it came down. He now had his right hand round Simon's left ankle, and his left hand was clutching Simon's right wrist.

Simon screamed and pulled away, but Brat hung his weight on the wrist. He had the confidence of a toe-hold, but Simon had nothing to brace himself against. Simon tore at the hand that was hanging on to his knife-wrist, and Brat, with a great heave, took his right hand from Simon's foot and caught Simon's left hand with it. He had now got Simon by both wrists, and Simon was bent over like a bow above him.

"Drop that knife!" he said.

As he said it he felt the turf at the quarry edge settle a little and slide forward. It made no difference to him, except to press him out a little from the face of the cliff. But to Simon, already bent over by the weight of Brat's arms and body, it was fatal.

Horrified, Brat saw the dark mass come forward on top of him. It struck him from his toe-hold, and he fell down with it into darkness.

A great light exploded in his head, and he ceased to know anything.

30

BEE sat in the dingy café with a cup of slopped coffee in front of her and read the sign on the other side of the road for the hundredth time in the last forty-eight hours. The sign said: MOTORISTS. PLEASE REFRAIN FROM USING YOUR HORN. THIS IS A HOSPITAL. It was only seven o'clock in the morning, but the café opened at six, and there was always at least one other customer having a meal as she sat there. She did not notice them. She just sat with a cup of coffee in front of her and stared at the hospital wall opposite. She was an old inhabitant of the café now. "Better go out and have a meal," they would say kindly, and she would cross the road and sit for a little with a cup of coffee in front of her and then go back again.

Her life had narrowed down to this pendulum existence between the hospital and café. She found it difficult to remember a past, and quite impossible to visualise a future. There was only the "now", a dreary half-world of grey misery. Last night they had given her a cot in one of the sisters' rooms, and the night before that she had spent in the hospital waiting-room. There were two phrases that they used to her, and they were as sickeningly familiar as the sign on their wall: "No, no change," they would say, or "Better go out and get a meal."

The slatternly girl came and pushed a fresh cup of coffee in front of her and took away the one she had. "That one's cold," said the slatternly girl, "and you haven't even touched it." The fresh cup was slopped over, too. She was grateful to the slatternly girl but felt outraged by her sympathy. She was enjoying the vicarious drama of her presence in the café, and its implications.

MOTORISTS. PLEASE REFRAIN FROM USING—— She must stop reading that thing. Must look at something else. The blue checked pattern of the plastic tablecloth, perhaps. One, two, three, four, five, six—— Oh, no. Not counting things.

The door opened and Dr Spence came in, his red hair tumbled and his chin unshaved. He said "Coffee!" to the girl, and slid into the seat beside her.

"Well?" she said.

"Still alive."

"Conscious?"

"No. But there are better indications. I mean, of a chance of his regaining consciousness, not necessarily of—his living."

"I see."

"We know about the skull fracture, but there are no means of telling what other injuries there may be."

"No."

"You oughtn't to be living on cups of coffee. That's all you've been having, isn't it?"

"She hasn't been having that," said the slatternly girl, putting down his full cup. "She just sits and looks at them."

A wave of weary anger rose in her at the slatternly girl's appropriation of her concerns.

"Better let me take you down town and give you a meal."

"No. No, thank you."

"The Angel is only a mile away, and you can rest properly there and——"

"No. No, I can't go as far away as that. I'll drink this cup. It's nice and hot."

Spence gulped down his coffee and paid for it. He hesitated a moment as if reluctant to leave her. "I have to go back to Clare now. You know I shouldn't leave him if he wasn't in good hands, don't you? They'll do more for him than I ever could."

"You've done wonders for all of us," she said. "I shall never forget it."

Now that she had begun drinking the coffee she went on drinking it, and did not look up when the door opened again. It would not be another message from the hospital already, and nothing had any importance for her that was not a message from the hospital. She was surprised when George Peck sat down beside her.

"Spence told me I should find you here."

"George!" she said. "What are you doing in Westover at this hour of the morning?"

"I have come to bring you comfort that Simon is dead."

"Comfort?"

"Yes."

He took something from an envelope and laid it in front of her on the table. It was weatherworn but recognisable. It was a slender black stylograph with a decoration consisting of a thin yellow spiral.

She looked at it a long time without touching it, then looked up at the Rector.

"Then they have found—it?"

"Yes. It was there. Do you want to talk about it here? Wouldn't you prefer to go back to the hospital?"

"What difference does it make? They are both just places where one waits."

"Coffee?" said the slatternly girl, appearing at George's shoulder.

"No; no, thank you."

"Righteeo!"

"What—what *is* there? I mean, what—what is left? What did they find?"

"Just bones, my dear. A skeleton. Under three feet of leaf mould. And some shreds of cloth."

"And his pen?"

"That was separate," he said carefully.

"You mean, it—had been—that it had been thrown down after?"

"Not necessarily, but—probably."

"I see."

"I don't know whether you will find it comforting or not—I think it is—but the police surgeon is of the opinion that he was not alive—or perhaps it would be more accurate to say not conscious—when he——"

"When he was thrown over," Bee said for him.

"Yes. The nature of the skull injury, I understand, leads him to that conclusion."

"Yes. Yes, I am glad, of course. He probably knew nothing about it. Just ended quite happy on a summer afternoon."

"There were some small objects in the cloth. Things that he probably had in his trousers pockets. But the police have kept these. Colonel Smollett gave me this," he picked up the stylograph and put it back in its envelope, "and asked me to show it to you so that you might identify it. What news from the hospital? Spence was driving away when I saw him."

"None. He is not conscious."

"I blame myself greatly for that, you know," the Rector said. "If I had listened with understanding he would not have been driven to this *sub rosa* proceeding, to that crazy night-time search."

"George, we must do something to find out who he is."

"But I understand that the orphanage——"

"Oh, I know. They made the usual inquiries. But I don't suppose they were very persistent ones. We could do much better, surely."

"Starting from the pre-supposition that he has Ashby blood in him?"

"Yes. I can't believe that a resemblance like that could exist without it. The coincidence would be too great."

"Very well, my dear. Do you want it put in hand—now?"

"Yes. Especially now. Time may be precious."

"I'll speak to Colonel Smollett about it. He'll know how to go about it. I talked to him about the inquest, and he thinks it may be possible to manage without your appearing. Nancy told me to ask you if you would like her to come in to Westover to be with you, or if it would only worry you to have someone around."

"Dear Nan. Say it is easier alone, will you? But thank her. Tell her to stand by Eleanor, rather. It must be dreadful for Nell, having to toil with unimportant things in the stables."

"I think it must be a soothing thing to have to devote oneself to the routine demands of the animal world."

"Did you break the news to her, as you promised? The news that Brat was not Patrick?"

"Yes. I dreaded it, Bee, I confess frankly. You had given me one of the hardest tasks of my life. She was still fresh from the shock of knowing that Simon had been killed. I dreaded it. But the event was surprising."

"What did she do?"

"She kissed me."

The door opened, and a probationer, flushed and young and pretty, and looking in her lilac print and spreading white linen like a visitor from another world, stood in the dim opening. She saw Bee and came over to her.

"Are you Miss Ashby, please?"

"Yes?" said Bee, half rising.

"Miss *Beatrice* Ashby? Oh, that's nice. Your nephew is conscious now, but he doesn't recognise anyone or where he is; he just keeps talking about someone called Bee, and we thought it might be you. So sister sent me across to see if I could find you. I'm sorry to interrupt you, and you haven't finished your coffee, have you, but you see——"

"Yes, yes," said Bee, already at the door.

"He may be quieter, you see, if you are there," the probationer said, following her out. "They often are, when someone they know is there, even if they don't actually recognise them. It's funny. It's as if they could see them through their skin. I've noticed it often. They'll say, Eileen?—or whoever it is. And Eileen says, Yes. And then they're quiet for a bit. But if anyone else says yes, nine times out of ten they're not fooled at all, and get restless and fractious. It's very strange."

What really was strange was to hear that steady stream of words from the lips of the normally silent Brat. For a day and a night and a day again she sat by his bed and listened to that restless torrent of talk. "Bee?" he would say, just as the little probationer had recounted to her. And she would say: "Yes,

I'm here," and he would go back reassured to whatever world he was wandering in.

His most constant belief was that this was the time he had broken his leg, and this the same hospital; and he was torn with anxiety about it. "I'll be able to ride again, won't I? There's nothing really wrong with my leg, is there? They won't take it off, will they?"

"No," she would say, "everything is all right."

And once, when he was quieter: "Are you very angry with me, Bee?"

"No, I'm not angry with you. Go to sleep."

The world went on outside the hospital; ships arrived in Southampton Water, inquests were held, bodies were consigned to the earth, but for Bee the world had narrowed to the room where Brat was and her cot in the Sister's room.

On Wednesday morning Charles Ashby arrived at the hospital, padding lightly down the polished corridors on his large noiseless feet. Bee went down to receive him and took him up to Brat's room. He had hugged her as he used to when she was a little girl, and she felt warm and comforted.

"Dear Uncle Charles. I'm so glad you were fifteen years younger than Father, or you wouldn't be here to be a comfort to us all."

"The great point in being fifteen years younger than your brother is that you don't have to wear his cast-offs," Charles said.

"He's asleep just now," she said, pausing outside Brat's room, "so you'll be very quiet, won't you?"

Charles took one look at the young face with the slack jaw, the blue shadows under the closed eyes, and the grey haze of stubble, and said: "Walter."

"His name is Brat."

"I know. I wasn't addressing him. I was merely pointing out the resemblance to Walter. That is exactly what Walter used to look like, at his age, when he had a hangover."

Bee came nearer and looked. "*Walter's* son?"

"Undoubtedly."

"I don't see any resemblance, somehow. He doesn't look like anyone but himself, now."

"You never saw Walter sleeping it off." He looked at the boy a little longer. "A better face than Walter's, though. A good face." He followed her into the corridor. "I hear you all liked him."

"We loved him," she said.

"Well, it's all very sad, very sad. Who was his accomplice, do you know?"

"Someone in America."

"Yes, so George Peck told me. But who would that be? Who went to America from Clare?"

"The Willett family went to Canada. And they had daughters. It was a woman, you know. Perhaps they finished up in the States."

"If it was a woman I'll eat my hat."

"I feel that way too."

"Do you? Good girl. You're an admirably intelligent woman, Bee. Nice-looking, too. What are we going to do about the boy? For the future, I mean."

"We don't know yet if he has a future," she said.

31

ONLY the Rector, Bee, Charles, Eleanor, and the firm of Cosset Thring and Noble knew, so far, that Brat was not Patrick Ashby.

And the police.

The police, that is, at what is known as "the highest level".

The police had been told everything, and they were now engaged in their own admirable fashion in smoothing out the mess to the best of their ability without breaking any of the laws which they were engaged to uphold. Simon Ashby was dead. It was to no one's advantage to uncover the story of his crime. By a process of not saying too much, the ritual of the Law might be complied with, leaving unwanted truths still buried; a harrow dragging over earth that held below its surface unexploded bombs.

The coroner sat on the poor bones found in the quarry, and adjourned the inquest *sine die*. No one in the neighbourhood had ever been reported missing. Tanbitches, on the other hand, was a favourite camping ground for gipsies, who were not given to reporting accidents to the police. Nothing remained of the clothing but a few scraps of unrecognisable cloth. The objects found in the vicinity of the bones were unidentifiable; they consisted of a corroded piece of metal that might once

218

have been a whistle, another corroded piece still recognisable as a knife, and several coins of small denominations.

"George!" said Bee. "What became of the pen?"

"The stylograph? I lost it."

"*George!*"

"Someone had to lose it, my dear. Colonel Smollett couldn't; he's a soldier, with a soldier's sense of duty. The police couldn't; they had their self-respect and their duty to the public to consider. But my conscience is between me and my God. I think they were touchingly grateful to me in their tacit way."

The adjourned inquest on Simon Ashby came later, since it had been postponed until Brat was capable of being interviewed in hospital. The policeman who had interviewed him reported that Mr Ashby could remember nothing about the accident, or why he should have gone there with his brother at that hour to climb down into the quarry. He had an idea that it was the result of a bet. Something about whether there was water in the old quarry or not, he thought; but could not take his oath on it since his recollection was vague. He had serious head injuries and was still very ill. He did know, however, that he had found out from Abel Tusk that there was no water there; and Simon probably had said that that was highly unlikely, and so the contest may have arisen.

Abel Tusk corroborated the fact that Patrick Ashby had asked him about water in the quarry, and that it was an unusual thing to find the floor of an old quarry dry. It was Abel Tusk who had given the first alarm of the accident. He had been out on the hill with his sheep and had heard what he took to be cries for help from the direction of the quarry, and had gone there as fast as he could and found the undamaged rope, and had gone down to the blacksmith's and used his telephone to call the police.

Bee, replying to the coroner, agreed that she would most certainly have taken steps to put an end to any such plan had she heard about it. And the coroner expressed his opinion that it was for that reason that the thing had been done *sub rosa*.

The verdict was death by misadventure, and the coroner expressed his sympathy with the family on the loss of this high-spirited young man.

So the problem of Simon was settled. Simon who, before he was fourteen, had killed his brother, calmly written a note on

that brother's behalf, tossed the pen into the abyss after hi
brother's body, and gone home calmly to six o'clock suppe
when he was chased out of the smithy. Who had joined th
night search for his brother on his pony, and some time durin
that long night had taken his brother's coat to the cliff-top an
left it there with the note in the pocket. Who was now to b
mourned by the countryside as a high-spirited young man o
memorable charm.

The problem of Brat remained.

Not the problem of who he was, but the problem of his future
The doctors had decided that, having against all probabilit
lived so long, he was likely to go on living. He would nee
long care, however, and a peaceful life if he was to recove
properly.

"Uncle Charles came to see you one day when you were ill,"
Bee said to him when he was well enough to keep his attentio
on a subject. "He was astonished by your resemblance t
Walter Ashby. My cousin."

"Yes?" said Brat. He was not interested. What did i
matter now?

"We began inquiries about you."

"The police did that," he said wearily. "Years ago."

"Yes, but they had very little to come and go on. Onl
that a young girl had arrived by train with a baby, and gon
away by train without one. The train had come from th
crowded Birmingham district with all its ramifications. W
started at the other end. Walter's end. We went back t
where Walter was, somewhere about twenty-two years ago
and began from there. Walter was a rolling stone, so it wasn
easy, but we did find out that, among his other jobs, he was i
charge of a stable in Gloucestershire for a couple of month
while the owner was away having an operation. The house
hold was a housekeeper and a young girl who cooked. She wa
a very good cook, but her real ambition was to be a hospita
nurse. The housekeeper liked her and so did the owner, an
when they found she was going to have a baby they let her sta
on, and she had her baby in the local maternity home. Th
housekeeper always believed that it was Walter's child, but th
girl would not say. She did not want to get married; sh
wanted to be a nurse. She said that she was taking the bab
home for the christening—she came from Evesham way—an
she didn't come back. But the housekeeper had a letter fror

her long afterwards, thanking her for her goodness and telling her that the girl had realised her ambition and was a nurse. 'No one knows about my baby,' she said, ' but I have seen that he is well looked after.'"

She glanced at Brat. He was lying with his eyes on the ceiling, but he appeared to be listening.

"Her name was Mary Woodward. She was an even better nurse than she was a cook. She was killed during the war, taking patients out of a ward to safety in a shelter."

There was a long silence.

"I seem to have inherited my cooking talents too," he said; and she could not tell whether the words were bitter or not.

"I was very fond of Walter. He was a dear; very kind. He had only one fault; he had no head for drink, and he liked drink very much. I don't believe for a moment that Walter knew about the girl. He was the kind who would have rushed to marry her. I think she didn't want him to know."

She had another look at Brat. Perhaps she had told him all this too soon; before he was strong enough to be interested. But she had hoped that it would give him an interest in life.

"I'm afraid that is as near as we can get, Brat. But none of us have any doubt about it. Charles took one look at you and said, 'Walter'. And I think myself you look a little like your mother. That is Mary Woodward. It was taken in her second year at St Luke's."

She gave him the photograph, and left it with him.

A week or two later she said to Eleanor: "Nell, I'm going to leave you. I've taken a lease of Tim Connell's stud at Kilbarty."

"Oh, Bee!"

"Not immediately, but when Brat is able to travel."

"You're taking Brat there? Oh, yes, of course you must go! Oh, that is a wonderful idea, Bee. It solves such a lot of problems, doesn't it? But can you afford it? Shall I lend you money for it?"

"No, Uncle Charles is doing that. Lovely to think of Charles supporting horses, isn't it? You'll need all you have to pay death duty, my dear. Mr Sandal has broken it to the bank that the place belonged to Simon all the time."

"What shall we do about letting people know about Brat? I mean, about his not being Patrick."

"I don't think we'll have to do anything about it. The facts will inevitably *ooze*. They always do. I think we just do nothing to prevent the leak. The fact that we are making him part of the family instead of starting prosecutions and things will take a lot of the fun out of it for the scandalmongers. We'll survive, Nell. And so will he."

"Of course we will. And the first time someone mentions it boldly to me, I shall say: 'My cousin? Yes, he did pretend to be my brother. He *is* very like Patrick, isn't he?' As if we were discussing cream-cakes." She paused a moment and then added: "But I should like the news to get round before I'm too old to marry him."

"Are you thinking of it?" Bee said, taken aback.

"I'm set on it."

Bee hesitated; and then decided to let the future take care of itself.

"Don't worry. It will get round," she said.

"Now that Uncle Charles is here, and is going to settle down at Latchetts," she said later to Brat, "I can go back to having a life of my own somewhere else."

His eyes came away from the ceiling, and watched her.

"There's a place in Ulster I have my eye on. Tim Connell's place at Kilbarty."

She saw his fingers begin to play with the sheet, unhappily.

"Are you going away to Ulster, then?" he asked.

"Only if you will come with me, and run the stable for me."

The easy tears of the newly convalescent rose in his eyes and ran down his cheek.

"Oh, Bee!" he said.

"I take it that means that my offer is accepted," she said.

Agatha Christie

Popular Reading

These and other PAN Books are obtainable from all booksellers and newsagents. If you have any difficulty please send purchase price plus 7p postage to P.O. Box 11, Falmouth, Cornwall.

While every effort is made to keep prices low, it is sometimes necessary to increase prices at short notice. PAN Books reserve the right to show new retail prices on covers which may differ from those previously advertised in the text or elsewhere.